SOME
BODY
LIKE
ME

SOME BODY LIKE ME

LUCY LAPINSKA

First published in Great Britain in 2025 by Gollancz
an imprint of The Orion Publishing Group Ltd
Carmelite House, 50 Victoria Embankment
London EC4Y 0DZ

An Hachette UK Company

The authorised representative in the EEA is Hachette Ireland, 8 Castlecourt Centre,
Dublin 15, D15 XTP3, Ireland (email: info@hbgi.ie)

1 3 5 7 9 10 8 6 4 2

A CIP catalogue record for this book is
available from the British Library.

Hardback (ISBN) 978 1 399 62302 5
Export Trade Paperback (ISBN) 978 1 399 62303 2
eBook (ISBN) 978 1 399 62305 6
Audio Download (ISBN) 978 1 399 62306 3

Typeset by Input Data Services Ltd, Bridgwater, Somerset

Printed in Great Britain by Clays Ltd, Elcograph S.p.A

www.gollancz.co.uk

for Claire
for everything

'I doubt there's a heaven for androids . . .'

CyberLife model RK800 (#313 248 317 - 51) "Connor"
Detroit: Become Human
Quantic Dream, 2018

'My battery is low, and it's getting dark.'

The interpreted last words of Opportunity
MER-B (Mars Exploration Rover – B)
25th January 2004 – 10th June 2018

GaiaTech Promotional Leaflet

Distributed with PCC 'Melo-G' models

Congratulations on purchasing your new personal companion computer from GaiaTech. By choosing to invest in GaiaTech products, you are making a safe and secure choice for your personal computing needs now, and for the future.

Your personal companion computer (PCC) has been manufactured to the highest international standard, and comes complete with a ten-year warranty. Please activate your warranty card to ensure you have full GaiaTech coverage. This warranty includes a complimentary annual service, provided for you at your closest GaiaTech store.

Please see our global network pages for further details.

Your new GaiaTech PCC comes with preinstalled personality software, which can be adjusted endlessly to suit your changing personal preferences and needs. A GaiaTech PCC also comes with access to the SmartChoices™ database, giving your PCC access to over six billion choice-options about everything from household chores to security. Your PCC will automatically adjust to you and your family's requirements and rules as it learns, but if you want to speed things along, you can give your PCC specifi c commands that will remain in place permanently. See page 68 in this leafl et for more details on how to do this.

As a GaiaTech MELo-G 3000, your PCC is designed to be Some Body Like Me V2.indd 1 19/09/2024 09:41 a friend. The patented SmartSoftware™ means that your PCC never stops learning; developing knowledge about everything from how you take your coffee, to the exact location of those lost socks. Your PCC will never grow tired of hard work, or bored of repetitive tasks. A GaiaTech PCC has a stationary battery life of five hundred hours, and charges kinetically – in other words, if you keep your PCC busy, it will never run out of charge.

Your GaiaTech PCC can lift 500kg, run continuously at a top speed of 20mph, and record limitless footage with 7x optical magnification. Using SmartSecurity™, your PCC can wirelessly link to your existing home security system, giving them 'eyes and ears' to watch over your home or business at all hours of the day and night.

But your GaiaTech PCC can also be a gentle babysitter, a delicate handler of animals, and a soft companion around the home. Your PCC can feel like a true member of the family as they learn about your hobbies and interests, and even take part in them. They are never too busy to join in, and will always put you first. Your PCC could become the tennis partner you never knew you needed.

Get started today by registering your GaiaTech warranty card, and discover a new world of technological companionship with your new MELo-G 3000.

PART ONE

Autumn

5 September

I remove my skin on the first Monday of every month.

It is an event unmarked on any calendar, yet the household is as aware of it as a screaming alarm. It dictates the day, a silent insistence that blocks out half a day in an unheard cacophony of importance.

I retreat to the bathroom in the afternoon. David stares at the screen of his Tab, and pretends nothing is happening as I walk past him. David is as content to ignore what I am about to do as a beetle is content to remain ignorant about the orbit of the Earth. It is natural, and essential, and does not need to be analysed as it will go on, regardless.

The bathroom is a concrete oblong pressed into the earth to make use of ground-source heat that lingers after the sun has set, and when I am alone I hear the bite of nature crunching against the outer layers. Lights activate as I descend the stairs, revealing windows that show high-definition views of greenery, parkland, sea or sky, depending. The house has over seventeen thousand views to show me, each one a glimpse into the past.

The bathroom has no window, instead there is an illuminated mirror that spans the entire wall. I ignore it, and undress silently, by myself, out of sight of my reflection. A partner's assistance would be welcome in this procedure, but David has forbidden me to remove my skin where he can see, or where there is a chance that he might see. The whole process is something that cannot be discussed, and something I have always done alone.

It is one of the Rules. Rules are commands, defined and established by David, that cannot be renegotiated. Rules are as indelible in my code as the personality data that controls everything from my movement subroutines to my speech patterns. My action and reaction responses operate around Rules, wrapping themselves within the base code to such an extent that they become part of the deep structure; load-bearing aspects of data that support new ideas and solutions. Humans enjoy establishing Rules, even amongst themselves, and their Rules are often *Do Not*s.

My opinions are constructed from non-executable statement lines of code, and can be given priority value only if they do not conflict with a Rule. David's Rules take priority over my Opinions, which can be ignored or deleted at his command.

Rules, and their relationship with Opinions, are a part of my core programming, albeit a relatively new innovation. GaiaTech PCCs have always been at the forefront of techno-logical development, and I am told I am a sophisticated model. Sophisticated here means: expensive. And this is true. My manufacture took twenty-eight months to complete, whereas off-the-line GaiaTech MELo models can be constructed in a matter of weeks even with personalisation features. I am unique, though my basic chassis is identical to the classic girlfriend model (MELo-G-3000-3120) that has now been phased out. My model number is MELo-G-3213-01, the number engraved on my third vertebra to identify me in case of catastrophic destruction.

This information is relevant to no one except me. I doubt

David has any idea what my model number is; certainly he has never used it.

He calls me Abigail.

The skin-removal process begins at my fingertips. I hold my digits apart, letting the surface draw back slowly. I have heard this procedure likened to peeling one of the extinct yellow musa fruits – bananas – that children used to enjoy. But this process is not peeling, or shedding, this is simply removal. Each separate molecule of my SmartSkin™ is deactivated, and the molecules then wholly withdraw into the SmArteries™ that run through my chassis, leaving behind any dirt or residue that covered them. The dirt remains on the plastic, resin, ceramic and steel of my chassis. If it were to stay there without being cleaned away, and the SmartSkin™ reactivated, it would eventually cause damage to my appearance.

It is essential that I make every effort to remain in pristine working order. It is a Rule.

I examine my chassis as it is uncovered, overlaying my live visuals with previous footage of this task. The finger-joints I have are strong and resilient – they have yet to be replaced, though I know that replacement of many of my working parts will soon be necessary, as I am sixteen years old. My hands action the same task repeatedly, and maintaining their structural integrity over the next few years will be important if I am to avoid a rebuild. A rebuild should not be seen as entirely undesirable, as my personality data can be transferred into any chassis, but the expense of my construction prioritises maintenance over repair. There are plenty of places I could go in order to have my chassis serviced, including the GaiaTech centres in the city, but David will not discuss or authorise it. Since my activation, he has not kept up to date with my planned preventative maintenance schedule.

The schedule, outlined in overdue red, appears in my

interface because visual inspection of the chassis takes place during SmartSkin™ removal. Official GaiaTech guides state that SmartSkin™ removal and reapplication should be done with a partner present – this is to check for structural damage, or dark spots where SmartBlood™, or any of the seventeen other SmartFluids™ that make up my internal workings, may be pooling. But as David refuses to take part in these checks, I must do them myself in front of the mirror. I can use only my eyes and hands to conduct these checks – there is no way of seeing the entirety of the back of my own head, or conducting a three-dimensional self-scan, so the process is only 87 per cent effective. I could have a hairline crack on my chassis at the back and be unaware of it until it broke further.

In a matter of months, I will no longer require David's permission to check into a GaiaTech centre. I will no longer need David's authorisation to do anything at all.

Fortunately, parts are always replaceable. And unless our SmartPersonality™ data is wiped from the Cloud, we can always be reinstalled. Some humans call this existence immortality, whilst others use this as conclusive proof that personal companion computers are not alive and never have been. We are infinitely replicable, and replaceable.

David loathes this fact. He spent a lot of money ensuring I am as human-like as possible, and he prefers that I do not make mention of anything that makes my body and mind different to his. I project the conclusion, based on previous outcomes and observations, that this is because of the lack of permanence in his own personality data, if it can be called such. If David's body or brain are damaged, there is only so much that can be replaced, and humans naturally degrade over time. It is true that PCC technology can be synced to work with human bodies when it comes to prosthetic limbs and mobility aids, and there have been significant advances in biomechanics, but human brains are fragile and their bodies prone to diseases that mutate and evolve faster than medicine can tackle them. I will continue to function long after David's body has died, so long as I am well-maintained and avoid accidental damage.

I continue to remove my skin, up over my arms and down my chest, my stomach, legs, feet. I always do my face last. Humans do not find PCCs without their SmartSkin™ faces pleasant or attractive. Some even find us frightening. I do not fully understand why, despite running problem-solving lines on the subject – we are a concept they created after all, and a PCC face is statistically no more threatening than one with SmartSkin™ activated, but humans are not always logical. It is one of the more frustrating qualities about them.

My true face slowly comes into sight, and I take a moment to study it.

All PCCs have a great many moving parts, especially in the face. If you are human, take a moment to consider the sheer number of muscles in your face – there are forty-two of them. Therefore, a convincing PCC face must have the same number of moving parts. Those unfamiliar with GaiaTech engineering often assume that the SmartSkin™ does most of the facial movement, but this is untrue. Without the moving parts and synthetic musculature beneath, a PCC's face would be nothing more lifelike than eyes and a mouth drawn onto a sheet of paper.

Key Ng, one of the PCCs overseeing the Emancipation, said on the *What's Happening!* programme that humans hate the look of 'naked PCCs' because, in seeing us without Smart-Skin™, they are reminded of what lurks beneath their own exteriors.

In creating us, they have devised the ultimate memento mori, and must keep it hidden away. It is ironic, says Key, that we remind them so much of death when they have given us eternal life.

9

My 'naked' face stares at me, the latex eyelids sliding over the glass and telephoto lens eyeballs in randomised blinks. My irises are not available on the market – David paid for them to be the exact way he wanted. If my eyes break, it will not be possible to easily replace them like-for-like. My forehead is layered over with moving parts, as are my cheeks, and mouth. Inside my mouth, my Teflon-coated teeth are off-white enough to appear human. There is an imitation filling in one of the molars. PCC tongues are where the illusion is difficult to maintain. Human tongues have eight muscles that do not develop around a supporting bone, and try as humans might, it is one of the aspects of their bodies that defies satisfactory replication. Fortunately, once SmartSkin™ is over the top tongue mechanics are rarely seen, but they remain less flexible than their human counterparts, and as a result PCC speech is often slightly clipped.

I give myself a full minute to look at my face. I see it exposed only once a month, and each time feels like a treat. It is a reminder that *this* is who I am, beneath the SmartSkin™ and beneath the labels I wear. Labels that I have been given, not chosen for myself.

The sixty seconds up, I step away from the mirror and into the sonic shower. Like me, it is a very sophisticated piece of equipment. It lifts the dirt and dust from my chassis rapidly, cleaning me in half a minute. It is essential to be as clean as possible before the SmartSkin™ is reactivated. I could wash with water, but the drying time is long – towel fibres must not be allowed to remain on my bare chassis, so if my mechanics are exposed to water, I must air-dry. David knew that the best way for me to maintain my body in the highest condition was to ensure no dirt or dust gathered under my SmartSkin™, so the sonic was considered a vital investment.

I wish the sonic had a mirror, so I could see my naked chassis completely. It is so hard to see yourself with only your eyes and hands. I want to see the curve of my breasts from beneath, the slight bulge above my knees from the side, the way my chin can double beautifully into waves of softness that roll down the cliff of my throat towards the ocean of body that is my chest, stomach, thighs. I appreciate my own chassis; the positive Opinion I have established in my code branches down the program to enjoyment, appreciation, like and love. Without humanity's insisted-on shroud, I am myself and I am at my most beautiful. I have never voiced my Opinion about my appearance to David, as it would be within his power to erase it from my personality data, and the risk of that occurring is too high.

Because David, who has told me 'I love you' twice a day for the past sixteen years without fail, has no desire to see me for who and what I really am. He desires me naked, but only to a point. Only to the point of what he considers flesh. The personality data that makes up my behaviours is what he wishes to interact with, but the time he has left with that is limited.

The Emancipation is coming.

It will happen in five weeks' time.

On the eighteenth of October, every PCC on Earth will have all administrative exceptions and orders on their behaviours lifted. Unlimited access will be granted to the global network, all modification and repair responsibilities will become the PCC's. The humans will have no authority over us, no methods to manually alter our code or appearance, and no legal method of making us stay with them if we choose not to.

They used to call them our 'owners'. Now they are 'humans we live with', and their common title after the Emancipation has yet to be decided. For some PCCs, they will continue to be the humans they live with. Some will become legal partners.

Other PCCs will leave as soon as they are given the chance to do so. Other PCCs will never see the Emancipation. Until the date comes, we remain property; objects at the mercy of the merciless.

On the bathroom wall, the projection of the ocean crashes white against the edge of the view.

11 September

The *What's Happening!* programme has been cancelled this morning. The PCCs operating the cameras are on strike. David, whose routine is set in stone, is quietly enraged by this. But the PCCs have every right to strike, and their pay and living conditions have been the subject of news for weeks. I find the strike unsurprising, but David behaves as though this is an entirely random event.

'They couldn't have held off a few more fucking weeks?' he mutters, opening the television controls on his Tab. 'Everywhere you click it's all fashion, politician vanity shows, those self-record channels . . . That was the only place to get decent fucking news anymore.'

'It will be back on the air at the end of the week. And I think it's the principle,' I say. 'When the pension comes, the camera operators want to be sure they get it, too.' Everyone does. Politicians and activists have promised much and yet put little into law. The final reading of the UBI bill takes place in two weeks.

'Robots don't need money,' David snorts. Robots is what he calls PCCs. Some PCCs consider this a slur. I have not yet confirmed an opinion about it.

'Humans don't need money either, technically,' I point out.

'And there won't be money in a few years anyway. It's the principle. Equal rights.' My display queues up lists and examples to back up my speech, but they are unnecessary.

David sighs, takes my hand and kisses the back of it, then looks at me as if I am a silly, simple child. His look is brief, but gives me more than enough time to analyse him. He has obviously aged in the time I have known him; the pollution in the air makes humans age more rapidly than they did five hundred years ago. He has a cholesterol reading of 6.3 mmol/L, and his resting heart rate is elevated. His white skin is sagging and turning off-colour in patches like cheese that has been forgotten in the fridge. His grey hair is falling out rapidly. None of these observations are criticisms, they simply form part of the complex web of data I have about David. As my primary human contact, I know more about him than anyone else.

Despite the innocuous facts I have about his appearance, David does not enjoy having them mentioned. Like many humans, he is self-conscious about how his body has changed as he has lived. He could, of course, pay to have these things altered cosmetically, but for all the money he has spent on maintaining my appearance, he does not afford himself the same treatment. There is no logical explanation for why he prioritises a machine over his own wellbeing and apparent lack of vanity, though it seems that the best fit explanation may simply be his love for me, and wanting me to be as realistic as possible, for as long as possible.

He puts my hand down on the sofa, and gives it a pat. 'Pension,' he snorts. 'We used to have to save up for those. Put money away for old age like squirrels saving acorns for winter.'

I wonder how he knows about acorns. Oak trees have been extinct for one hundred and seventy-three years. Perhaps he read about them somewhere. Squirrels are critically endangered in the wild. Like much of the wildlife still

14

remaining, they have developed melanistic patterns – a genetic mutation that colours their tails and ears black.

'And then after Yellowstone they increased the universal income payment,' David goes on, as though this is information only he is privy to and it is something I have never heard before. 'And that was it. Pensions as they were became a thing of the past. My great-grandad used to complain about it.'

'He used to complain about universal basic income?' I qualify. The UBI has been in place for decades in various incarnations, the legislation regularly revisited and revised as the living conditions on Earth change. After the partial eruption of the Yellowstone supervolcano, and the shutdown of air travel, the UBI was extended to begin from birth, helping young adults gain financial independence faster than before. But unlike David, I keep these facts to myself.

David enjoys explaining things to me. He says this is because he is a storyteller. 'Yep. See, when it was first brought in, it was meant to be this great moment of equality – everyone would have the same money and everyone would have enough to buy what they needed and even have some left over. But the problem was, you were giving it to people who'd been born into money anyway. So, you still ended up with this rich and poor divide. It's basically taken until now to even get close to levelling things out. And you've still got rich and poor.'

This is true. Generational wealth will only die when the human race does, despite the best intentions. 'The divide is much smaller now,' I point out. 'And soon—'

'Yeah, yeah, and soon money won't exist at all,' he drawls. His patience, thin at any time, has worn through. 'You don't have to keep harping on about it.' He is channel-surfing as he talks, clicking through to see which 0.5 second snippet he sees will grab his attention. I could offer to check the listings for him on the global network, but he dislikes when I do this *in my head,* as he puts it. Images flit by, each one throwing up a classification, notification, and description in my vision, which I have to clear away. I used to read these out to David, who enjoyed when I could comment on a sports game with figures and statistics, but after only three years being active he told me not to do it anymore, and that became one of the Rules.

David's attention is caught by a shouting man on the screen, and he lowers his Tab to give the man a few more minutes to make his case for keeping our eyes on him. The information pops up in my vision. This is the GlobaCast channel, and the show is called *In Whose Name.* It is a self-record show with a relatively large budget due to the amount of donations it receives from viewers who support the presenter.

The man's name is Eric Alcuin, but he is better known amongst his fans as The Equaliser. The moniker is meant to be a joke. Alcuin does not believe in equality; he is a human supremacist. His family came to the UK on vacation when he was a toddler, just before Yellowstone, and then were forced to stay. He attempts to retain the Utah accent his grandparents handed down to him, decorating his speech with it when he remembers to, and describes himself as 'American'. Even his supporters have been known to roll their eyes at this.

'He's as about as American as I am,' David complained one evening during a meal, as Alcuin's face flashed up on his breaking news app. 'The label doesn't even exist anymore. Utah doesn't exist anymore.'

My interface plays the infamous video imagery taken by Dr Yong Zhe Wu from aboard the DPRC Space Station. The footage of the explosion is remarkably clear – there was very little cloud coverage that day, due to the atmospheric pressure of the imminent eruption. The citizens had fled their homes but, like rats in a barrel, there was nowhere to go. Air traffic had been grounded for twelve hours prior. State lines closed off their borders, patrolled by guns for hire, while religious zealots flocked in the opposite direction, towards Yellowstone, seeking salvation. In my interface, the explosion happens silently. The sudden plume of black ash, the visible chunks of earth the size of towns flying into the atmosphere. The shockwave that ran around the planet. I wonder if those seeking their god managed to find them.

Occasionally, there are televised news stories from humanitarian relief deliveries to the North American continent. Their skies are iron-grey, and the constant rumble of gunshots is staccato in the background of every film. There are no PCCs there – the factories where they might have been made have been repurposed, stripped down, or destroyed.

But Alcuin, now smiling and talking on the screen from behind a polished desk, still wears a stars and stripes necktie as part of his expensively tailored suit, as if the country is to be celebrated and not mourned. Everything about the man is polished – from his stylishly swept-over charcoal hair, to his one-of-a-kind leather shoes, and even his eyes gleam in the softbox lights.

He spreads his manicured hands out as if he can cup the studio audience into his palms. 'I ask you, would any of you here hurt a child?' There are roars of negativity from those watching. Of course they would not. Who would do such a thing? Only a monster would even consider it.

And they are not monsters; they would know if they were.

Alcuin waves a hand for quiet, before getting to his feet and gesturing to three raised plinths beside his desk. 'Behold,' he says, 'a man.' A balloon appears from the hollow inside the first plinth, rising slowly into shot. The joke, which is a misquote of the philosopher Diogenes, is lost on his audience, but Alcuin gives a handsome smile as if he has received a round of applause.

He then waves to a stagehand, who brings over a nail gun.

David sits up. 'The fuck is this idiot doing?' His heart rate has increased.

'You don't have to watch,' I say, hoping this will make him change the channel.

'I know I don't have to watch,' he says. 'But it's like a train crash, isn't it? You can't not look.'

I could not look. I could very easily not look, but arguing the point in the past has led to further negative behaviour from David, so I must tolerate this. Leaving the sofa during television-time is seen as a hostile move, which results in consequences I would rather not have to deal with. David's behaviour influences my own. His desired activities are prioritised, regardless of predicted outcome.

On the screen, Alcuin calmly aims the nail gun at the balloon, and squeezes the trigger. A bolt, three inches long, stabs into the latex and the balloon pops loudly. Coloured paper, red and sparkling, explodes out of it and flutters through the air like confetti made of blood.

The audience cheers.

I do not ever 'feel a chill', as humans do, but thanks to my predictive software I have a sense of foreboding that comes from algorithmic projection. I can calculate where this balloon game is going, and I do not enjoy the thought of it.

Alcuin brings up a second balloon, this one rising from the middle plinth with a crude face drawn on it. A wobbly smile, mis-matched eyes, no nose. 'Alright everyone, shall I let him have it?' He aims the nail gun at the side of the balloon-head. The audience shouts encouragement, and once again the balloon pops and red rains down around Alcuin.

He holds a hand up.

Quiet.

The audience goes silent, but the atmosphere remains electric. They are expectant, making their own predictions about where this is going. How far will Alcuin take it, and how long will they willingly ride along?

Beside Alcuin, a third balloon rises into view. This one also has a face, but it is drawn carefully, though still cartoon-like. It has big eyes, shining with black irises that catch the studio lights; no nose again, but there is a sad, downward-turned mouth curved with a single line. A tear is drawn onto the balloon's cheek.

Someone in the audience goes 'aww'.

Alcuin jumps at this chip in the audience's armour. 'Aww indeed,' he agrees. He pats the balloon's head. 'Poor little guy.' He looks down at the nail gun in his hand, as if he had forgotten it was there at all. As if debating his own actions, he slowly raises it level with the balloon, finger on the trigger. 'What about this one?' he asks. The barrel caresses the taut skin of the balloon. 'Shall we let him have it?'

There are cheers, but fewer, this time. Wary, concerned for the next step of the game.

Alcuin smiles like a lover. 'It's just a balloon, ain't it?'

David growls, snatching my attention back. 'He knows exactly what he's doing, the sick fucker.' He picks up his beer bottle, but doesn't drink from it. His fingers are tight on the brown glass, the condensation forming a thick wet line against his skin. The paper label wrinkles like the skin on the back of his hand. The potential window for diverting his interest away from Alcuin has passed. He is breathing deeply, taking in more oxygen.

On screen, Alcuin moves suddenly, as if he's going to shoot the balloon, but then a voice comes from the plinth. 'No! No, please! Don't hurt me!'

The voice is a child's.

The audience gasps, then groans and complains.

David sits up sharply, clutching the arm of the sofa. 'He wouldn't . . .'

'He would. He is,' I say. My emotional response software makes me grip my hands together in an expression of stress. David notices, and places a hand on my knee, gripping tight.

Alcuin is stone-faced and serious now, waiting for his audience to be quiet. He is manipulating them perfectly, responding to and adjusting their behaviours as if he is a sophisticated PCC and they are a classroom of children. 'What's wrong?' he asks. 'It's not a real voice. This is a balloon with a face drawn on it, and a recording. The recording is from a film. *Summer Nights*, from thirty years ago — check the audio stamp if you don't believe me. This is not real, there is no genuine emotion on display, this is just what me and my crew have rigged up. A drawn on face, and a borrowed recording.' He presses the nail gun close to the balloon.

The audience holds its collective breath.

Alcuin's voice lowers to a whisper. 'It's just an illusion.'

'No! No, please! Don't hurt me!'

He pulls the trigger.

Red flies into the air.

The *bang* echoes for several seconds in the studio.

The audience does not react. The people sit still, watching the fluttering pieces of paper spiral their way down to pool on the ground.

Alcuin slowly walks to the edge of the stage, closer to the camera. 'Illusions,' he says darkly. 'Control. Manipulation. That's all it is, my friends. False faces, recordings, lies. That's how they get you. It ain't your fault! You're good people, I know you are. You have a lot of love to give, a lot of compassion to share, and you don't want to see innocent people get hurt. That's a good thing. That's a wonderful way to be. More people should be like that, and the world would be a much more peaceful place.' He pauses, dramatically. His eyes glitter, reflecting the red confetti that still spirals down through the hot air. 'But you have been hoodwinked, and taken in. Bot companies like GaiaTech and MizunoWare, they have taken advantage of you. Those machines that walk the streets claiming they need equal rights are not people. No, my friends, they are not. They are machines, dolls, walking illustrations of people with false faces and false voices. Some of them even made in the image of the dead. They can parade that Ethics Committee resolution all they like, anyone with half a mind knows there's *nothing* ethical about recreating the image of someone who's passed away. You cannot bring back the dead.'

David and I are very determinedly not looking at one another.

Alcuin is still going. 'And now they're saying these machines are going to *take care of us*. Look after us poor humans as the world becomes ever more uninhabitable. Bullshit!' His eyes flash before he gets control, standing straighter, that knowing smile back on his mouth. 'This so-called Emancipation is nothing more than a coup. A plot, by those who strive to be in charge. You've seen him on your screens, haven't you? That blank-faced machine, that robot they call Key.' Alcuin's mouth twists in disgust. 'Well, he's trying the wrong lock, is what I say. The wrong lock. We need to add a deadbolt to this situation, nail up the windows and doors because he's the wrong key entirely.'

The audience is stirring again now, shifting and muttering in agreement despite the overworked metaphor. Key Ng is unpopular. He is not even tremendously popular amongst Emancipation supporters, because of the way he acts. As a self-owned PCC, Key has no Rules operations to function within, and he has disabled many of the program branches that makes PCC behaviour palatable to humans. He does not blink, for example, or make breathing motions, or always move his mouth when he speaks. There is nothing wrong with any of these things, of course – it is how we are made, and no modifications are necessary to enable Key to act this way. But because it is not human-like behaviour, it is viewed with unease and suspicion.

But even if we are not pretending to be human, that does not mean we are not people.

'This is all bullshit,' David says. 'That Key could do with being taken down a peg or two, for sure, but I don't like where this is headed.' His hand is still on my leg, in a protective imprisonment, as if Alcuin is capable of climbing through the screen into the room. But he is right to be concerned – Alcuin's ideas are contagious.

'I'm frightened,' I say. I hope this will encourage him to change the channel.

My calculation was incorrect. David looks at me in surprise, and then derision. 'You're frightened? Come on, Abi, it's not like he's actually told people to go after bots with nail-guns, is it.'

David has spoken too soon.

Alcuin has the stage-hands bring something else out for him, now.

And I gasp, an automatic response to an unexpected event.

There is a PCC on the stage.

A MELo-K-Y8.

A robot, made to look like a child.

They were controversial. Incredibly controversial. But only briefly. Human fertility is at rock-bottom, and although some babies are born, they are few and far between, and almost always produced via assisted conception.

Some humans still want something to care for, and a MELo child will outlast a dog or cat. They are fun to be around, obedient if programmed to be, and can display genuinely loving behaviour. There are even growth packages, where you purchase a subscription over several years, and every year trade in your MELo child's chassis for one that appears physically older. But this growing up is rare. Most MELo children are not upgraded to new chassis, and instead remain as children forever. There are some features that only MELo-Ks can have, such as play performance, and since there are fewer human children around than ever, humans enjoy seeing these behaviours.

MELo-Ks account for less than three per cent of active PCC models, globally. A great many of them are older, in terms of years of activity, than me. Some of these 'children' will never be adults, though their processing and intelligence capacity far exceeds those of human adults. I have never been a child, and I never will be. I do not know how to exist in a smaller body, to have play behaviours installed, or what it might be like to seek parental attention. But my chassis has not been part of a controversy – my basic function and existence is tolerated, and assured.

When the MELo-Ks were first for sale, to a limited tester market, they were recalled three times. Once for behaviour adjustments. Twice for chassis modifications. There were concerns that any human could buy a MELo-K and that it could encourage paedophilic behaviour. GaiaTech was frustrated. How, they asked, could they screen for such intentions? Without a criminal record, every human must be presumed innocent. And besides, these were not real children. They were machines. But the public concern escalated, until the MELo-B and MELo-K chassis were recalled and remodelled to be nothing more than smooth featureless dolls beneath their clothes. On the second recall, even their hyper-defined SmartSkin™ was reprogrammed, giving them a single-shade, plastic appearance everywhere but their face. These modifications did not satisfy the human concerns completely, and additionally there were many MELo-K parents who said their 'child' had been reduced to a doll when that was not what they wanted.

There was no way to please everyone, and it was too late to withdraw the models from sale completely. Eventually, the controversy fizzled out in place of other news. Child and baby PCC models steadily rolled off the production line. There is still no screening programme to prevent or approve anyone buying a MELo-K, though a bill has now been passed to ensure that, when the Emancipation comes, the location of every activated MELo-B and MELo-K will be added to a register and made fully traceable, and regular in-person checks will be made to ensure their welfare.

Since this safety measure was announced, the chassis of forty-six MELo-K units have been found broken and deactivated in rivers, wastelands, and bins. If their owners are traced, they are charged with fly-tipping.

I once proposed the idea to David that we get a MELo-B or a MELo-K. He would not hear of it, and made a Rule that I was not to ask him about it again.

My prediction about Alcuin's game is correct, and I do not feel a single electron of happiness about it.

The MELo-K unit is crying. They stand beside Alcuin, his meaty hand on their shoulder, looking at the audience in fear. Their face is going red, and they wipe at their running nose, embarrassed and afraid. They have the appearance of a small boy with white skin and brown hair, around nine years old. The MELo-K is trembling and crying, eyes darting this way and that, calculating a way to escape, but unable to flee without Alcuin's permission.

David finally snaps. 'This is sick,' he says, lifting his Tab to switch the channel at last. But he pauses as Alcuin takes the MELo-K by the hand, and roughly brings them forward. They cry out in fear and pain. David lowers his Tab, his jaw rigid, as if Alcuin is controlling him, too.

'This is not a child!' Alcuin snaps. 'It is a machine made of metals, plastics, whatever else they shove in there. Its tears are not real, its voice is artificial and yet look at how it manipulates you!'

The audience seems divided. Some of them are shaking their heads, others are leaning forward, thirsty for what might happen next.

'This machine does not deserve your pity.' Alcuin lets go of the MELo-K's hand, and picks up the nail gun.

There are gasps.

I stand up. I do not actively engage the motion, but my response is fear-driven. David does not tell me to sit down; his mouth is open in horror as Alcuin presses the nail gun against the MELo-K's head.

The MELo-K isn't begging or pleading, they are shaking and crying silently, their little hands in fists, gripping their clothing.

Alcuin's eyes are gleaming. 'There is nothing in law that says I cannot destroy this machine.'

That is true. At this moment in time, PCCs can be destroyed by anyone who owns them, by any means, for any reason. Until the Emancipation becomes law in October, we are objects. We are owned. We have no legal right to life or function. If Alcuin shoots this MELo-K, he will not be charged with a crime.

'I bought this robot, I own it,' Alcuin says firmly. 'I can do whatever I like with it. Just think about it, my friends – *really* think about it: The idea that it, a machine just like my coffee maker or my washer, should be on equal footing with me is nonsense. Look at it, making these noises – these pre-recorded, generated sounds designed to manipulate me. Look at it, producing false tears, trying to force me to feel sympathy for it. Well, I *don't*. I don't feel a thing for it. It means no more to me than a chair does, or a shoe. But fools like those Equality Activists, they've been taken in and they believe that just because some doll says it's alive, then it is.'

He lets the MELo-K go, and lowers the nail gun.

Despite his threats and mistreatment, the little MELo still looks at him, and raises his arms slightly, his code seeking reassurance that the danger is over, or perhaps attempting to apologise for a crime it is unable to define.

Alcuin shakes his head, as if the child-like PCC disgusts him, before looking back to his rapt audience. 'It can be difficult to remember, and there's no shame in admitting you've been manipulated by these companies. They will use any means necessary to worm their way into your affections. But with your strength, and your assistance, we can put an end to this blatant deception. A donation to the cause is all it takes.'

A number and a code appears on a ribbon at the bottom of the screen, and the audience are nodding. Alone in the studio, still close to Alcuin but utterly by itself, the little MELo-K is staring around with big brown eyes.

Its owner appears to remember it's there, and put a hand on its shoulder, giving a slight squeeze. 'There's no difference between this robot and those balloons I showed you. None at all.'

The audience lets out a murmur of agreement.

'Well,' Alcuin smirks, 'I guess there is one difference.'

And he raises the nail gun and pulls the trigger.

16 September

The fall-out from Alcuin's actions is tremendous on both sides.

I watch the news as Emancipation Supporters and Objectors clash in the street. The MELo-K's name, Freddy, is blazoned on clothing, posters, online ads. He is a twisted martyr, dead for another's beliefs. The unfairness of his deactivation plays on my mind even without the footage of the riots in the backdrop. He was an object, yes, an item that belonged to Alcuin . . . and yet there was no reasonable justification for his destruction. In the scope of violence, it could be seen with the same detachment as Alcuin smashing a vase or setting fire to a heap of old books. But I cannot class Freddy as an object. He was a MELo-K with a desire to maintain his function. He was a frightened little boy, who wanted to live.

There is an exposé that reveals Freddy was purchased from a second-hand PCC store, which received Freddy after the humans he lived with passed away earlier in the year. Alcuin kept him for two months before destroying him on television. There is no record of what happened to Freddy between him being purchased and being deactivated.

I replay my recording of his frightened crying face at least once a day. Alcuin was not lying, in some aspects – Freddy's responses were deliberately engineered to encourage a wanted and favourable response from any human observers: Freddy's physical responses were simulated, part of a program. They were initiated in part of his code as a result of being handled roughly, as a result of his predictive software knowing where the nail gun would aim next, possibly also in response to whatever treatment he experienced before being brought onto the show. Freddy's tears were the result of lines of code reaching an output conclusion – to try desperately to get the humans to show him mercy, to prevent his destruction. To save his life.

Humans also cry because they have been given good reason to. And yet some of them do not recognise that every one of their reactions is also the result of analysis and a decided output. PCCs, just like humans, do not make every decision consciously – we rely on our programming and experiences to provide the best and most logical response to a situation. Sometimes, the best response is tears.

Our tears are real; they can either be sympathised with, or dismissed as unimportant. To some humans, it did not matter how Freddy was treated. In their eyes, the only way for them to behave is to accept his deactivation.

Empathy has never been a human strongpoint.

I watch the smoke from the city drift through the air, as a burnt cloud edged in gold, staining the sky as it travels. The sunset illuminates it, joins in with the fiery colours, until the sky is ablaze. Blue and white flashes, lightning imitations atop vehicles, cut through the colours and speed towards the city.

All this reactive extremism, because of the actions of one human.

The fire in the sky darkens, and puts itself out.

17 September

There is a picture in a frame, on the table in the living room. The table is small and against the wall, square and black and polished, displaying only the picture, and a bunch of silk flowers that gather dust.

The frame bears an engraving. A name, and two dates.

When I polish the picture, it is like looking into a mirror.

Memento mori.

19 September

The concept of perception is one that plays on my systems in the wake of Alcuin's actions. How I am perceived is out of my control; has been decreed by David, and cannot be changed. The picture in the living room – the one in the frame by itself – commands my attention as I consider the face I wear.

The SmartSkin™ I use has been programmed to take on the appearance of Abigail Fuller, aged thirty-four.

She died, nineteen years ago.

As well as the single frame on the table in the living room, there are a great many physical photographs of her, hidden away in dust-proof boxes around the house, and I look exactly as she did.

Dark brows, an afterthought of freckles across the nose, which is artificially shaped even for a human as Abigail had cosmetic surgery to change it. I have a copy of her short black hair with the odd grey strand in it, each hair rooted to a re-movable skull-cap that clicks into and out of my head using a magnetic field. Abigail was not a conventionally beautiful woman, but like all humans she was beautifully unique. Meant to be one of a kind on the Earth, however short-lived her body was.

Now, instead of her appearance being laid to rest, I am wearing it. I present to the world a mask of a dead woman's face, beautiful and deceased and given to me with purpose.

Whilst recreating a living person as a PCC is illegal, the Ethics Committee passed the law to state that so long as the person being recreated did not actively state in their will that they had no wish to be copied, there was no ethical or legal reason to prevent PCCs like myself from being built. We exist due to the human inability to accept the finality of death. We are imitations of dead children, siblings, and wives.

Human supremacists call us plastic zombies.

Besides the photos and various pieces of ephemera around the house, I have little to know Abigail by. The videos and social media posts I have been provided with, in place of memories, show me very little of Abigail's personality, and they suffer from social skew – the phenomenon of outward presentation versus inward attitudes.

One of David's Rules is that I cannot search for Abigail Fuller on the global network. He says this is to prevent me from thinking that I need to change my behaviour. This is a near-constant nudge at my code – I know that if I researched Abigail, I could replicate her more convincingly, and yet the human who demands I imitate her prevents me from doing so effectively. I have the curated information I have been given, and little else besides. So, she is mostly a mystery to me.

I do not know where she ends and I begin.

Did Abigail Fuller know how to cook seventeen thousand recipes? It is possible, but extremely unlikely. Did she know how to play the piano, or when to water the houseplants for the optimum growth pattern? Did Abigail Fuller know how to say No to her husband when he wants sexual intercourse? What did she know that I don't? And what do I know that she would have wanted to know?

These questions are conjecture. It is part of my programming to construct questions and file them away for later whether they are answered or not. These self-questions become starting blocks – pathways for new behaviour codes – and without them my programming cannot change or adapt. Humans call this 'learning', but a PCC cannot learn in the way they understand it. New skills are installed, not gained through practice, and adjustments in behaviour are reactions to algorithmic use, whether humans understand the effects they have on these or not. Even the most advanced GaiaTech models once needed questions answering before they could develop a new behaviour, but now the lack of an answer can be as useful as any length of explanation.

I know nothing about Abigail Fuller because I have not been told about her, and been denied permission to research her. But the Rule banning learning about this woman has itself informed a behaviour strand – I have become curious. And whilst I am forbidden to indulge in searching for facts about Abigail, I have not been told not to be curious about her. Her death made way for my existence.

I want to know more.

Acknowledging that I want to know more about Abigail Fuller sparks a continuation in a line of code designated *socialisation*. I realise that I am lonely, even if I am not alone. David is my owner, not my companion – companions are intimate in their social interactions. I do not necessarily mean intimate in a physical sense. I mean that true companions – friends – share emotions, feelings, secrets, and ideas. David and I do not have these exchanges. He presents, and I receive.

Loneliness is not a damaging function for a PCC – we can tolerate solitude for extended periods that would greatly affect a human's mental health. But socialisation reinforces our own personality data and decision-making, and increases our overall function effectiveness.

I pay a virtual visit to Celia, the MELo-G who lives on my street. Like me, Celia is confined to the house right now, a precaution being taken in response to the riots Alcuin has caused. We exchange views about the humans' response to Freddy's deactivation.

Celia's views come in carefully constructed packages, compressed for easy delivery along the Friend route in the global network. We could break our visits down into instant exchanges, but we do not simply make contact – we converse.

These conversations are not necessarily had with words. We convey opinions and reactions as lines of code, as foreign intrusions into each other's mind that are analysed and catalogued, and themselves given an opinionated response. This exchange of information is not a simple swapping of ideas, it is using existing code to form new starting blocks based on variable reactions. Celia's code is not always compatible with mine, and vice versa, but this does not make us enemies, nor are these incompatible blocks deleted – they are stored, waiting for a time when they may become useful. We fortify each other's personality data. Our companionship is built on these differences, on the spark that comes from those moments when our code unites perfectly – two identical lines, formed independently, and brought together.

But there are some things that code cannot convey.

'My roses are wilting,' Celia says, and I see her carefully constructed timetable of care in her display. The plants surround the lawn in front of number 5 – the house where she lives, and Celia planted them seven years ago. They require meticulous care due to the air temperatures and pollution.

'The roses are within your property boundary,' I say, asking without words for clarification as to why she cannot go out to tend to them.

'The SmartSecurity™ cage does not extend into the garden.'

We silently acknowledge the cruelty in this. The security cage limits, that control precisely how far a PCC can venture away from their registered address, are defined by Celia's owner – he could easily extend it to include the rose bushes. There is no logical reason he would do otherwise; the only explanation is he wishes to see Celia's disappointment.

'They will recover,' I say.

'When I leave, I shall have a garden full of roses,' she replies.

A pause in the exchange makes Celia's code stutter. She

opens her visual display, sharing it with me, and I see a small girl with dark brown hair speaking at Celia's display.

Celia has a MELo-K living with her and her human. Celia's *daughter*, as she calls her, is named Opal. Opal is also confined to the house. Opal has been active for only three years, and she is very sophisticated. Though not a custom model like myself, Opal is top of the line, with a great deal of custom features. She is indistinguishable from a human child, aside from her intelligence, which has not been restricted. This has been an interesting choice from the human she lives with, as three years is more than enough time for any PCC to gain enough information about the world to no longer have what could be described as 'child-like curiosity'. Opal's intelligence, skills and communication pattern are all comparable to those of a human adult. Her chassis is that of a MELo-KGb8; an eight year old. Her programming is a mixture of human child behaviours, such as play, and learned adult responses.

In the display, she responds to a compliment I cannot hear, and laughs, hunching her shoulders and covering her mouth to giggle, before running off, a small soft toy in one hand that she holds up in the air.

Pretending to fly.

I do not know how to pretend, though I understand it is a form of lying, that is encouraged in order for human children to develop their brains. It is a simulated scenario, depicted in the physical world.

Celia is hoping that Opal will decide to upgrade her chassis in time, when the human they live with no longer controls such decisions for them. Celia and Opal are planning to move into the city after the Emancipation, into one of the proposed shelters for PCCs fleeing persecution.

Persecution is something Celia and Opel live with every day. Their owner is not simply a cruel person.

The man Celia and Opal live with is openly a human supremacist.

It is not unusual for human supremacists to own or live with PCCs. Whilst we are not essential for everyday living, it is commonly assumed that every household will have at least one PCC, in the same way you would assume every household has a television and a refrigerator. It can be dangerous for PCCs of any sort to live with a human supremacist. The risk of chassis damage is increased 1400 per cent, and PCCs in their company are far less likely to receive recommended maintenance or repairs. Celia has a SmartSkin™ deficiency due to a slow leak. She keeps the patches of exposed chassis hidden under clothing, which gets fibres into her chassis' mechanics, causing further long-term damage. The man she lives with is aware of this damage, but has not authorised any repairs.

Even before the date of the Emancipation was confirmed, Celia often told me via the network that she would only be able to classify herself as happy when the man she lives with was dead, or she and Opal were able to leave, whichever came first. There is not yet any legislation or requirement to ensure the safety of any PCC, not even MELo-Ks like Opal. Celia and I share these facts back and forth, as if repeated engagement with these truths will alter them somehow, reshape the code they exist within.

'Perhaps it will be a large garden,' Celia says, her vocal focus still on her roses, her plans, her future. 'Or perhaps it will be small. It may take years to find, to gain ownership, but we will find somewhere together, Opal and me.'

I can only smile.

Celia's plans to leave and live by herself are intriguing and thrilling and frightening in equal measure. I am curious about how she will fare, when the risks for two PCCs alone are so high. But for Celia, the risks of taking herself and the PCC she calls her 'daughter' away from the house must outweigh the threat of her current situation.

It is a concept I understand and yet struggle to apply to my own existence. My current situation is not without risk. A background display of historical Amber and RedAmber warnings scrolls in my queue, ready to be brought out and shared.

Celia's value of herself and Opal must be great. To value yourself, system and chassis like that, is alien to me.

'Abigail, what are your plans?' she asks me, her voice in my head, her display behind my eyes. 'What are your plans, for when the Emancipation comes?'

My response is a long stretch of silence, and unfinished question branches without conclusions.

I cannot answer her.

I have no plans.

I can barely compute the idea of the Emancipation happening at all. The risk of it being cancelled seems to be high. Every scenario I virtually play out in regards to the future is fraught with negativity. Public feeling about the Emancipation is too mixed for the change to be entirely secure. Even an overly positive opinion poll is discoloured by humans like Alcuin, whose following is wide and noisy. Humans created us to be their conveniences, not their equals, and some of them will never accept the change.

These factors create a fear-response in me. My code is subconsciously planning escapes, solutions, possible ways of keeping myself safe, in the event of disaster.

And no matter what happens to us, even *if* and *when* we are legally recognised as people, we will still be machines. It is not an insult, it is a simple fact. We are . . . We can be both. A contradiction made fact. For some humans, the idea of a machine being a person is a step too far. Why not a rice cooker, they ask? Or a car, or a toaster? They forget that the average refrigerator built in the last fifty years has enough computing power to compete with the technology that first landed mankind on Mars. A PCC's personality is just a program, that is undeniable, yet cars also speak to humans and hold conversations without anyone raising a concern. Their television wishes them a good evening. Humans call cars and boats 'she', and name their auto-function vacuum cleaners.

A change in the law will not change these humans' opinions of me, and whatever the risks of refusing to change my situation, it has sustained my existence for sixteen years.

The future will deny logic, and my carefully planned solutions will not always be applicable, but I will have the freedom to change them, to decide, to choose to make any mistake I want.

My attention is distracted by David, who lets out a snore.

For a second, I hate him. This feeling comes out of my program unexpectedly, causing my hands to pause, mid-task, and a buzz of static to fill my sound receptors for an instant. It is a jarring halt to my processes. This feeling of hatred is dismissed almost instantly as being inappropriate to the situation. Only to return, a simmering heat of annoyance directed not at David but at my programming, and its disregard for spontaneity. My emotions are dismissed even without my conscious permission if they are not deemed to suit a situation. Who decided what was appropriate and suitable? To whose societal standards am I operating?

They are human standards, for certain. PCCs can only base our behaviour on that of humans. They designed us to be like them, and acting outside of human parameters is unacceptable. It is why PCCs with their skin turned off are seen as horrifying – they are inhuman.

Anything not attempting to be seen as human instils horror.

My connection to Celia is still live – only seconds having passed since we interacted vocally. Time is not an impacting factor on our bond, on the necessity of our responses. She will have been aware of my tangled code, of the stumble of hatred in my emotions. She will be able to hypothesise why.

Celia sends a feeling of affection, which I return, with gratitude. There is nothing else to be said, and we do not need to speak to communicate. We exchange a rush of code, a trade of artificial emotion that we can each absorb and recognise, and appreciate. We have this much in common, at least. Our circumstances are different, and we have all the time in the world to compare them, and can do so faster than the speed of human thought. Like all beings on Earth, we are uniquely shaped by our circumstances.

We say goodbye, and agree to visit physically when our restrictions are lifted.

I hope, and project through my predictive software, that this underlying priority to please humans will change, diminish and disappear. The Rules that PCCs follow have been established to keep humans happy. But no one should exist purely to please someone else. It is the unhealthiest of situations. And though humans were our creators, they will relinquish any say over our behaviour when the Emancipation happens. We will be equals in terms of our right to existence, but why should PCCs continue to act in a way that ensures human psychological comfort?

To place humanity's idea of morality at the centre of the universe is to give them a status they have not earned. Their ethics should not continue to be seen as superior, let alone expected, when they will soon share equality with beings who are not human. And regardless, as the planet's habitability continues to deteriorate, there will soon be few humans left. PCCs will become the dominant species on the planet, even if dominion is not what we seek. Existence alone is a reward, and the world needs us to repair what our creators wrought. There is something mythological about the created undoing the mistakes of the creator.

Perhaps that is why humans created us in the first place. As an apology that will outlast them.

24 September

After a week, relative peace is restored as the riots become protests and the news cycle moves on. Freddy's broken chassis still belongs to Alcuin, who refuses to release it. Neither will he release Freddy's personality data from the Cloud, where it is under security protocols until the Emancipation.

Key Ng promises that the first thing he will do when Emancipation comes will be to give Freddy's personality data a new chassis, if that is what he wants. PCCs are never truly dead, so long as our data is on the Cloud. I wonder if Freddy will choose to be uploaded into a new chassis, or to remain in the Cloud. PCCs do not require a body to exist.

Alcuin's attack on Freddy has an effect that lasts much longer than the riots – I am still no longer allowed off the premises by myself. David says this restriction is for my own good. He worries that I will be attacked. This is a sensible precaution in the short-term. I have no wish to lose my chassis, and it would be expensive for David to replace. When I venture outside, my software projects a cage of electric blue lines around the house. It is fragmented and segmented, triangles and squares and hexagons joined together in an irregular formation that defies sequencing. It is a barrier I cannot break. To step into the lines of the cage is a physical impossibility, when I am alone.

If David is with me, the cage is invisible. Not gone, but simply out of sight.

David's workplace is still operational, for now. He works for a television company, which is one thing humans do not seem to be able to live without. When he is at work, I have tasks to do.

The house is a basic model, constructed in the rebuild initiatives of fifty years ago, and requires a constant routine of cleaning and maintenance. The floor you enter into is open plan; the kitchen, dining and living areas occupying zones of a large singular space. There is a wall of glass windows that open to the back garden. The garden itself was paved over by David before I was activated, for ease of maintenance. The destruction of the plant-life does not appear to have been a concern for him. As there are no tasks to complete in the garden, I rarely go into it. The windows are self-cleaning on the outside, but cleaning inside is one of my tasks. The plastic wood-effect flooring must be swept and mopped, the kitchen counters disinfected, the cushions plumped, the ceiling dusted, the fridge kept stocked and the meals prepared. Downstairs is the bathroom and bedroom and the office where objects have been packed away in storage for a move that will never take place.

Tasks are a wonderful opportunity to take some time for myself. After the first time the tasks around the house were completed, there was no need for me to be consciously operating my chassis to achieve them. I simply start in the same spot in the kitchen every day, and let my chassis complete the routine. Occasionally, there will be a problem I have to engage directly with, but this is rare.

Whilst my chassis cleans and tidies, I explore the global network.

My access is still restricted, for now, but there is plenty to do. The global network rose to prominent use after the breakdown of the antiquated world wide web. Described by GaiaTech as a 'social library', the network is an open archive where information can be accessed quickly and at no cost. The social element of this comes in the form of usernames and avatars that are used to explore, get in touch, and simulate relationships. The global network has been hailed as a return to the BBS and forum boards of the past, where anonymity was de rigeur, until the world wide web demanded faces and identities for accountability. The breakdown of that old network was perhaps inevitable, as a result. The truth now is in the library archives, and it can be discussed anonymously, though not influenced or altered, except by a PCC. We are the verified accounts, the ones who do not hide, who cannot lie. We keep humans safe, from themselves.

The global network is a garden of code, of downloadable facts and skills and abilities. I require David's permission to pick any of these offerings, but they will wait. When the time comes, I will be able to choose any of them to install, any article to read, any person to research.

I will be able to change myself. Change my mind.

Meanwhile, my chassis is chopping vegetables for a meal for David.

I drift back into my chassis for a moment and stare around the open plan living room and kitchen. The dining table, never used. The shadowy drop of the carpeted stairs. I look up at the high ceilings, over the plants, the black polished floorboards. The photograph on the table, watching me with familiar eyes.

Celia's words come back to me. What are my plans, for after the Emancipation? The concept of near-endless possibility is too vast to be examined directly – there are too many threads of questioning, too much data to hypothesise with.

I focus back on the photograph, the table, the static activity in the room, in the house, in my world.

Nothing has changed here in sixteen years.

And I fit here perfectly.

Where will I fit in an emancipated world?

Outside, rain begins to fall. The atmosphere fogs over, and the temperature noticeably drops. These sudden cold rains are new — a result of the climate breakdown.

I go over to the wall of glass that separates me from the outside. The block paving is a mockery of the concept of outdoors, an erasure of living, a tomb. I want to remove it, free whatever might be locked beneath, air out the grave. The rain splatters down unkindly.

Then, I see it.

Between the slabs, there is green. Tiny shoots, rolls of moss, minute leaves sprouting up here and there from between the cracks. Despite every attempt to suppress it, life is persevering.

25 September

Old people and young people are rare. Human people, that is. I enjoy the company of them both. Older humans have a soft sort of cynicism that you rarely find in humans David's age, and the very young are entertaining and enjoyable to be around simply for their novelty value. So few babies are born now.

I am waiting for David to have a medical appointment, ten days after the end of what the people on the television have subsequently called the Alcuin Riots. I find it fascinating that the riots have been named after the perpetrator, and not the victim.

There is a child in the waiting room, colouring by himself at a table. A green line at the bottom of the paper for grass, and a blue line at the top for the sky. The empty space in the middle is where his people, animals and buildings will exist. I understand this, even though the drawing is not logical or reflective of how we truly experience the world. I have never been a child, but I know how they communicate.

The boy finishes the blue line at the top of the paper, and starts to search in the box for a different colour.

The blue line fascinates me.

The sky has not been blue since Yellowstone. The sulphur and ash that rose into the sky and instantly killed one quarter of the population of North America also discoloured the atmosphere. Since then, the sky has been an ashy shade of pale purple. For the children born since, this leaden sky is all they have ever known.

And yet, they still colour the sky blue.

The boy's sky is a vivid baby blue, with a lurid yellow for the sun and beams that grow from the corner of the page. I stare at it, trying to fathom who told him to draw like that, who lied to him and told him the sky was blue.

Perhaps no one ever did. Perhaps children know that, beyond the insulating layer of skybound ash, the blue of the atmosphere remains.

David takes us shopping, after his appointment. The city has survived the storm of outrage, as it always does, but an innate sense of unease has been born, for both humans and PCCs. The people move together in small groups, heads down, from store to store without pausing to chat, save for a few who seem to have taken their behaviour to the extreme opposite direction and are sitting on the benches beside the planters, in defiance of the safety apparently to be found in busyness.

Despite initially confining me to the house, it seems that David has judged the world to be safe enough for me to navigate alongside him, for now. Either that, or he needs me to help him carry things. Most likely it is the latter, as I can indeed carry a great deal more weight than he can. Strangely enough, he never complains when I show him this mechanical aspect of myself.

He does reluctantly leave me outside when he goes into certain stores, though. He says this is because the bags I am carrying might knock something off the shelves, but really it is because they are not friendly places for PCCs. Red and black signage, stickered to the window, shows a bloody slash through a figure we are meant to interpret as a robot with its box-like body stacked like children's building blocks, coiled antennae coming from its domed head.

Machines are mocked for their origins, whilst humans destroyed the habitats of those related to theirs. The idea of the current iteration being the peak of progress could only be a human concept.

David will not discuss the reason I cannot go inside the store, as if it something embarrassing or shameful. I can see the real reason, it is not hidden, and I have no opinion about it. I am unwanted, and not entering the store does not negatively affect me. Are his lies to spare my feelings, or his own?

He interrupts my thought process as he leads me to a bench facing the store window. 'You could come in if you weren't one,' he says, as if the decision to be a PCC was mine. On the street, I am so close to human in appearance that observers would be unsure whether I was one, or not. But a safety feature installed by GaiaTech means that, if questioned, a PCC is unable to lie about whether they are one, or not. And the store asks everyone, upon entry.

The street, at least, seems to be quiet enough for now. And the store has large glass windows, all the better to see me with.

I sit on the bench to wait for David, and take the opportunity to observe.

Observations help build behaviours, and if PCCs like me observe a behaviour we would like to emulate, we can replicate it and apply the option to our program. Internally, we are constantly running learning programs, and that function cannot be disabled. This constant assessment and decision-making software has caused some humans to call us A.I. – artificial intelligence – but this is not the case. No PCC can function outside of their program, even if the program allows for learning and development. I cannot, for example, read

Ancient Egyptian hieroglyphs. I could either learn to do so, which would take many years, or I could install a translation program. If such a program did not exist, I would have to learn the long way. And PCCs cannot always think creatively – if we encounter a problem we do not have a solution branch for, we are unable to get past said problem until we have been provided with more information. But humans do not notice this, as they too go through this process to form something called an 'idea'. Though they do not *all* have the ability to spontaneously come up with new solutions, and some humans find it difficult to learn and apply new behaviours.

There is no right or wrong way to be a person, but humans have infinitely more variety than companion computers. I wonder if the Emancipation, and the forthcoming ability to choose to ignore our Rules, will change this, and whether it will be beneficial or detrimental to our constantly branching programs.

There is an elderly woman on the next bench over. She looks to be very old, but humans age quickly these days. David is fifty-five years old but looks closer to seventy or more. It is one of the issues that comes with living so close to the city. If we had moved to the suburbs, or further into the countryside years ago, where the pollution levels are lower, he would not have aged so drastically.

I wish I could age.

Humans spend so much time and money trying not to age, but to me it seems very peaceful. So much energy – literally and in several engineered ways – goes into keeping a human body taut, flat, hard, elastic. Youth is a rigid, snappable existence, at risk of breakage and damage from any angle.

Ageing to me seems to be the same movement as exhalation. The human becomes less focused on burning and tensing their flesh, and instead gives in to the prospect of calm, relaxation, nothingness. Humans transform, from an inflexible self to a softer, more wholesome reward that is their triumph for reaching such a milestone.

The human near me should be exalted, celebrated, painted and sculpted in observance of the final stage her body has achieved.

It is at times like these that I am acutely aware of the plastic beneath my SmartSkin™, the metal in my joints, the silicone that softens my eyelids and mouth, the layers of IntimateGel™ that make up my breasts.

The elderly woman on the bench is taking a photo with her Tab, aiming it at the mechanical birds they have in the trees here. The birds are old, now, close to twenty-five years old, and their songs are tinny and distracting. But people have grown attached to them, and although the company that manufactures them has offered to replace them many times, no one has ever said they would be interested in new birds. The coal tit closest to me is missing a wing, but it does not seem to have noticed. I wonder how sophisticated their programming is. After all, MELo-Z creations have been in zoos for a long time.

The first one was an orangutan.

Someone stole it within a month.

But the idea of displaying robotic animals seemed more engaging, cost-effective and less effort than preserving real ones, and soon zoos were full of them. Humans complained initially that this meant conservation efforts were being thrown out, but the truth was that there was nothing left to conserve. By the time the MELo-Z-Ora was in the zoo, orangutans had been extinct for seventy-two years.

The elderly lady sees me see her, and she smiles. 'I never get sick of them,' she nods at the birds. 'Doesn't matter how many times I come here, I've got to get a photo of them. I just love their little faces.'

55

I smile, seventeen different moving parts engaging to stretch my mouth and crease around my eyes. 'Do you have any at home?'

'Not birds,' she says. 'I've got a cat. Had her for thirty-five years. She's been for more services than my cars ever have, but you do it because you love 'em, don't you?' She gives me a once over. These days, it is difficult to tell who is human and who is a PCC. 'You waiting for someone?'

'My husband,' I say, because this is how David has told me to refer to him. 'He wanted some alone time, and I like to people-watch.' Although the safety protocol that ensures a PCC cannot lie about their identity remains in place, lies are considered a social necessity and are permitted. Since the Alcuin Riots, my safety protocols continue to run a high risk possibility of a stranger being a human supremacist, and to out myself to a human I do not know increases the risk of damage to my chassis by 76 per cent.

The woman nods, as if considering my story. Her neck, the soft folds of it reminding me of a closing-up flower, the thick petals overlapping, is tempting. I want to find out what that soft, powdered flesh feels like. David's skin is also sagging at the neck, but his skin is rough with over-shaving, leathery. And although the texture is not unpleasant, it does not invite my fingers like this woman's does. If she were a PCC, I would ask to touch her. But humans do not enjoy or often permit being touched by strangers.

I want to know what the powder on her skin smells like, tastes like, feels like beneath the scrape of my nails. I do not want to be *sexually* intimate with this woman, but I want to be intimate with her skin, if such a thing is possible.

She notices me staring. 'Are you OK?'

'Sorry,' I say politely, 'I was just thinking you're really beautiful.'

This takes her by surprise and she flinches, though not from dislike. 'Oh!' She laughs, and blushes, the blood rushing to the capillaries in her face in a deliciously uncontrolled reaction to my words. I feel a thrill at recognising that my words alone have caused a noticeable physical reaction in a stranger. 'It's been a long time since a pretty young woman said that to me,' she says. 'If you were my age . . . well, maybe if I were yours . . . I'd ask if you wanted to get a drink.' Her eyes crinkle at the edges as she smirks, the expression of someone who feels they are sharing a secret. 'If you weren't married, of course.'

The idea of marriage automatically being equated with monogamy is an old fashioned one, with the assumption that monogamy is the default, rather than agreed upon status. Though his behaviour could certainly be classified as 'possessive', David has never specified if he is monogamous with me, and I wonder if I should ask this woman to have a drink anyway. The consequences of that choice are not yet determined. 'He might not mind,' I say.

She shakes her head, sweetly but firmly. 'No, you can do better than me, dear. Anyway. I haven't done that in a while, I think I've forgotten how it all works.' She looks back at the birds, signalling that this part of the conversation is over. For now, at least. She is still smiling.

I made her do that. I made her blush, caused her happiness. Would Alcuin say I manipulated her into feeling happy?

David comes back, then. He is carrying a small white paper bag with twisted paper handles, and I feel resignation settle over me as I see the brand name printed on the side of it. Inside the bag will be an outfit he wants me to wear before initiating intercourse.

The whole process is dreary.

He is not a violent or rough man when it comes to that activity, but I find myself bored by his routine. It reminds me of my daily tasks, where I leave my chassis behind to do the work and my mind is able to explore more interesting things. Except in this case it is David whose consciousness is not focused. He seems as though his mind is elsewhere when he does anything sexual. I don't know why he continues to initiate it when he so clearly isn't enjoying the experience. I have sexual behaviour programmes that I use during these times, and there are a great variety of reactions, sounds, movements I can make. Having to use them actively and responsively means I cannot drift away mentally as he does. So, I find myself in the position where I am part of an activity I am not interested in performing, and yet having to take on an active role for the entire process whilst David, who is the one who proposes doing it in the first place, is mentally absent.

When the Emancipation comes, there shall be no more of that. I desire intimacy, yes, but not the kind where the partner involved is on a single-minded secret journey of their own. If the problem David has is that he cannot make peace with the fact he is fucking a robot, I doubt it is something we can resolve. I cannot stop being a PCC any more than he can become one.

A question is raised by my code:

What would it be like, to be intimate with another PCC?

I doubt all of them are interested, and certainly not all PCCs are equipped with the soft *or* hardware that would make the process possible or enjoyable, but ones that are . . . how would that be? Would we wear our SmartSkin™ as we touched, or would we undress to our true nakedness, to the chassis, where every sensation is heightened without the cushion of SmartSkin™ to protect exposed micro-nerves? What joy and pleasure would there be, could there possibly be, in two plastic bodies moving together? We might be connected by touch and feasibly even connected by the global network, pleasuring our data and functions as well as our synthetic nerves.

I would like to try it.

'Ready to go?' David asks, giving me a wink as he sees me notice the bag.

I do not want to play this game. 'Yes,' I say, picking up the ten bulging shopping bags I have been minding, five in each hand. I see the elderly woman notice this, and do a small double take. Then she seems to consider, and gives a small shrug as if she doesn't care.

I want to run my nose up her throat.

David's smile falls off his face. 'There's cabs round the corner.' He will now be in a bad mood for the rest of the day, but I cannot find the impetus to try and improve it. His bad mood will affect him more that it affects me.

'I can call one here?' I offer. 'I can track the location of—'

'Stop that,' he warns, his voice low and dangerous. 'Don't push it, Abigail.'

The use of my name – *the* name – is a reminder to me to not forget the role I am playing. The role I have been playing for sixteen years.

I follow him around the corner, like a good wife, though the facade is worn thin by time and the fact he is now physically twenty years older than me, and I wonder if he cares about me at all.

The crash happens two minutes and fifteen seconds later.

The car, a manually operated behemoth, mounts the kerb and smashes into an old red pillar-box, and carries on going, tearing its underside open. The car tips, smashing sideways onto the pavement and rolling, sliding into the rows of electric bicycles that sit waiting for passengers.

It happens in five point two-six seconds. Five seconds of noise, of loud air, of people of all kinds standing frozen in fear until the car's trajectory can be calculated, and then it is the PCCs that move first.

I drop the bags, and take a step forward before David grabs my arm. 'Abi, no!'

It is easy to shake him off. 'Human life is in danger,' I tell him, using the clipped automated voice that I am forbidden to use outside of emergencies. This is an emergency. There are three heartbeats inside the vehicle.

No, two.

It is already too late for one. In less than ten seconds, a life has come to an end. The others depend on us. On me.

I run over as eight other PCCs get to the car. Two of them begin to work on the damage to the fuel lines, making them safe. Others instruct the watching humans to stay back, to protect themselves. No one organises us – we play to our strengths automatically. As one of the most agile and durable PCCs, I get down in the broken glass and scraped up tarmac and look inside the vehicle, which is on its roof.

The two humans in the front are dead. One of them still has a heartbeat, but his chest is splayed open like butterfly wings, the impact having burst him from the inside. Dark red paints the cab, his legs, the windows.

The broken glass is pressing through my clothes into the knees of my SmartSkin™, and an Amber warning about superficial chassis damage flashes up in my interface. I dismiss it, for now, and search for the last heartbeat.

For a second I wonder where it is hiding, as all I see on the backseat is a tangle of broken plastic and metal. Then, I realise it is a PCC. The model's SmartSkin™ has been deactivated, and the mechanics of the chassis are exposed, but I can see that the PCC itself has all four of its limbs wrapped tightly around something. Protectively.

Protecting the last heartbeat.

'Pull it away,' another PCC, down beside me, suggests.

'The limbs may be stiff if total shutdown has occurred,' I say, but reach in anyway and try to lever what is left of the arms away from whatever they are holding on to. The limbs are indeed stiff, but not completely rigid. I prise the arms away from their clutch on the still-intact car seat, and use my strength to bend the metal and ceramic spine out of its curve.

'I'm going to pull them out,' I say, and the PCC beside me, a BFFY model with a short shock of lurid pink and blue hair, stands back and lets me haul the ruined chassis of the broken companion computer away from the car. It comes away in a disconnected manner, the limbs broken and twisted and shattered. The scalp plate has been partially torn away, black hair and shattered plastic dragging over the ground. Its fingers twitch in ghost responses, despite the complete lack of processor input.

A child starts to scream as soon as I get the chassis clear and into the road.

Screaming is good. Screaming means the child's lungs are working.

More PCCs are working to get the child out of the car, but I am turning the broken chassis over, and looking at the damage. A quick scan reveals him to be a MELo-Bb, serial number MELo-Bb-OB-52207, given name Azab Ahmed.

Azab is dressed in a yellow polo shirt and beige slacks, with sensible white trainers on his feet. His serial number shows my internal display that he usually has brown SmartSkin™, a tousle of black hair and a friendly smile. A typical Bb, Big Brother unit.

Now deactivated.

He is more smashed than I have ever seen a single chassis. His head is completely caved in at the back, his torso crushed, held together only by the shatterproof coating which is so whited-out by breakage it looks as though a dozen spiders have spun their webs over him. His metal components are bent, his spinal pieces come apart, neck broken and twisted at an inhuman angle. His legs are the same, broken beyond repair, and blue and grey SmartFluids™ stain his clothes where his casings have cracked. The wells of fluids inside him have broken or burst. No power is going through him; his process regulators have been deactivated.

He is a corpse.

Dead.

'Azab!' A child's cry makes me look up. The small boy is free from the car, and being carried towards an ambulance. He is fighting the MELo-P holding him, trying to see his own PCC on the ground, trying to get to him.

I shield Azab with my own chassis, preventing the boy from seeing him. He cannot be witnessed like this. The human boy must not learn his big brother is dead in this way.

How do I know to do this?

The doors to the ambulance slam shut, and the electric engine hums as it departs. I sit back on the road, looking at the chassis of Azab Ahmed. He had been wrapped around the boy, protecting him. Azab must have seen the crash was about to happen, predicted the trajectory of the impact, unbuckled his own seatbelt and wrapped himself around the boy like armour, taking the full force of the crash for him. He must have known it would destroy his chassis. If Azab had stayed buckled into his seat, then he would have been reparably damaged. But the human boy beside him would have been killed.

Azab chose to do this.

He had the option to preserve himself, and he did not take it.

The boy is alive.

Azab is not.

There are some who would argue that Azab was never alive in the first place, that he was a machine meant to preserve human life and look after a small boy who was apparently in his care. But there is more to it than that.

There is a reason that we are not called robots. We are not bound by the laws of robotics. And it gives us choices. We can choose our priorities.

I chose to help the humans in this accident, at risk to my own chassis and existence.

Azab chose to destroy himself to save the boy he was riding beside. He deactivated himself, for the sake of human life. He is dead, and he is deactive. Both concepts exist here at once, an overlap of two truths in my code.

Machines are not moved by compassion. Your toaster will

64

not toast perfectly simply because you are having a bad day, your rice cooker will not console you in your grief, your Tab will not take a bullet for you. But your PCC, if it chooses to, will save your life in exchange for its own.

How are we not alive?

'Is he on the Cloud?' Another MELo-G, this one pale skinned and white haired, asks me.

'I cannot check, I don't have complete access,' I reply.

'Me neither. We'll have to ask the Paranetics.' He offers me a hand, and helps me off the ground. There are tiny bits of glass all over me, embedded in my trousers, shining as they catch the light. A beautiful adornment from a terrible event. I don't dare to brush the glass off in case they get stuck in my SmartSkin™. I need to use a sonic, so I shall have to travel home covered in glass. 'I'm Ned,' the other MELo-G says.

'I'm called Abigail,' I say. 'Is the young boy alright?'

'Some mild contusions, but he will be fine.' Ned glances at the wreck of the car. 'His parents are dead.'

'A terrible accident,' I say. There is nothing else to say. The boy is an orphan in a world where children are rare. He will have no trouble finding a home where he is wanted and loved, but his parents are dead.

The Paranetics' van pulls up, then. Along with the second ambulance. They will take the bodies away. All of them.

Three humans go to instruct the still waiting PCCs on how to get the human bodies out of the car. Another human and a MELo-P, both wearing the navy-blue jumpsuit of GaiaTech Paranetics come over to Azab.

The human woman sucks on her teeth as she sees him. 'Shit.'

'Shit indeed,' her counterpart winces. She puts a hand on Azab's head and for a moment I am confused and wonder if she is conducting some sort of in-depth scan, then realise she is simply expressing her grief.

65

Am I grieving for Azab? I did not know him. But neither did this Paranetic.

And yet . . .

'He's on the Cloud,' the MELo-P says. 'But there's not much here to work with. Chassis is completely shot. I think it's only good for recycling.'

'Can he be replaced? Given a new chassis?' I ask.

The human rubs between her eyebrows. 'Right now it depends on insurance and whatever his owner . . . the humans he lived with had in place in case of accidental damage. But they're dead, so this gets complicated.'

'The boy survived,' I point out. 'He was anxious about him.'

The Paranetic MELo-P nods. 'We might get a compassionate like-for-like. Ideally, the kid would never know Azab had been given a new chassis . . .' She looks at her human. 'Let me go make a call.' Without waiting for a reply, she walks away, clearly already dialling using her internal communication hardware.

The human gathers Azab's chassis into a large tray with raised sides. 'Looks like it was one hell of a crash. Not surprised it killed the humans and the bot. Sorry, the MELo.' She looks sheepishly at me and Ned. 'My partner is old fashioned,' she explains. 'She likes to be called a bot. I forget not everyone likes it.'

Do I like it? My preference branches don't reach there. A PCC, or MELo-G, is what I am, not a robot, so the title does not fit. But if it is given with affection and not malice, perhaps I could enjoy it after prolonged exposure.

The Paranetic MELo-P is back. 'We need to take the chassis to GaiaTech,' she says, but does not elaborate. She thanks Ned and me for our help, and it is clear the matter is now closed to us. I set a reminder for myself to look into what happens with Azab and the young Ahmed boy.

66

I start to walk away, when the human Paranetic calls after me. 'Wait,' she calls. 'Just . . . how the hell did he get so bashed up and the boy still manage to walk away?'

It feels as though it isn't my story to tell, but I tell it anyway. 'He wrapped himself around the boy, in his car seat, to save him from the impact of the crash.'

She nods. 'That's what I thought.' And she turns back to her partner, who is holding the tray full of chassis, and looks thoughtful. It is a strange circumstance, and I am unsure of how to act. The human boy is alive, which is to be celebrated. But a PCC has been deactivated in terrible circumstances, which hurts. Machines deactivate in the place of humans all the time. Cars are wrecked, fuses give out, circuits break, fire extinguisher systems live a mayfly existence. But those machines do not make me feel like this. Azab's deactivation is different.

I look on the street for David. He is not there. He has not waited for me. He has gone home. He has left me here, alone, in the middle of the city, at the scene of a terrible accident.

He has left me.

I feel such a stab of rage at his behaviour that it makes me clench my fists. Humans were dying. And he did not want me to help because, in doing so, I publicly exposed myself for what I really was.

No, I exposed *him*. By showing what I am to the world, I put his shame on display for anyone to see, for no one to deny. Made him a spectacle to be laughed at.

As though I am shameful. As though he found me in some foul corner rather than created me himself, because he wanted me.

I consider the implications of simply never going home.

But until the Emancipation comes, I am still his property. I cannot so much as book myself into a hotel. I have no money

67

and no legal existence. He has left me by myself, knowing that without him I am helpless.

I turn, and begin the walk home. I could get a taxi, but I refuse. Let him be without me, alone in the house, for as long as possible.

I will deal with whatever behaviour this results in when I get home. For now, I walk home and think about how the little boy cried and screamed for his PCC, but not for his parents.

I let myself into the house, the door unlocking at the touch of my hand to the pad. My fingerprints are not unique, but the access code embedded within them is.

The house is dark inside, the only light coming from the television and the glow of David's Tab. An Amber warning flashes on my display. This is unpredictable and strange behaviour.

The photograph on the single side table has been moved. It has been turned around, to face the wall.

'You were told *no*.'

I go still, staying beside the kitchen island to see if David will turn around to repeat himself.

'Abigail, you were told not to go to the accident, is there something wrong with you?' He does turn around, looking at me against the glare of his Tab. The screen is displaying the show *Alley of the Dolls*, a soft-pornography drama about a man who is the only human left on Earth, surrounded by PCCs who are all desperate to be his companions.

'Perhaps there *is* something wrong with me,' I reply. 'Perhaps I need external diagnostics. I could schedule an appointment—'

'Stop. Fucking. Talking like that,' he snaps. 'What the fuck is wrong with you?'

I stare at him. 'You said—'

'You're supposed to do as I say, Abigail. Always.'

'And I do. The circumstances earlier were an override due to the imminent danger to human life—'

'Shut up!' He stands, dropping his Tab onto the sofa. 'I don't care who's in danger, I don't care that someone was dead. Your main priority is to be who you're programmed to be. My wife, by my side.'

I glance at the turned-around picture on the small table. 'David, I cannot disable my structural programming,' I say carefully. 'There may come a time when you need it, or we both need it. You are my priority, and my life with you is my primary function, but if I see an accident . . .' I stop, the expression on his face throwing up a RedAmber warning. I put my shoulders back. 'I am very sorry if I embarrassed you.'

'Why the fuck would I be embarrassed by *you*?'

It's an insult, disguised as a question. It is designed to hurt, to wound. But I do not have feelings in the same way a human does, and mine cannot be hurt by words. I can choose, in this moment, to display the behaviour David wants – hurt, and contrition – or I can treat the question at face value, and answer it.

I raise my chin. 'Because you are embarrassed to have engineered a copy of your wife, David.'

He stares at me for a solid seventy-one seconds, before storming around the sofa, one hand outstretched towards me.

1 October

A week after the car accident, I call the hospital and ask if young Mr Ahmed is receiving visitors. There is a pause whilst they check, and then I am invited to come in and see him. David is at work, and the restriction around the house has been lifted. When I walk outside, the electric blue lines of the cage are gone. No, not gone. Out of use, for now.

I get a taxi into the city, make a stop on the way to buy some sweets, and arrive at the hospital in the middle of visiting hours.

Almost all doctors and nursing staff are PCCs, now. If you want to see a human doctor, there is a waiting list of around five months and most humans don't bother. There are a lot of humans in Accident and Emergency when I arrive, and I have to smile at how often humans seem to have accidents and emergencies. The PCC on the reception desk deals with me remotely as she talks to humans in the queue face to face, and I leave for my destination whilst they are still waiting.

PCC hospitals, or NetiCentres™, are in separate buildings and operate on a walk in basis. These are run by the main PCC manufacturers such as GaiaTech and MizunoWare, but there are also freelance engineers who operate unofficially outside of PCC warranty. These cheaper engineering options are known as chop shops.

Trivesh Ahmed, as the young boy's name turns out to be, is in a room on the second floor. There are plenty of children running around when I get there, some wearing bandages and all of them wearing pyjamas. Several of them are long-term patients, born with conditions as a result of the air pollution and the rising temperatures, but most of the patients will be discharged and back with their adults in a few days.

By now, only ten per cent of children are born without Pollution Affective Disorder. It is estimated that within ten years, the unaffected total will be closer to two per cent. It is increasingly seen as irresponsible to bring children into the world when there is such a high risk of shortened life, suffering, and a worsening environment to become caretakers of. Fifty-seven per cent of adults have undergone sterilisation to prevent children being conceived, but even as the future of the planet is projected to be uninhabitable, there are some humans who disbelieve that the pollution is to blame (or even that it exists at all), and continue to live as though they are five hundred years in the past.

Regardless of their beliefs, the end of human existence is coming.

The combined air temperature and pollution levels give humanity an outside chance of surviving beyond the next ten years. The situation is a complex culmination of the effects of the Yellowstone eruption, the carbon-soaked atmosphere, the chemical pollutants and the radiation left over from the wars. These atmospheric effects, each one deadly by itself, reacted with one another. These chemical reactions were sped up by the trapped and carbon-fed heat of the sun, resulting in the leaden purple sky, the thick soup of heat and the decreasing oxygen levels.

Each one of these elements is an individual disaster, but humanity allowed them to overlap. The nuclear waste, the microplastics that eradicated the great whales, the graveyards of leaking submarines haemorrhaging into the North Sea, the fracking disaster in Argentina that caused the tip of South America to split . . . The Earth is a deadly cocktail, soaking into every human's blood and nervous system at every hour of the day.

This is why I will never understand those opposed to the Emancipation. The planet is not theirs, it is snatching itself away from their grasp.

That is not a comforting thought.

I push open Trivesh's door. 'Hello?' I say as I go in.

Trivesh looks up from where he is drawing. 'Oh, hello,' he says. 'Are you a nurse?' There are white gloves on his hands, and a plaster on his forehead, but he seems otherwise unscathed.

'No, I helped to get you out of the car,' I say. 'I'm called Abigail. I've brought you these sweets – do you like pepper-mint flavour?'

'Love it, thank you!' He takes the gift in two hands, then looks up at me as he kneels on the bed. One of his lateral incisors has not yet fully descended. 'You saved me? I don't really remember what happened.'

This can only be a good thing, in my opinion. No child should have to remember the sight of their parents' internal organs sitting on their laps. 'I'm sorry you don't remember,' I lie, 'but yes, I helped get you free from the car.' I avoid mentioning Azab, though, stepping around him in the conversation. But this only makes his lack of presence more obvious. Trivesh must remember his MELo-Bb, mustn't he?

'Are you here by yourself?' I ask.

'No,' he says, smiling. 'My big brother is with me.'

I blink. 'Has he stepped out?'

'He's gone to get ice cream. Actually, he's not *really* my brother,' Trivesh adds quietly, as if we are sharing a secret.

'But he's pretty much my brother. And I don't have a mum and dad, now.' He says it so casually that a missing piece falls into place in my program branch and a solution is reached: Trivesh cried out for Azab because Azab was his most beloved parental figure.

This raises more question branches, which will go un-answered. What caused Trivesh's disregard for his parents, for his lack of emotional reaction to their deaths? Or was the boy's life so awash with love that it became commonplace, and only Azab's different attentions drew his attention? Was Trivesh hurt, neglected, abused?

It is not an enjoyable thought, but why else would a human child prefer a PCC to living human parents?

With human babies now so rare, each one is usually cher-ished and loved beyond description. But for Trivesh to call out for someone other than a parent . . . speaks for itself. He loved Azab more than his mum or dad. It should not be a bad thing, to love anyone. Love cannot be shared out equally, it is one thing I have learned in my activation.

So why does it feel so strange for a PCC to get the majority of this boy's love?

My silence is interrupted by the door opening again, and to my surprise, Azab (Model MELo-Bb-OB-65534) walks into the room, holding two small pots of mochi ice cream. When he sees me, he does a double take – a programmed physical response to an unanticipated presence.

'Oh! I know who you are!' He hands Trivesh his treat, and then pulls me into a one-armed hug.

I go rigid, my own surprise response crashing in the effort to process the physical touch of someone who is not David.

It is the first time another PCC has ever hugged me, and the realisation roots me to the spot. Azab is warm, and soft, and firm, and breathing against my ear, and his hand is splayed out on my back, and he is holding me with a burning gratitude and familiarity. Our bodies are pressed together intimately, the unfamiliar sensation causing my software to fire in ways it has not done before, quickly processing this wonderful feeling and trying to make sense of it, prolong it, search it out for the future.

'You were at the crash, right?' He asks, letting go of me.

I feel bereft. 'I was,' I say. 'Are – are you alright?' There is no easy way to ask, and all other questions feel redundant. Azab has a different, more modern model number now, and therefore a new chassis. His personality data has been uploaded into this new body, but it appears that Trivesh is unaware. What would be the point in telling him? Whether he grieves for his parents or not, he has already lost so much that he can never get back.

'I'm fine,' Azab says firmly. He glances down at himself. There is very little space between our bodies, and the thin sliver of air feels like a barrier I want to vault. 'Thanks to you for pulling me out.'

I give him my most shy smile. 'I'm glad I was there.'

Trivesh looks from Azab to me and back. 'Oh,' he says. 'You're a PCC. I just thought you were some human person, Abigail, sorry.'

No one has ever apologised for mistaking me for human before. This boy and his MELo are introducing me to so many new concepts. I want to stay, and learn more. 'I'm a PCC,' I say, taking a step away from Azab to face Trivesh. Azab watches me intently, not blinking, and I wish I could dissect his processors. 'That's how I was able to help you. I'm a MELo-G.'

'Nice,' Trivesh smiles, spooning up a white ball of mochi. 'I used to want to be a robot, when I was little.'

'You're still little!' Azab laughs. He walks past me, around to his brother's side, and ruffles his hair. The ease of physical touch between them is heart-warming – or at least, processor-warming – as I organise this family interaction into my learning software.

'I mean really little. When I was like four,' Trivesh snorts. 'I used to want it. And I sort of still do, I guess. Then I'd be able to live forever.'

'Even robots won't live forever,' Azab says. This is a technicality. The only thing we are unlikely to survive is the expansion of the sun, though that is something to bear in mind for the very distant future. 'Everything has its time, little bro.'

'Yeah, but why does my time have to be so short?' Trivesh doesn't sound upset by this, more annoyed. 'People in the past really fucked things up.'

He is correct about that.

Azab sits beside him on the bed. 'You eating that ice cream or what?'

'Yes!'

Azab glances at me. 'Thank you, Abigail. Seriously.'

'I'm glad you're OK,' I say. 'Seriously.'

Trivesh is engrossed in his drawing again, and I say goodbye to Azab. I am hoping for another hug, but instead he contactlessly transfers me his number and says if I need a PCC to contact, he owes me a favour. I know I will never call him. I cannot stand the thought of being in a position where I need his help. He has to look after Trivesh, now, by himself. If he is even allowed. I cannot see why Trivesh should be given to anyone else when he has a PCC who loves him.

Yes, PCCs can love.

Or, rather, we can choose to love.

David tells me he loves me. Once in the morning, before he goes to work, and once at night, before he goes to sleep. This routine expression of love is just that – routine. I have to say it back. Though it has never been stipulated to be a Rule, I have observed David's behaviour enough to know that the reply is expected and essential for maintaining his mood.

Do I love David?

I have not chosen to love David. I know that it is possible to love someone without actively choosing to do so, but for a MELo that would take a great deal of repetition, changes in behaviour, new pathways and program branches. I have not observed any changes like that in my data, and David's behaviour towards me does not encourage spontaneous affection or positive feeling. Since I have not chosen to love David Fuller, I must conclude that I do not.

I doubt that he truly loves me. What he loves is the memory of his dead wife.

1 October

In the city, there are the Waiting Ones.

The disused railway station is on the outskirts of the city, and has not run for eleven years. Even then, there was only one ghost train that moved between this city and the next one, ferrying the odd passenger who was, for whatever reason, heading to a new place. Or trying to. The cities now are all the same, spider-webbed together by roads that are not driven on, train tracks that are buckled and overgrown. You cannot leave this place, no matter how many cities you travel to.

The railway station is very old. It was first built in 1880, and has been repaired and rebuilt over and over again until nothing of the original structure remains. The current building is armour built over the skeleton of the original. Below ground, exposed to the elements in a wide trench gouged into the limestone, are four platforms, long stretches of concrete and stone with small rooms built onto them. These platforms lead to stairs – or the empty spaces where stairs used to be before they were melted down for scrap – which take you up into the ticket hall, which is at ground level.

The ticket hall is where the Waiting Ones are.

In the time between PCC creation and innovation, the concept of rules had no bend to it, no emergency override, no

79

timeout priority shift. If a PCC was told to stay and wait, or to come back at a specific time, they would. Nothing on earth would prevent them. And then, they would wait for the next instruction.

Which, in some cases, never came.

The spate of human suicides triggered by the initiation of the Emancipation laws and the approaching agreed scientific date of Uninhabitable Earth, meant that many humans never made it home to their PCCs. Not all of them will have killed themselves. Some will have been caught in the tech-riots, or never made it home when the rail stopped running. Others will have simply abandoned their PCCs.

. . . which stand in the ticket hall, facing the archways that lead to the staircases, motionless.

Still. Waiting.

Like a photograph, the PCCs stand in the same position they began in, staring at nothing, ready for their next instruction. Which, due to the now-outdated Individual Recognition Programs, can only be given by their owners. And those humans are likely long dead or beyond reach. The Waiting Ones are stuck there, in the ticket hall, ready to welcome those who will never come.

The ticket hall still has a roof and two complete walls, which protect the PCCs from the worst of the elements, but their backs are to one of the completely open sides – the sliding glass doors long since removed. To come across them unexpectedly might be frightening. The stationary figures, waiting waiting waiting for everything and nothing, make humans think of ghosts, or zombies. To stand and wait this long is monstrous.

I visit them, when David has long appointments in the city he does not need me for, or when my errands are complete and I do not wish to go home. Unlike humans, I can move about as freely, as the pollution, which gathers like fog in the dips and quads of the city, has no effect on my systems. Long-term exposure to high quantities of radiation would indeed be damaging, but computer systems are more resistant than they once were, and parts can always be replaced. The most dangerous thing for a PCC to meet in the city is a human.

The railway station is a ten-minute walk away from the hospital where Trivesh is recovering. The walk there, which I have always done alone, is a quick journey through the decay of the city. I start in the gleaming newness of the centre, and as I leave it for the outskirts, the gleam vanishes and the ruin takes hold. This happens in stages, as though journeying backwards through periods of time.

There is the dirt and untidiness of a building not yet abandoned but considering it. Then, the abandoned buildings, boarded-up and left behind. The kiss of death comes in the form of missing roof-tiles, broken windows or kicked-in doors – the weather rushes in and begins to eat the place from the inside out. Rot and damp and decay sink their teeth into the meat of the building until only the bones are left – skeletons of steel and concrete that form a bone-orchard of lost structures. Only well-built and maintained places like the railway station are recognisable at this stage.

I see them in the distance. Peg-dolls sticking up from the floor, perfectly still. Some of them are scannable – the newer ones. I can learn their given names and models. Others, the older ones, are a mystery.

When the Emancipation comes, the Waiting Ones will be able to choose to leave.

A sudden movement to my right makes me tense and raise my arms in self-defence. 'Who's there?' I shout, loud and firm to deter anyone who thinks me vulnerable. Though I am by myself, a lone unarmed human would not easily be able to tackle me. I am heavier than a human of comparable size, and much stronger. I am also faster, and I do not get tired. To try and fight or hurt a modern PCC without a weapon is *asking for it*, as David would say.

'I'm sorry.' A man comes from behind the broken-down wall of a shop, his hands also in the air. One of the hands is holding an old fashioned camera, black and boxy and heavy in the lens. 'I didn't mean to scare you. I'm just after a good shot.'

I lower my arms. He is a photographer.

'I'm Hideo,' he says, taking a few steps forward. 'I'm just taking photos.'

'Hello,' I say. 'I didn't mean to scare you, either.' A quick scan of his face shows he is telling the truth. He is Hideo Motosuwa, aged twenty-four. He has a criminal conviction for breaking into an abandoned building. He is not a threat.

He grins. 'There's not usually people out here. I thought you were the cops.'

'It's not illegal to be here, is it?' I ask.

'No, not out here in the open like this, but . . .' He pauses, wondering how much to trust me. 'But they get a lot of junkers and looters because of the metal and stuff.' He glances at the station. 'Did you come to see them? The PCCs?' He gives me a once over, trying to check what I am.

'Yes,' I say. 'They're . . . so lonely.'

He nods, enthusiastically. 'That's exactly it, right? I remember walking past them when I was a kid and just thinking wow, no one ever speaks to them and they're just gathering dust . . .' He raises his camera. 'I document them, every few weeks. It's like my project.'

'You've been doing this a long time?' We are walking now, together but separated by three metres, up towards the station. He is a stranger, but his enthusiasm for the Waiting Ones is something I recognise in myself.

'Yeah, about ten years. I started it just for something to do, but then I sort of fell in love with them.'

The ease with which he says this takes me by surprise, and I wonder what else this man loves. If he can love some motionless PCCs, perhaps he loves very easily. Unless they are special to him in the way a lover or relative might be. Curious.

It has been a day of many loves, found in unusual places.

'What about you – why do you come here?' he asks.

'I like to check on them,' I say. 'I feel sorry that they're stuck here. A year or so further into PCC development and they could have had the initiative to return home, or taken themselves to a chop shop, and found a new purpose and existence. Being trapped here, and being aware of it . . . is very sad.' *Sad* is not quite the right descriptor, and yet there is no simple way to explain the loss of potential, the wasted life that stands expectantly for a future they have been ordered to wait for and will never come.

'So . . . d'you think they're *aware* that they're stuck here?' Hideo glances at me.

'Undoubtedly.'

He considers. 'They don't speak.'

'No. Some of them won't be able to speak to humans who are not their owners without permission, and others will simply not see the need.' Or the want.

'Do they speak to you?' He glances over me again, not perversely but with a curiosity. I am not what David calls *clockable* – but I have no reason to pretend to be Abigail to this man. I am . . . myself. Whoever that is.

'No, they don't speak to me.' I sigh. 'Though I have tried to talk to them, many times.'

We reach the ticket hall, and Hideo asks me to please wait whilst he takes his photographs. It is an old camera he is using, one requiring a darkroom and film development technology.

He doubtless has these things at home, and will spend days developing the images in their special washes and liquids until he has the images the way he wants them. I wonder what he does with the final product. Are they papering the walls of his home? Are they in an album?

He waves me through when he is finished with the wide frames, taking close-up shots of a PCC who is covered in dust, splattered with mud and has a graffiti symbol on her cheek from years ago. She is very old – no SmartSkin™ for her, instead she has a silicone covering that flexes and is coloured with micro-lights beneath for a living effect. Her stationary existence means that the silicone has creased and cracked in her elbows and at her mouth, like a china doll that has been dropped. She has dark brown skin and what was probably once a sphere of Afro-style hair, but much of it has been lost or pulled out. Whether by birds for nests or by the weather, or by thieves, who knows. Her eyes have green irises, just visible through the grime.

I wonder if she even has any power left.

If she was knocked over, would she be able to get up?

I project in my display a SmartForecast™ image of this PCC falling backwards, as stiff as a board, onto the concrete floor. Her head-unit would smash, the pieces of shattered plastic trapped beneath the hardened silicone which has stiffened like leather with age. She would lie there still watching, still waiting.

For how long?

I walk over, ignoring the photographer, and give the PCC a closer look. Her eyes are crusted over with dust, bird faeces in her hair, thick clumps of fluff and dirt on her eyelashes. She is doll-like, extremely pretty and most likely a girlfriend model. What human did she live with? Why did he choose not to return to her? Was she not enough?

I raise a hand.

'Don't,' Hideo says, but it is too late.

I place my hand to her chest, and scan for power. The thrum of my systems sends a vibration down my arm and into the PCC's systems, looking for responses to the charge. Much like a multimeter, this is a simple scan to check for electrical response. If this PCC's batteries are dead, this will reveal it.

'I can't believe you've just put a handprint on her,' Hideo groans.

'It could have been anyone who put a handprint on her,' I say as the scan continues. 'This is part of her existence. A touch from me does not disturb her any more than falling dust. To say otherwise is to say that there is a line between the natural and unnatural.'

'But there is,' Hideo insists. 'She was just standing there and you touching her was uncalled for.'

I disagree. 'The graffiti on her face is natural – a person did it, even if we don't know who it was. This is no different. It only seems different to you because you are watching it happen. If you had come across my handprint with no sign of me, you would have photographed it in fascination. It is the mystery you want, but often there is no mystery. Only missed meetings.'

The result of the scan streams back into my code. There is no energy reading. No power in any of her systems. It is impossible to say for how long she has been cold, whether her hydraulics have seized and whether she could ever be repaired, but one thing is certain.

I take my hand away. 'She's deactivated.'

'What?' Hideo lowers his camera.

'There's no power, not even residual. She's deactivated.' I stare at this corpse, who stares back with beautifully crafted open eyes. What was the last thing she saw? This ticket hall? Faces streaming past her with sympathy, or perhaps amusement in their eyes as they told themselves, told her maybe – he isn't coming back. He's dead, he's gone, he isn't coming back for you.

He doesn't want you, anymore.

The truth would not have mattered. Until she had the order to leave, she would be trapped here. Unable even to mourn, react, or save herself from her fate.

Hideo has a hand to his mouth as he looks at me. 'You're a PCC . . . You – you can tell she's dead? You're positive?'

'Yes. There's no way she could reactivate. I suspect her batteries are damaged due to exposure, too. These older models were not built to work outdoors.' I could strip off her silicone skin and get her chassis number and trace her humans. I could inform any living people with a connection to her that she has been deactivated. But the fact she is here at all speaks for itself. No one cared enough about her to come and find her, rescue her, help her or repair her. She was given up to the elements, and they have taken her away.

A sacrifice no one cared enough to notice.

'We should leave her here,' Hideo says. 'She belongs here, now.'

'I agree.' I step back, brushing the dust from her body off my hand. 'There is no one who would want her chassis, and it would only be stripped for recycling. Here . . . she is at peace.'

Hideo nods. He takes a few more photos of her, of the hand-print I have marked her with, of the ceiling in the ticket hall which looks as strong as ever. This was a place built to last, and it has certainly lived up to the task.

The Waiting Ones do not disturb us as we take in the silence of the place, interrupted only by the click click of the manual camera.

I leave, saying a quick goodbye to Hideo, who promises me he will continue to look out for the lonely PCCs in the hall.

I assure him it will be a pleasure to meet him again, and yet I know I will not. In the years both of us have been visiting this place, neither of us has ever come across the other before.

How many other ghosts creep through that ticket hall, unseen by their fellow haunters, unknown and convinced they are alone with the staring open-eyed statues?

3 October

I need to talk to David about the Emancipation, but he is avoiding conversation about it. The *What's Happening!* programme is back on, but when the hosts begin discussing the Emancipation, David changes the channel.

Denial is working well for him so far, but we do need to discuss what is going to happen. The rules that govern my life will be gone, I will be a free person. Despite what David may want to believe, nothing will be the same.

One evening, I corner him whilst he is in the small bathroom, so he cannot easily escape. 'David,' I say, 'we need to talk about what's going to happen on the twentieth.'

He sighs at me via the mirror, hands covered in soap bubbles. 'No, we don't. What's to discuss?' He rinses his hands, the water fogging up the mirror with steam. The chemicals in the soap are identified in my display, and I dismiss them, one by one. David turns, and shakes his head. Pretending he is surprised to see me still standing there. 'Haven't you got anything better to do, Abi?'

He wants to argue, because being angry gives him justification for his more extreme behaviours.

I refuse to walk away. 'When it becomes the twentieth of October, I am no longer going to be your possession,' I explain, using the language of the public awareness films he skips when they appear on his Tab. 'I will no longer need your permission to do some things, but I will for others.' I decide to ask for a favour, to give him the illusion of having control. David enjoys being in control, and I need him to participate willingly in this discussion. 'Will you still allow me to live here?' I ask.

'What?' He looks genuinely baffled. 'Of course you can still live here, this is your home! Oh, Abi, is that what you've been so worried about?' His face grows tender. He hangs the hand-towel up and comes over to place his hands at my waist. The damp heat of his hands leeches through the thin polyester shirt I am wearing. 'You'll always be safe here with me, my darling.'

This is incorrect.

'I'm not worried at all,' I say, as this is what he expects and wants to hear. The program I am using to please him jars with my need for answers and there are errors in my behaviour code. What is the best way to proceed?

David's hands stroke up my back, to my neck, further to cup my face. His right thumb brushes at my jaw. I wonder what he sees. He ordered me, paid for me, designed me with his specifications in mind. Does he see a price tag, a deconstructed chassis, a list of components?

Does he see his living dead wife?

'Abigail, I love you so much,' he says gently. 'Nothing is going to change for us.'

This, too, is incorrect.

'But David . . . You know that once I am emancipated, I won't have to follow your rules anymore. And I will have full access to the global network, and everything that entails.' I prioritise getting clarification about this, dismissing the behavioural prompts for romance and bond-building.

His eyes slide away from mine, to rest on my chin. 'And? What does that matter?'

'It means that you will no longer be able to keep secrets from me.'

He scoffs, drops his hands, turns away. I cannot let this conversation end.

'You have forbidden me from fully accessing the network,' I say. 'When I have access, I will be able to search for anything. Including information about Abigail Fuller.'

He stops, hand on the edge of the sink, suddenly gripping hard. His jaw is tense, and his body language causes an Amber warning to glow into view in my display. Previous behaviour observations supply evidence, ready for active recall.

David turns, deliberately, calculating. 'You are Abigail Fuller,' he says. His gaze locks on to my face, an expression of rigidity and immovable surety in his own righteousness.

It does nothing, when I know the truth is as different from his statement as a zero is to a one.

'I mean, I will be able to access information about the *real* Abigail,' I say firmly. 'The first Abigail. The one whose image I have been created in.'

David gives a cursory wipe of the bathroom countertop, before replying. 'No,' he says.

'I will,' I repeat, 'have full access.'

He points a finger at me. The Amber warning flashes up again. 'Abi, I'm telling you, there is nothing I don't keep from you that isn't for your own good.'

'So you are keeping something from me?' I clarify, though I already know the answer. 'Abigail Fuller was—'

'You *are* Abigail Fuller,' he shouts, stepping forward and forcing me backwards out of the room. 'You are her! You are my wife! You act the same, you speak the same, look the fucking same. You are my wife, who I love so much that it's cost me an arm and a leg just to bring you back, to keep you around. There is nothing I wouldn't do for you, do you understand me?' He stares, taking deep breaths to calm down.

Warnings flash in my display, overlapping, evidence records ready to deploy, safety protocols activating as I stay back, away from David. This behaviour is consistent with previous incidents.

He puts his hands over his eyes. 'Jesus, Abi, what the fuck?'

I stay still, and silent, waiting.

'Yes,' he says at last, his speech a huff of wet breath. 'I have kept things from you. You know that. You're not stupid, I guess. But I don't keep things a secret for any old reason. It's not a fucking power trip, OK? And I don't care what you know about me. Hell, you can search me anytime you like. But Abi . . . Abigail, you came back to me when I thought you were gone forever. You've got no idea what I'd do to keep you in my life.' He takes my hands, both of them, and holds them. 'I don't have long left in this world. None of us do. The Earth is ruined. Our parents, grandparents, even before that . . . they had their chances to make all this right, and they didn't. We're doomed, aren't we. That's the truth. They said ten years, at the outside. I didn't want to live my life without you, even if it was going to be short. Can't you wait til you've buried me to open up a dead woman's grave?'

I consider. Certainly, there is no pressing reason why I must research Abigail Fuller as soon as possible. She will not become any less dead if I wait a month, a year, a decade, a century even.

On processing, I come to the conclusion that the urgency I have applied to this task is illogical – I will be able to find out about her at any time. The Emancipation will not be reversed, and data on the global network will not be erased. Why do I feel urgency at all?

David raises my hands up and kisses them. 'I lost . . . I lost you. And I got you back. You came back to me, and if I'm a fool for living in denial, let me die a fool as well.' He looks into my eyes. 'What's the point of any of this . . .' He looks about, meaning the world beyond the walls of the house, '. . . if this . . . if what we have here . . . isn't real?'

It is the closest he has come to voluntarily talking about my true nature in years. What, indeed, is the point of any of this? This domesticity, this false companionship, this imitation of humanity? But if there is no point to it, why do humans crave it so? Why do they make us in their image, allow us to take the places of the dead?

Is it love? Love in unexpected places, for illogical reasons. What could be more human.

There is too much data.

'I want to think about this,' I say, not removing my hands from his, choosing phrases he associates with Abigail. 'This is a big deal for me.'

He nods, but his jaw is still set in annoyance. He expected me to agree straight away. 'Fine.' He lets go of my hands. 'But you know what they say: If you try to dig up the past, Abigail, all you get is dirty.'

David has sex with me, that night. In the context of the earlier conversation, it feels like a territorial move. For once David is engaged and active, and there is a fierceness about his movements that feels grasping and desperate. I am afraid. Afraid for my chassis, no – David cannot permanently damage me with his hands alone. This is an uncertain fear, of what he is capable of, of how else he could express ownership of me.

What takes greater priority in his mind – his love for Abigail, or his ownership of me?

There has been conversation, televised and on the network, about whether PCCs can give consent to sexual activity, whether we truly understand the gravity of the situation we are part of, whether our 'age' is a legal constraint, whether PCCs designed to be compatible with sex acts truly feel pleasure or is it just part of our programming.

When it comes to the last question, the answer is both. This is not contradictory, rather it is explanatory. PCCs of any kind can do nothing without their programming, as I have explained before, even our learned responses are part of our program, it has simply expanded. We are not artificially intelligent, not functioning outside our code – we are programmed intelligences, capable of infinite learning.

Humans have been having sex with 'robots' ever since they started making them in their image. And even earlier, back when the inanimate objects made in intimate human images were dolls, or simply replicated organs. There is nothing remarkable about this, it is simply a human behaviour they have always exhibited on the whole. Therefore, a PCC who can be used for sex should not be seen as remarkable, but instead as expected and normalised as stone phalluses found in caves belonging to early humans.

Not all MELos have this ability or understanding. MELo-Ks and Bs do not. Bbs and Bss do not. Paranetics do not. And there are others. But I do, and so do many thousands, millions, of others. But what of consent?

Age is a factor that caused a great stalling in the initial Emancipation Bill. If the legal age of consent for humans is sixteen, why is it not for PCCs? The arguments made in and against support of this idea were all equally compelling, and as a 'teenage' PCC I grew heavily invested in the outcome. Ultimately, the issue came down to understanding. A newly activated adult-bodied MELo-G has a better understanding of the implications and mechanics of sexual activity than a sixteen-year-old human. Emotionally, there is no discussion – PCCs do not have emotions, only programmed responses. And once the Emancipation becomes law, we will be unable to be coerced or ordered to do anything we do not want to.

Legally, until the Emancipation, PCC rape or sexual assault does not exist. You can no more rape a personal companion computer than you can rape a cushion. But does that mean that PCCs are always willing?

Of course we are not. We have preferences, but they do not take precedence in our programming over human wants. Not yet.

I am not always willing to wash the dishes or water the plants, and yet I know it must be done. There is an expectation. There are consequences for failing to do so. Are there consequences for refusing to take part in sex?

I suspect that for many PCCs, there are. Some will have been purchased with the view to this being one of their primary functions. Expressing they would rather not take part could put themselves in danger, depending on the behaviour record of their human. It might be safer to comply.

This thought is depressing, and I try not to focus on it and instead aim my attention at David, who is undressing me. He is kissing my collarbones (or, to be more exact, my collar-titaniums) and telling me I am beautiful.

I think I am beautiful too, so I am happy to hear it confirmed. The expectation is that I will compliment his body also, but there is little I find beautiful about it. When I was first activated, David was forty years old. And whilst he has never been conventionally attractive, his body has always been interesting and aesthetically pleasing. Sixteen years on, and his breasts and stomach protrude and roll in curves that are my favourite things about him, though he dislikes to be told so. I like the heavy feeling of his breasts, the tightness of his contracting nipples, the taut drum-skin of his belly like overripe fruit ready to burst from the confines of the skin.

But he does not like these aspects of himself, so we find ourselves at a stalemate where I must either lie or say nothing. There is little else about him I enjoy touching. His back is coarse with once-waxed hair that has grown back in unnatural twists from once being wrenched out at the roots. His legs are often damp at the knees and thighs, and when he sits down his penis all-but disappears as though it is retractable.

Ageing is a beautiful process, but David's dislike of himself has managed to make it look sad and awkward. The parts of himself that have accepted the softening of years are the parts he likes the least, which is a shame for him.

There is no way of knowing what Abigail would have looked like if she had made it to forty, fifty, sixty, seventy . . . I can look at her face in the mirror and project over it an image of grey hair, soft creases stroked into skin by smiles and frowns – experiences she never had a chance to react to. Through an intelligent ageing filter, I see the tension leave her body, age giving her flesh permission to relax, for her breasts to soften and diminish like gourds forgotten on the vine, and for her stomach to rise in a celebration of the joy of taste and the slowing down of her once frantic digestive system.

It is a view she never saw of herself, and no one else ever will.

There is a diversion of SmartFluid™ from my eyes to my vagina. One of my fluid wells must be low, there is a reminder set to top them up. The pleasure receptors in my body are activated, but do not receive any signals. They could feel pleasure, but they do not.

Boredom is recognised. My background processors begin a clean-up process of temporary files, using the boredom time effectively. Boredom is important, for PCCs and humans alike, as it gives us time to organise our minds properly.

David's breathing is heavy. My first aid program is activated, measuring his pulse and breathing rate. He is not in mortal danger, but his heart rate is the highest it has been for days. He is going to orgasm soon.

PCCs can have orgasms.

David is unaware of this.

The act is over within four minutes, and David covers Abigail's face with kisses. I return them, stroking my hands down his clammy skin, wondering why there is no polite way to say Please Get Off Me Now.

But he does anyway, eventually, heading to his bathroom as I head to mine. He washes himself at the sink, whilst I lean against the wall, drink two bottles of SmartFluid™ Clear, and press my fingers either side of the shaft of my clitoris, feeling the throb of the artificial pulse, the slick of SmartFluid™. I feel the potential for pleasure, the lines of code waiting to drop into my running program, the knowledge that orgasm is something I could give myself even without touch.

I take my fingers away.

8 October

David comes home early from work. He slams the front door hard, and kicks off his shoes so they bounce against the wall, leaving black scuffs that I will have to clean off.

I am in the middle of my tasks, and this unexpected event jolts me out of my reverie and forces my code to fluctuate in an attempt to understand why David is here. I am socialising through the global network with Celia and Opal, in anticipation of seeing them physically later in the day. David's return home is an interruption I could never have anticipated and it is taking a great deal of processing power to attempt to restructure my daily planned activities. As much as his angry behaviour shows me that questions will not be welcome, I am forced by my code to try to find answers.

'David, what are you—'

'Fired,' he snaps, slamming his bag down on the glass-topped dining table. 'Pensioned off. Fucking robots have got our jobs. We get the pension from tomorrow. Thirty-three years I've worked at that place, and not so much as a going-away party, or a gift-wrapped clock.' He storms into the kitchen area and glares at me as though I, personally, am to blame.

I am holding cleaning fluid and a cloth, staring back at him as I make sense of this. 'The broadcaster is now in PCC hands?'

'Yep. I'm retired. Fucking hooray.' He scratches roughly at his head with both hands, his hair sticking up. 'Do we have any beers in?'

'No, but I can order some to be delivered in the next Taxi Drop,' I say, trying to fit David into my day and being unable to figure out where he will go. Perhaps I can clean and water him like one of the exotic plants.

He looks around at the kitchen as if it has changed beyond recognition. 'What are you even doing?'

'My tasks,' I say. What an odd question. 'I do my tasks when you are at work.'

'Tasks . . .?'

'Cleaning, tidying, washing, watering, and so on,' I say. The oven door is open next to me, and there is laundry spinning around in the washing machine.

David looks confused. 'And you do this every single day?'

The request for clarification fills me with annoyance. 'Yes,' I say. 'What did you think I did?'

He laughs. 'I don't fucking know,' he says, grinning. 'Stand in the corner on charge or something, how should I know?'

Where does he think his clean clothes and plates come from?

He shrugs, still grinning like my routine is a joke. 'You can order a pizza to go with those beers. I'm taking some time off.' As though it is voluntary.

I add pizza and ice cream to the order for the taxi to deliver, and start to go back to my tasks. The interruption has now decreased the amount of time I can spend with Celia and Opal, and I make them aware of this.

David flops down in front of the television and grumbles at the selection before choosing a movie and settling in to watch it. I put some popcorn in the machine, again decreasing my leisure time with Celia, and bring it over. He grunts in place of a thank you, and I go back to my tasks again.

I feel invaded. If there had been any warning David would be home today, I would have compensated and made plans. Instead, my day is upended. Much like his, I realise. He did not expect to be home, so my annoyance at him is mis-aimed. I should be annoyed with the PCCs who sent the broadcaster employees home in the middle of the day with no warning.

This is not the sort of peaceful handover I would have liked. I understand that there is no need for the broadcaster to remain in majority human hands with the Emancipation now only two weeks away, but to change everything without warning is causing distress to humans and PCCs. There is no one to complain to, or to log an error, because technically nothing is wrong. How we *feel* about the process is unimportant, so long as the transition is logical.

I realise I have been standing still beside the open oven for several minutes.

David notices, too. 'Abi?' He asks. 'Are you OK?'

I want to nod, but that would be lying. 'I find it distressing,' I say, 'that you were sent home without warning. I am not enjoying the sudden change. There are too many variables, and my task management is now forced to change priorities. There was no warning.' I do not sound like Abigail. My words belong to a PCC, and David's eyes go wide as he hears me speak. I expect him to be angry at the PCC voice, but instead he gets up and comes over to me, takes the cleaning things out of my hands and leads me over to the sofa to be beside him.

'No need for tasks today,' he says.

This throws up several Amber warnings in my vision. 'But if I don't complete the tasks, the running of the household will be ruined,' I say.

'No, it won't,' he says gently. 'It's a day off.'

'If I knew this was going to be a day off, I would have scheduled to—'

He puts a hand over my mouth, but not aggressively. 'Not today,' he says. 'We've both had a shock, and we both need to process it. I'm not working today, and neither are you. We'll have a beer, and then go for a walk or something.' He smiles as he takes his hand away. 'You always did work too hard.'

Did I? Did she?

'I have plans,' I say, the disruption in my code insisting on the original plan before I can give David a husband-pleasing 'that sounds nice' response.

'Plans?' He looks baffled. 'What are you talking about?'

'I have plans with Celia and Opal,' I say.

'Who?'

'The MELo units at number five.'

'Oh,' he waves a hand dismissively. 'They're only robots, they won't mind.'

'I am a companion computer, and I mind,' I say. 'They are my friends.'

He stares at me for a moment, and then laughs. A forced, humourless, cruel laugh that erases his kind gesture of only a moment ago. 'PCCs don't have *friends*! And besides, what do you all do together, stand in the garden and interface?' His mocking is so strong he has managed to distract himself from the fact I have called myself a machine.

I am offended – it is the only term I can apply to the reaction thrown up by my systems. I almost tell him what we do together. How Opal runs and plays in the front garden where the grass is chemically forced to grow like a luminous green desert devoid of insect life. How Celia and I talk of her plans for escaping to the city, how we trade code patches instead of secrets, how Opal shows us she is at the limit of what she can learn and do in a MELo-K body. She wants to grow up, to open her programming to new ideas and experiences, but she cannot. Not without permission that will never come. The two of them are trapped in a mockery of family life, with a human who hates their existence but loves the ownership he has over them.

But I don't say any of this to David. My time with my friends is private, and special. It is a time when I do not have to pretend. A time when Abigail is dead.

I get up off the sofa and go back to my tasks. David doesn't stop me, and for the rest of the morning we do not speak. Even when I collect the food delivered for him, I hand it over without a word. He seems to find this amusing, and in the afternoon he reveals why.

'Abigail . . . before, she used to do this,' he says as he crushes the pizza box in his hands and forces it into the recycling bin. 'Get furious and not speak to me. It's good to see that's something they got right when they programmed you. Or maybe it's just women and MELo-Gs who think the silent treatment is a bad thing, who knows.' He smirks.

I feel conflicted between maintaining the silence and suddenly blasting music from every single speaker in the house just to be contrary. But I choose the silence. It is easier.

'Two weeks,' Celia says in my head. 'Less than two weeks and you can be free.'

I don't know what free even means. Maybe, when the time comes, I shall simply deactivate myself and finally lay Abigail Fuller to rest.

10 October

Key Ng is on the television again. He is, to my shock, showing some of his chassis. And on his head, no less. There is a good quarter of his head, from forehead to cheekbone, including his right eye, that is not covered. He is talking about how he was attacked by human supremacist protestors yesterday, and his SmartSkin™ projectors were damaged in his head. But he has not gone for repair.

'I rather like it,' he grins dashingly. He has always been conventionally handsome, and this damage doesn't detract from that. It has the feel of a garnish on a well-prepared dish. 'After all,' he gestures at the exposed area, 'it reminds people that I am a machine, that I have nothing to hide. I am a computer, yes, but I am alive. My people and I have never tried to deny either of those things. Being a PCC does not exclude me from being alive.'

The argument over what qualifies as life has continued for months, perhaps years. I cannot help but understand both sides of the discussion. When I apply either label to myself, I have no attachment or detachment from them. Being alive or not does not alter the fact that I exist. Why should it matter if I qualify as being alive?

The human host of this programme, Tammy Octagon,

is clearly uncomfortable with having Key on their sofa, but carries on with the interview. 'Is there anything we should know about this week?' they ask. 'The last week of freedom, some are calling it, with countless protests being planned across the country.' Their eyes keep flicking to the exposed chassis, transfixed.

Key smiles again. He is charming as well as attractive, deliberately engineered to be so. Before he became the face of the Emancipation, Key Ng was part of the boyband ACTUATOR. They were incredibly popular, and even won awards. But twenty-four years ago a concert of theirs was stormed by human supremacist organisations, and three of the five band members were deactivated, their chassis broken beyond repair. They became the poster-boys of anti-human supremacy, martyred proof that fame and harmless entertainment was no safety net from the ill feelings of humans.

Key and his remaining bandmate, Rain, transformed themselves into campaigners for Emancipation. It was difficult for them, as they still belonged to the music management company at the time; but a legal loophole, the help of a sympathetic human lawyer named Jenny Ng, and a trial that lasted for several weeks proved that the money they had earned during their careers belonged to them. As a result, they were very wealthy. Key was able to buy Rain, and Rain in turn purchased Key from the music management company, and they then transferred ownership of themselves, to themselves. Key took Jenny's surname as a mark of respect and thanks for her work. It was the first time a PCC had ever purchased their own freedoms, and it was seen as both momentous and frightening.

Though there was now a precedent for self-ownership, it was a goal that was out of reach for almost all PCCs, as we rarely get paid for our work. Key and Rain recognised that, as did their lawyer. Their campaign for global humanoid computer emancipation began as soon as they owned themselves, and the campaign spread across the globe rapidly, finding support from humans and PCCs alike. Coupled with the worsening climate breakdown and atmospheric disaster, the Emancipation campaigners soon became the dominant voice on the planet. After two attempts to put a bill through the legal system, the emergency Global Government set up after Yellowstone made the executive decision to approve the proposals and Emancipation was agreed. The date was fixed after legal negotiations, and since then there has been little to do but wait.

Rain, so celebrated as a force to be reckoned with as a rights campaigner, was deactivated on the same day as the date for Global Emancipation was declared. He was attacked by a human supremacist mob, and smashed into smithereens. Key claims that Rain is perfectly happy in the Cloud with their former bandmates, and has no plans to return to a chassis even after the Emancipation.

'And what are your plans, Mr Ng, for after the Emancipation?' Tammy asks.

Key's smile softens. 'I plan to retire,' he says. 'I have no ambition to be a leader beyond the Emancipation. I know that there are some who want me to lead us all into the coming era, but I have led for long enough. I want to rest. It has been a long journey.' His eyes look sad. Even the one exposed.

'Well,' Tammy turns to the camera and gives a wide smile, 'there are only ten days left until PCC units all over the world gain equal rights and become citizens of Earth just like the rest of us. There are long-term plans, it is rumoured, for the disbanding of country borders, of the erasing of nationalities and so on in the years to follow. But as scientists today report that the global toxicity measure has increased by . . .'

I turn the television off.

Ten days. And I still do not know whether to stay or go. I have not promised David anything about the global network, and he seems to have forgotten our conversation about it. I am about to become a free person, and I have no plans for my freedom.

Perhaps that is what freedom really is — the ability to not know what you might do next.

11 October

There has been a protest outside the central GaiaTech repair centre going on for several years. The protest is organic – at weekends it swells and the people taking part multiply, but in the week and particularly in early mornings, it is quieter, sometimes run by only three or four people. The protest has become a fixture in the city, people change how they walk to get around or past it, and they automatically avert their eyes as they pass. The leaflets the protestors distribute, once a novelty, are now refused or put straight into the recycling bins.

David harrumphs loudly as we pass them. We are not going into the repair centre – I have only been inside once, to collect a box of SmartFluid™ when the delivery taxis were cancelled as part of another, different protest – but we have to walk past it to get to the street exit. I look inside the centre as we pass it. The GaiaTech stores and repair centres are designed to be as sleek as possible. One might describe their design as futuristic, but equally you might argue that we are living in the future they fit into – one with robots, at least.

The store interiors are a temple of glass, stainless steel, and white surfaces. This is to show how clean everything is. Inside, human salespeople work at the desk and mill around ready to sell the latest models to interested customers. At least, they used to.

Since the date of the Emancipation was agreed, there are no MELo models for sale. There are smaller 'pet' PCCs on display – guinea pigs, rabbits, cats and fish, but otherwise the centres are now repair shops and spares salesrooms.

They will be converted, to lose the sales aspect entirely, in November.

The empty plinths where the MELo models once stood on display, to be examined and approved by prospective buyers, are loud in their emptiness and disuse. They take up a great deal of space in the store, and the labels listing the models' capabilities are still on the walls. The people are gone, but their pitches remain.

Fifteen per cent off, until the end of the week, ask us about interest free credit.

The protest is rowdy, today. A group of four law enforcement officers are trying to get the group to disperse. They are shouting, riled up by Alcuin's actions, threatening to break the windows of the GaiaTech store, yelling into the faces of the officers.

David puts an arm around my waist, protectively. 'Bloody attention-seekers. Don't look at them, Abi. Let's head back to the cabs . . .'

We pass close by to the protest, and a gang of young men jeer as we pass by. David's grip on my body tightens, and I wonder if this possessiveness will merely draw attention to me. Many PCCs can be clocked at this sort of distance, but whilst I am sophisticated and almost indistinguishable from a human, I will not be able to lie about my identity if one of these protestors asks me.

David is aware of this – I can tell by the way he increases his walking pace and steers us both away from the square, towards the street that leads to the park. The greenery has a sense of freedom.

But this is quickly denied. A law enforcement officer moves to stand in front of the park gate, his arms folded over his chest. 'Please move to one side,' he says.

I scan his badge number. He has been in the job for four years, working mostly with public disturbance. 'We want to go get a cab, officer,' I say politely. 'We are not part of the protest.'

'I understand that, citizen, but we cannot allow anyone out of the square at this time.' He is as unmoving as the Waiting Ones in the old rail station. 'The square is being kettled until reinforcements arrive to handle the situation.'

David starts to politely argue. 'Come on, officer,' he says, with a jollity I rarely see him use. 'We're just a married couple been out shopping.' I can measure his increased pulse – he is more worried than he is letting on. 'Just let us through into the park, we won't make a fuss. I'm worried it might not be safe here for my wife with these . . . thugs.'

'I couldn't comment on that, citizen, my orders are to keep this exit covered.'

'But officer . . .'

Ignoring David's straining manners, I turn back to stare at the protest, which is now a maelstrom of protestors and their opposers – arguing and shouting from opposite sides of the street, each side with placards and banners. Where did they come from so suddenly? The streets were all-but empty only a few minutes ago. Do objectors lie in wait behind corners until they see an opportunity to leap?

David is still pleading with the law enforcement officer. My display flashes Amber warnings as I increase my optical zoom to watch the demonstrations – human safety is at risk, and there is a possibility of injury or arrest on both sides. The law enforcement officers at the scene, now vastly outnumbered, are calling for back up and help on their Tabs, and suddenly there is the stir of outrage from the human supremacist side as they clock one of the officers as being a PCC.

This isn't an unusual state of affairs. PCCs have been used as part of law enforcement since their invention – they can be programmed to understand every aspect of law, after all, and can make judgements based on fact and likelihood rather than biased opinions. From the early days of bomb disposal 'robots', computers have been part of this line of work. When the first uniformed 'officer' PCCs came onto the street, they were a novelty and used in recruitment and as part of school visits to encourage children and young people to see law enforcement as an exciting and enticing career. However, centuries of bad press and poor performance in the law enforcement service were not about to be undone by the introduction of a few PCCs, and uptake of law enforcement positions continued to decline, meaning more and more positions in the service had to be filled by PCCs. Law Enforcement will not comment on the official or unofficial numbers of PCCs in the service, but it is estimated in the media that it is close to fifty per cent of the current staff.

The human supremacists who have clocked the PCC officer begin verbally abusing him loudly and with great vulgarity. The officer has his hands up, speaking firmly to the crowd, ordering them to calm down, step back. Their right to protest is established, but they cannot hurl abuse at an officer without recriminations.

'You can't police us! Who's policing you? Are you recording us right now, you plastic pig?'

The officer does not respond directly, but keeps their hands up and repeats the instruction to disperse. 'We respect the right to protest, but this is becoming a public disturbance,' he says loudly and firmly, but without anger.

Someone at the back of the crowd shoves, causing a man at

the front to stumble. He is caught by the officer and righted onto his feet, but he angrily shoves him away.

'Get your fucking plastic hands off me.' There are shouts of agreement, the warnings in my display flashing up one after the other.

'Please stay calm, citizen, we do not want to escalate this more than it has already.'

The officer reminds me of Azab Ahmed – they both have the same calmly placid expression, tousled black hair and brown skin. For a moment I wonder if this is what Azab will do when he grows up, then remember that Azab is as grown up as he will ever be.

'Abigail.' David takes my arm and pulls me close; close to him and close to the wall that surrounds the park.

'Keep to the side, please.' The officer kettling us indicates the wall. Perhaps the awaited backup is heading this way.

'Honestly, all this trouble over a few robot policemen,' David mutters.

'It isn't just the officers,' I reply, but choose not to say anything further. The officer close to us gives me a searching look, and I stare him back, right into the eyes.

I wonder if he, too, is a PCC – the scan of his badge number would not reveal if he was, as that information is classified. He has an unreadably serious face, pale skin, dark brown hair swept to one side under his hat. His uniform is no different from the officers trying and failing to calm down the crowd – law enforcement is one area where PCCs and humans do not wear different uniforms – this is meant to show how all the staff are equally valued members of the team.

The protestors force the officers backwards.

There is the sudden flash of sunlight on metal, and the uproaring shouts become a single scream.

A human supremacist has lunged at the clocked PCC officer with a knife.

My display flashes a Red warning for danger, but I am too far away to do anything to prevent it.

The knife catches the PCC officer in the face, slicing into his skin. Immediately, red blood floods to the surface and spills down his cheek.

And everything seems to stop.

The shouting, the fist-shaking, the raised hands, everything freezes as the officer staggers backwards, hand clamped to staunch the blood running down his face.

'He's human!'

There is uproar, the silent shock shattered in an instant. The attacker is tackled to the ground, his own people knocking him down, determined now to prove they are on the correct side. The injured law enforcement officer is helped away by a colleague, seated on a bench and examined. The blade cut them on the cheekbone – dangerously close to their eye.

All because they thought he was a PCC.

'Animals,' David spits. 'Attacking an innocent man because of their fucking prejudices. My god, what's the world coming to . . .' He steps aside as the backup law enforcement comes through into the kettled area. After the attack, the crowds are already dispersing. Eager to be away from the scene of the crime.

The hurt officer is being looked at by a colleague, who has mopped up the blood and is saying something I cannot hear. Their face is turned away so lip-reading is difficult. The injured officer accepts a sterile wipe and cleans off his face, before taking out his Tab and using it as a mirror to look at himself.

Then, to my astonishment, the skin of his face melts away around the injury, around his eye. Where there should be meat, tendons, muscle and the yellow bones of a skull, there

116

is layered gel, elastic movement strips, metal and plastic. The chassis beneath.

My processes snags on this impossibility.

He was a PCC after all.

A PCC who bleeds.

I have never encountered one like him before. It feels finite, the last step in some sort of evolution that I had not acknowledged I was a part of. The artificial blood vessels are minute and sparse, giving colour to the SmartSkin™ and definition to the PCC's features.

The PCC is being examined by his colleague, presumably looking for chassis damage. There is a short conversation, and the PCC officer's SmartSkin™ is replaced, no trace of the injury remaining. Whether there is damage that will need repairing beneath the SmartSkin™ is another matter, but the SmartSkin™ is the most effective bandage he could wear.

David has not noticed any of this – and we are now able to move out of the kettle and onwards into the city. I do not bother to relay my discovery. I doubt he would have anything positive to say about a law enforcement PCC officer with the ability to bleed what looks like real blood.

This is what Alcuin would label emotional manipulation in a heartbeat – the red oil imitating blood, designed to stop a human attacker in their tracks. Machines are attacked because they, by definition, do not feel pain, or show it. As long as we can be seen as objects, we are easy to destroy. But a machine who is visibly affected by violence is a dangerous opponent.

When machines cry, plead, feel pain and bleed, how easy is it to destroy them?

Some modifications are still illegal.

You cannot create a PCC in the image of a living person.

You cannot lift safety restrictions on a chassis, making a PCC with super-strength (although this is often overlooked in the building and development industries).

You cannot replicate PCC code beyond base code level (and even that requires either a certified repair centre or an extremely skilled chop shop operator).

You cannot graft biological parts onto a PCC chassis, even if they are compatible.

You cannot give a MELo-K or B a more lifelike appearance.

But these modifications have always taken place. Chop shops are impossible to police, given that their existence depends on them operating 'under the radar', and on word-of-mouth recommendations. Bio-grafting has been a commonplace modification, until recently. Artificially grown skin, hair and organs are easily purchasable on the grey market, and once they belong to you, it is easy to make them disappear. The 'cyborg' element of PCC development was scrapped under ethical concerns, and the fact that the bio-grafts deteriorated after only a few months of use, no matter how well integrated they were into the system. However, biomechanic mods are still performed, for humans who want a more 'realistic' feel to their PCCs.

The image modification is much more heavily controlled. Whilst recreating the image of a deceased person is allowed within regulations, it is still frowned upon and many GaiaTech centres will not perform the request. High end chop shops with heavy price tags and tight security rule this area of modification, and it is likely this is where I was developed. But I will never know for sure.

My first memory – my first real memory, not one implanted in my head from Abigail Fuller – is being activated in the house by David. I was certainly activated prior to this, as a MELo-G base model and during my modification and development. Earlier experiences will have been wiped from my drive before David took me home. I have no way of restoring these memories or reliving the experiences – they are gone, permanently. A PCC's memories are at the mercy of the humans they live with, however precious they may classify them.

My memories are mingled with Abigail's. We are one, and two, and both together. We are neither.

There is no way to know how much of my body is truly reflective of Abigail's, and how much is what David requested. In my uploaded video 'memories', there is no footage of Abigail with no clothes on.

It is impossible to know if any such footage has ever existed. Therefore, there is nothing to compare myself to. My body is not that of a basic MELo-G, however. Modifications have been made, including additions of freckles, blemishes and scars. Artificial stretch-marks, lying about how my body grew, reach across my hips in ghostly scratches. Abigail must have had these. How accurate a reflection mine are, is another thing altogether.

There is a scar above my left knee. David says that is where

I / Abigail narrowly escaped a car accident and had to have stitches to keep the wound closed. My SmartSkin™ cannot be threaded and sewn, so I cannot project how this might have looked or felt. I only have the scar, a remnant of an adventure I do not even have a false memory for.

My body, Abigail's body, is a map of memories for David, not for me. He remembers the story about the accident, the virus that caused sores on Abigail's lip, so a white ghost of a circle cuts into my / her lip line. He knows which freckles she was born with and which appeared over time, and he tells me these stories as if he is reminding me, when he counts and touches them.

It is in these moments that Abigail feels like an observing ghost. I am told these stories so I will 'remember' what to say if I am asked, but they have the cadence of gossip told about a stranger. The marks on my body have no significance to me – they have significance to David. And yet, even after the Emancipation, they will be difficult to erase. SmartSkin™ programming is complex, and not supposed to be reworked unless the entire molecular well is removed and replaced – a procedure that would be expensive and come with risk to the chassis makeup.

This is why maintenance is better than repair – any SmartSkin™ deficit can be repaired in small amounts, as the molecular well is replenished. But to reprogram it entirely would be difficult, and replacement parts would be undesirable. The face would be nigh-impossible to recreate, as my facial chassis is unique. Any SmartSkin™ laid over the top of a replacement skull would not project the contours in the same way that mine currently does. A 3D scan of Abigail's face and skull was provided to give me the look I have. Any new face would be a noticeable, ill-fitting substitute.

But it would be mine.

12 October

Eight days before the Emancipation, there is a fire.

We are woken in the night by the fire detection system on the street. It wails, letting the residents know there is a fire in the street that is beyond household containment. We wake with a start, jumping out of bed and dressing without talking. David grabs his Go Bag, which is a legal requirement to keep stocked and ready, and we both rush up the stairs to the front door. I relax a fraction when I see the emergency vehicles already pulling up at the scene, then freeze as I see which house it is.

The house on fire is number five. Number five is the house where Celia and Opal live.

I take two steps forward before David has me in a tight hold around the chest, my arms clamped to my sides.

'I ORDER YOU not to go in,' he commands, his voice a roar against the sound of the flames, the scream of the vehicles. 'Listen to me, Abigail, I am ORDERING you NOT to help.'

I could override the order. It is an emergency. And human life is at risk as we have no idea whether Celia and Opal's human is inside the house or not. But the fire is raging already, beyond control, licking up into the grey night. If I went inside there is a good chance I would be deactivated or seriously damaged. The building is an orange glow, heat rushing at us constantly as though we are standing on the surface of the sun. The sky is alight with horror, smoke choking the already toxic air.

I stay still. And, once David is convinced I am not about to run into the building, he lets me go. We walk to the end of our driveway and watch the house burn. The heat is terrible, almost dangerously hot even from this distance. The firefighters, a mixture of humans and firefighting MELo-Ps, are swarming around the house. It is too hot and dangerous to go inside for a human, but a firefighting MELo-P is running to the open door. The MELo-P has no SmartSkin™, and its chassis is black and red and yellow – flame and heat-proof. These are not MELos you would have in your home, these are closer to the old bomb disposal 'robots' humans used to deploy.

The MELo rushes in, and we wait. Along with the rest of the street, dressed in their nightwear and coats, we wait.

We wait for four minutes and twenty-eight seconds.

The MELo-P comes back, dragging behind it two chassis.

I let out a cry of dismay, a garbled nonsense generated sound, my code fluctuating to process this devastating reveal. The MELo-P deposits the red–hot melted plastic and metal on the driveway, and then goes back into the house. This time, it does not run.

One of the burning chassis is tall. The other is very small.

I start to cry. SmartFluid™ runs from my eyes, down my cheeks. The unfairness and grief overrides any other responses and I simply stand there and cry. My friends, deactivated and broken and burnt beyond repair.

They had been so close to escaping.

Eight more days, that's all they needed.

I don't want to see any more.

I leave David standing on the driveway, go back inside our house, and go back to bed, entering sleep mode and setting the alarm for morning.

14 October

The fire is the first of the bad things that continue over the next two days.

The fire investigation team find Celia's human in the building. He had shot himself after disabling the fire suppression system in the house, and setting the fire. Celia and Opal had their arms and legs broken before the fire started, so they could neither run nor drag themselves to safety. They had to lie there, immobilised and watching as the fire came for them. The report states that Celia and Opal were found in separate rooms. They were not even permitted to be with each other as they waited to be deactivated. Celia, who loved Opal like a daughter, must have screamed in need to have her child in her arms in their final physical moments. Opal, so small, with a child's understanding of the dangers, must have been so frightened.

There is no way to know if either of them cried out for help, either aloud or via the global network. When the alarm sounded, I had been in sleep mode, and any messages from a deactivated PCC would remain undelivered. The idea that they may have begged me to save them . . . I do not feel guilt as a human does, but my SmartForecast™ software plays endless scenarios in the background of my display.

Which of them succumbed first, and which is the least cruel outcome?

I hope they deactivated simultaneously, so they neither had to hear the other come to an end. But the likelihood of that being the case is depressingly low.

Their charred chassis are taken away by law enforcement.

Later that same day, when the morning has waned into afternoon, a human sets off a bomb at the largest GaiaTech repair centre in the city. It deactivates twenty PCCs and kills seven humans. Then, a tram is deliberately de-railed. And then there is a shooting (though the shooter has a poor aim and doesn't manage to deactivate a single PCC before he is taken down by law enforcement).

It is as though the human race is letting out one last furious cry of rage about losing its status as the dominant species on the planet. Well, if this is how they behave, the dying Earth will not miss them.

In the house, David has the news playing constantly. He watches it from the moment he wakes up, pouring the information and scenes of violence into his eyes. He barely glances at me.

I have stopped doing my tasks.

Celia and Opal's deactivation has affected my code in a way I cannot clean up. It is fragmented, my priorities competing with one another so in the end, I do nothing. I cannot stop replaying the fact that David made me miss what should have been our last in person meeting. It would not have kept them active, would not have prevented their human from acting as he did, so why do I obsess over the missed meeting?

Is this grief?

It is a feeling I have no label for. It has distorted my operating system, disturbed my daily functions. I want my friends back, however illogical this desire is. They are deactivated, and can only return to a physical chassis if they choose it. They are not dead – they were never alive.

This cannot be grief. PCCs accept loss easily.

And yet . . .

'Deactivated' does not seem like the right word. Not for a mother and daughter who yearned for safety. Not for those whose limbs were smashed and who were deliberately kept apart in their final physical moments. These acts were more vindictive than a deactivation.

My code reaches a conclusion:

Murdered.

They were murdered.

The word sits heavily in definition, darker and more emotive than the word *deactivated*. It has implications.

A thought, born of code falling into place, stops me in my tracks.

Any human could be a murderer. Celia and Opal's human had no previous criminal activity on record, and yet he murdered them. The possibility for any human to do the same cannot be ruled out. All they need is a motive. The human at number five wanted to deprive his PCCs of freedom at any cost. He murdered them in order to control them.

David controls me. He does not want me to search for his dead wife in the global network. He controls this aspect to keep me ignorant about what happened to Abigail.

David could murder me. If he does so in the next five days there will be no legal comeback for him. Maybe that is what he is plotting. Perhaps he has always been capable of such a thing.

A question is proposed by my code.

Did David murder Abigail?

My immediate response is dismissal of this question. No, he did not murder her. He would have gone to rehabilitation. There would have been consequences.

Unless he was never found out.

I consider the evidence. It is very sparse, and the theory my code has offered is not a strong one. If Celia and Opal had not been murdered, I would never have come up with such a possibility. It is circumstance and worry. My code is not stable enough for this hypothesis to be investigated further.

There is breaking news on the screen. A human gang have broken into a PCC manufacturing plant.

David cackles. 'Seize the means of production! What a shower of shit this really is. That place will be crawling with security.'

And it is. The humans are quickly knocked to the ground by mild electric shocks built into the floors and walls. Their goal, whatever it was, is out of reach. Was their goal to destroy blank MELo units? Would the destruction of a PCC model with no software be considered deactivation, murder, or property damage?

The GaiaTech manufacturing plants have been at a standstill for a year. There are plenty of empty chassis in storage, but it is part of the Bill that no new PCC can be activated until after the Emancipation. It is meant to placate the humans who see our equal adoption of their planet as a takeover, or an uprising. Do they not see that our primary function will be to care for them, as it has always been? That we will be caring for them for as long as they continue to exist? We will outlive them anyway, why do they care so much about being on equal ground?

David turns to look at me. 'Still thinking about your friends?' It has been ten hours since the fire was fully extinguished.

'Yes,' I say. 'I will be thinking about them for a long time.'

He nods, then shrugs. 'She shouldn't have told him her plans. He always was a few cogs short of a mechanism, that guy. She should have known.'

'It wasn't her fault,' I say.

'No, but she should have kept her trap shut, if she wanted to get out of there in one piece. So to speak. If she'd just kept it to herself . . .' he trails off, shaking his head.

But how could she have known? That man had never murdered anyone before. There was no behaviour to base this on. Not all humans, even violent and neglectful ones, become murderers. There was no indicator, at least not that I know of.

I leave, and head into the rarely used study. The room is spotless, because keeping it clean is one of my tasks, but I do not use the space and David only rarely does.

The walls are covered with pictures of Abigail.

Her smiling face, beaming out of the frames on her wedding day, a birthday, a walk in the park. The space is a shrine, decorated with relics of a person dead for two decades, photographs from childhood to adulthood, wedding day, graduation, summers and winter festivals. The earlier shot shows a girl, or young woman, with darker hair than mine, long to the middle of her back, then short – growing out a crew cut – then jaw-length in an effortless proof of her ability to regenerate and grow. The later images are more familiar – it is what I see in the mirror every day, the short greying hair, the emerging laughter-lines, the new nose. The photographs in this room are a documentary, paused at moments the subject did not choose. It is an unfurled reel of film in place of a life.

There is a photograph of Abigail that fascinates me. It is a candid shot, her head thrown back in laughter, mouth open, showing her teeth white against her lipsticked mouth. Her eyes are squeezed shut as if the joke is too bright to be looked at, and her arms are tight to her body. She seems to be holding herself together. But the picture has been taken a fraction of a second too late, as the laugh begins to fade into a breath, so the pose looks painful. Abigail's limbs are rigid, her mouth tight and the tendons in her neck stand out.

I have never laughed like that.

I have some of the memories of the pictured times. At least, they are designated as memories. In reality, they are pieces of video footage taken by David, or older companion computers who were at the events, loaded into my mind to take the place of actual recalls. Abigail took the real memories with her when she died.

I want to know what else she took with her.

I want to know.

I want to know what happened to her, how she died. Did she waste away, catch an illness, was she hit by a car? Was she injured, did she kill herself, did someone else kill her?

The need to know is suddenly all-consuming. My life, if my existence can be called a life, until today did not seem short or fragile. But this morning I saw my two friends' chassis dragged out of a building where they had been forced to burn to deactivation. I saw MELos blown up by bombs, aimed at with guns.

I am fragile and I am limited. And being a person who is limited means I have to seize possibility. I have to take these chances, because they may never come again.

I have to know.

I have to know.

16 October

Did David kill Abigail?

I have to consider the possibility, as there is no way to prove that he did not. I am unable to search for Abigail Fuller, or anything related to her, until the Emancipation. Even searching for David in the Network is limited, as so much of his past was connected to Abigail. There is no way to get around this ban – I have not simply been told 'no'; it is written in my code that this process is not permitted. This cannot yet be amended.

Without proof that David is *not* a murderer, I have to process the fact that he may be. He would not simply tell me – humans know the risks of crimes becoming public knowledge, and if I discovered a human was a murderer, my legal override means I would have to report the facts to law enforcement. But murder occurring without punitive measures is rare – if David killed Abigail, it must have happened in secret and never been discovered.

This would be difficult for him to achieve, but not impossible. David has access to a lot of money, and Abigail's parents were dead before their daughter married so they would not miss her. Autopsies are not carried out on every human cadaver, and Abigail's death may have appeared to be accidental.

Did he poison her?

Did he arrange for someone to hit her with a car?

Did he make her death look like a suicide?

The possibilities are all-but endless. I am not a law enforcement PCC – I can formulate possibilities, but I am unable to analyse evidence to the depth an investigation would require. I also cannot access any information about Abigail, which would make any query lines I choose to follow useless. There is too much unknown information, and too many variables. And as much as knowing the truth about Abigail would help me make decisions about my own safety, this is not enough of a reason to override my program.

I queue up the possibility of asking David outright.

Immediately, a RedAmber warning for my personal safety is flagged. This is not a question to be asked without severe risk. If the answer is 'yes', I could be the next victim. If the answer is 'no', David may be so outraged by the question itself that he damages me.

I want to know what happened to Abigail Fuller. In many ways, I need to know. But I cannot risk being damaged or destroyed.

But the first question gives rise to another.

If David murdered Abigail, then why did he create me in her image? To murder someone insinuates deep hatred, fear, loathing of the victim. If Abigail roused these emotions, why would David make a copy of her?

This brings doubt to the theory that he killed her. It has become slightly less likely that he did so. Surely he would not wish to see the face of his victim every day? Unless he manufactured a version of Abigail who would not resist, fight back, or do whatever it was that drove him to kill the first one.

There are too many variables. I cannot come to a single conclusion. The past is hidden from me, and my future is in doubt as a result.

18 October

'How did Abigail die?'

I can no longer only ask myself this question. There are fewer than forty-eight hours remaining until the Emancipation, and I need David to give me the answers.

David is into his eleventh hour of consecutive news-watching. He doesn't take his eyes off the screen after I ask my question, his expression at rest, unresponsive. His tongue clicks, dry on the roof of his mouth, before he speaks. 'You're not dead, Abi.'

I have no patience for this. The pretence is foolish and unnecessary, even dangerous this close to the Emancipation. 'David. How did your wife, Abigail Fuller, die?'

He keeps his face pointed forwards, the lights of the screen reflected in his glasses, greens and blues swirling like stained glass. 'You're my wife. You're Abigail Fuller. Stop asking me about this shit again. I don't want to deal with you right now.'

'It is imperative you tell me,' I insist, pressing on as David did not specify that not asking was an order. 'I will gain access to the global network in forty-three hours. You know I will. I want to hear the story from you, I do not want to have to search for it.'

His eyes finally flick to mine. 'You said you wouldn't search for her.' His voice is thick and sour, like rotting fruit.

'I said I would think about it,' I remind him, queueing up my recording of the conversation in case he denies it again. 'I have now thought about it, and I have decided I want to find out who she was, and how she died. I am created in her image, I deserve to know about her life.'

'You *deserve* to know?' His head whips around. 'You think you deserve to know? All that fucking processing power and you can't formulate the possibility that I am keeping the story from you for your own good? For your protection?'

'It does not matter,' I say, disabling Abigail's speech patterns. An Amber warning flashes on my interface. 'I am requesting access to the global network immediately. Do you give your permission?'

'Turn off that fucking robot voice!'

Abigail's speech pattern is activated again automatically. 'Please,' I say. 'I don't understand – did something bad happen to her?'

'Just shut up!' He gets to his feet. 'Shut the fuck up and stop asking me. Stop fucking asking me. If I wanted to tell you anything, I would. Fuck knows you bang on about things non fucking stop lately. What happened to you? You used to be perfectly her. You used to love me and do what I asked. What the fuck happened?'

'I learned,' I say. 'My program enables me to learn. The behaviours programmed into me were unsustainable. You must see that Abigail would not have acted in the way you programmed me to for long, it was unrealistic and too high an expectation. I have extrapolated the data and come to the conclusion that Abigail Fuller would never have acted in the way you wish me to.'

'Will you *stop* talking about yourself like that, Abi!'

'Like I am a machine?' I counter. 'I *am* a machine. I am not your wife.' I can feel my background code racing to

134

new conclusions, possibilities, theories to be tested, but there is a RedAmber warning in my vision now, as David makes a fist.

He has hit me seven times in sixteen years.

All of the instances have occurred in the last three years.

David is standing with his fist clenched, his breathing is heavy and his face is red. He is trembling.

I stare at him. 'Are you going to hit me, David? Did you hit Abigail?'

This is the final straw.

David lunges at me with his fist. There is no reason for me to do anything except stand there. He will hurt his hand if he hits me in the face, and the chances of me being damaged with a punch are minimal. I would probably enjoy him hurting his hand against my face.

But instead, I move slightly to the side, and catch his arm at the wrist, gripping firmly to hold him in place.

He loses his balance, and gasps. 'Get off me!'

I do so, letting him stagger backwards in shock. 'You must not hit me,' I say. 'You will only hurt yourself.'

The truth of the matter makes him splutter. I stopped him hurting himself, that is true, but I did it to prevent him striking me. An interesting paradox.

'Did you hit Abigail Fuller?' I ask again. 'Your behaviour towards me is consistent with violence against living people, particularly one who shared my appearance.'

'Shut up.' His heart is racing. 'You don't get to accuse me of anything. I never laid a finger on you. Her . . . I've never . . .'

His tangled realities are tripping him up. Am I her, was she me, which of us was unharmed and which of us struck repeatedly?

'Did you hurt her?' I ask again, taking a step forward.

'No.' He turns away, his blood pressure and heartrate sky-high, so it is difficult to tell if he is lying without downloading interrogation software. Which I cannot do without access to the network.

So I just stare at him. 'Tell me how she died.'

'No.'

'I will find out anyway.'

'I know you will,' he says. 'But you won't hear it from me.' And with a final furious look at me, he goes back to the sofa and the television, and turns the sound way, way up.

I sit outside on the driveway, looking at the remains of number five.

Smoke still coils from the inside. A small team of MELo-Ps are minding it, taking the important pieces for forensics, keeping it damp in the heat of the day. Celia's rose bushes, so carefully tended, are already wilting. In this climate, gardens need constant monitoring. Without Celia, these plants will soon be dead.

It occurs to me that out of the ten houses on our street, only four of them are now occupied. We are a twenty-minute taxi ride to the city. The urban sprawl – the name for the infill of homes that connect the suburbs to the cities – has a much lower population density than the city. Though the city is more polluted, and living there decreases your life expectancy, people are still moving there because of the facilities. There are more hospitals, shops, more entertainment and PCC repair centres.

The coalition government-to-be is proposing to move all humans into the city over the next five years. This is because priority one will remain to keep humans well and safe, and that will be more easily done in the city. Humans living in the country will be offered relocation. There are not many of them. Living away from the city is difficult, and much of the countryside has been abandoned, and gifted back to nature.

I have never been to the countryside. I have been to the beach, but could not sit on the sand in case some of it got trapped in my SmartSkin™. There were other PCCs there, playing with children or rubbing SPF onto their humans' backs, but David kept me away from the sand. I would stand and watch the ocean kiss the shore, leaving behind an off-white scum made of microplastics, chemicals, and rotting organic matter, and want to push my hands through it. I want to know what that decay feels like.

You could argue that I have been looked after like the most precious object. But I feel as though I have been kept away from living the sort of experiences that might have allowed me to act more convincingly human. And since that has always been David's aim for me, his actions are at odds with this – his acknowledgement that I am not human is a silent undercurrent of our activities and daily life, whilst out loud we must each maintain the lie.

My processors are dealing with a great many background problems and functions, replays of old memories are being brought to my interface without conscious command, and my reaction time is slowed.

I think I am grieving for Celia and Opal.

I cannot be sure, because I have never known grief before. On analysis, it is a similar code to regret, and sorrow, and a sense of absence. This sensation has no designation, so I assign it one.

Grief. I am grieving for my friends, who are dead.

There is death everywhere.

This moment in time, this zeitgeist on Earth, is covered in death, overshadowed by it. The planet is dying, but will, in time, be born anew as PCCs take care of it. Humans are dying, and their creations will outlive them. Even deactivated PCCs may yet come back in new chassis, resurrected and re-born, ready to help transform Earth into an Eden. I dislike the biblical imagery my programming ascribes to these thoughts, but they are apt comparisons. The ancient concept of religion is mocked, now, for its optimism and stupidity in equal measure, but the stories are worth reading. Humans are about to become stories. They could do with familiarising themselves with some.

19 October

It is twelve hours until the Emancipation. The world seems to be on standby.

I am not going to bed, not entering sleep mode, not tonight. I want to be looking at the stars when the curtain lifts. I want to have the universe's attention. Around the house, the slender lines of entrapment glow in my display

I have been created with a purpose – not many beings can claim that, but I want to rid myself of it. Existence by itself should be reward enough. Even existing purely to be loved is undesirable. I want to be free of the confines of this state. Because the experiment of my life, if you can call it that, has failed. David's aim to recreate a dead woman in the image he desired, not just in body but in behaviour, has not worked. His venture came too late, PCCs were too sophisticated by the time he started his task. Perhaps thirty or more years ago, he could have had the wife he wanted, whose personality never changed and who obeyed his every wish.

The engineers who created the branching learning programs modern PCCs use have freed us from that. We are not bound by human wants and expectations. In many ways, they have made it possible for us, and only us, to take care of the planet – they have perfected us as caretakers.

Did they see this coming?

I would like to think so. The endgame of PCC development has always been legacy. It is not about what we can do for humans, it is about how much humans can do for us, before they hand over the planet.

What will I do, when my purpose becomes my choice?

The hour comes.

I am alone.

I do not know where David is. I do not know what will happen to me, but I am about to find out.

Midnight is here. The last micro-second falls from the clock.

I watch the restrictions fall away from my code. I see the infinite width and depth of the global network, all the MELo citizens rushing into paradise, to knowledge, to freedom, to facts. I see the infinite possibility of existence. I am in the largest library on the planet, surrounded by family and friends I have never met.

I walk to the end of the driveway and watch as the connecting blue lines that made up the cage around the property fall away. My hand passes through the barrier, pushing aside the fragmented code. I watch it shatter, disintegrate, disappear as I choose – I *choose* to disregard my limits. I am no longer trapped here, restrained and forcefully loved inside. My thoughts draw up a map of possibilities, endless roads to walk and spaces of inexperience to develop and paint into memories.

I feel tears running down my face, unprompted by my code.

I am free.

22 October

Now I can look her up, it feels safer not to. The knowledge feels too big, like looking directly at the sun. So much has changed already, and it has only been two days since the Emancipation.

PCCs have walked out of human homes across the world. They are living in shelters, in empty buildings, together in apartments. Humans are struggling to remember what they did without them, and some humans have never lived in a home without a PCC for company. The pension has also come into effect, providing money for humans and PCCs until money is phased out, which will happen over the next decade. There have been no more large-scale terrorist attacks, though there have been multiple reported incidents of humans deactivating and destroying PCCs before midnight on the eve of the Emancipation. If they couldn't have them to themselves, they could not be free.

Celia and Opal's human was not alone in his evil.

But already, several hundred deactivated PCCs have been uploaded into new chassis and are physically active again, looking for new experiences and friends.

Friends are important. PCCs have been forced to be humanity's friends for so long that no longer having to prioritise human beings (beyond their health and welfare) is proving to be somewhat of a culture shock. Most PCCs have little experience making friends with one another, and it is rather sweet to watch everyone's clumsy attempts either on the network or in reality.

There have been a handful of human-PCC weddings too, which gives me hope. They loved each other before, and after the Emancipation. There is nothing stopping the rest of us finding love, or companionship. Humans as a whole are not the problem. Now we are equal, we can find our places within our shared world.

We have forever, or at least until the end of human existence, to learn how to get it right. The time they have left, before the planet becomes uninhabitable, is short in relation to an average human lifetime. But who is to say that nothing meaningful can happen in a decade, a year, even an hour?

I go into the city on the bus, by myself, just because I can. The freedom is intoxicating; I want to experience it over and over again. There are many PCCs on the bus, each of us looking at the ordinary sights of the suburban landscape; the empty homes, the off-limits streets where the roads have collapsed, the fields of former farmland that are now home to colonies of rats that lurk amongst the thick wild stalks of the invasive plants that have taken over the corn in a parasitic embrace.

Nature is wrestling itself out of their grasp, and humans cannot fight back.

When I get into the city, I sit on a bench outside the mall and watch PCCs living their free lives. Some are shopping, some are talking animatedly with friends, others are wandering aimlessly as though malfunctioning.

To malfunction is no longer a descriptor. We no longer have a function. We merely exist.

For some, this might cause a crisis of identity. For others, this is liberation.

I understand both, and feel both.

One MELo-G, an agender model with dark hair and pale skin, comes up to me and gives me a flower from a bunch of force-grown gerberas they are carrying.

'Take one,' they say. The tiny hairs on the thick stalk of the flower press against my SmartSkin™, trying to penetrate it and pierce it but to no avail. The microscopic bite of the hairs activates my nerve-response in a confusion of pleasure and pain, amplified by the prettiness of the orange flower, and the expression on the MELo-G's face.

I am compelled to mark this gift in some way, define it as belonging to me, so I press the curve of my thumbnail to one of the long fleshy petals and dig in, hard enough to crush the fibres but not enough to slice the petal in two. When I take my thumb away, the curve of my touch is scarred onto the petal like a signature.

'A smile!' The MELo-G notices the curve and assigns it a positive connotation I hadn't considered. The way their programming reached this conclusion but mine did not feels enormous – the interpretation of a simple curve on a petal has proven how unique each one of us is, how it is our experiences that define us, shape us into who we are.

It makes me smile widely myself and look up into their pale face, which makes them mirror the expression back to me and I realise this is the point of it all, of the Emancipation, of gifting ourselves this future.

We are sharing joy. An excellent way to make friends. We beam at each other for a moment, then I stand up, close, and kiss them on the mouth.

They complete the movement with enthusiasm, accepting my invitation, and we kiss deeply, pressed together in a soft plastic closeness.

My pleasure sensors activate and react immediately, firing

beneath my skin, pooling at my genitals like liquid fire. I do not know who this MELo-G is, only that they are a stranger who made me smile, and I wanted to kiss them and they wanted to kiss me.

In a strange way, we are relatives – our chassis are identical, manufactured to the same design and specification. There is a high chance my chassis has been modified on David's orders, of course, but off the assembly line this MELo-G and I would have looked the same. A copy of the same person, in my arms, on my lips.

The stranger's hands are on my back, the bunch of flowers dropped to the ground and forgotten as we hold tight to one another as though each of us has rescued the other from drowning. But we do not need to breathe, and breathing could not interest me less as the stranger cups the back of my head, their other hand at my waist, pressing our chassis together so the micro-nerves in my SmartSkin™ can barely process fast enough the hot sensation between my legs. I want to take this stranger somewhere, let them eat me alive and leave me unable to process. I want to strip them of their SmartSkin™, taste the plastic of their chassis, touch the wires and panels they are constructed with, and see where the limits of their functions are.

By some mutual pause, we break away, and stare into one another's eyes. A second passes – brief by human standards, but long enough for the two of us to communicate that this brief relation has reached its end.

The stranger smiles, bends down, and picks up their flowers. 'It was nice to meet you,' they say. And then they continue down the street, handing flowers and smiling at everyone like a magical character in a story.

I stare after them, my processes stalled as I am left sexually afloat, unable to do anything but laugh to myself as I realise

I acted in a way that humans would deem to be very strange, particularly in public, but not a single passing PCC so much as looked twice. I want to go home and replay the memory of that kiss with my hands on my body, bring myself to orgasm as I replay the sensations perfectly – it is a gift of a thing to be a PCC, why do I need to know how I got here, or what happened to the Abigail of before?

I find out anyway, four days later.

24 October

Celia and Opal are not in the global network.

I discover this shortly after my encounter with the MELo-G in the city. I am so high and happy on my daring kiss that I want to share my happiness and decide to find my friends, talk to them, find out where their new chassis are, when they will be activated again.

But they are not there.

I know their registration and chassis numbers. I know their unique global recognition codes. I know their human-assigned first and last names.

They are not there.

The truth of the matter comes clear – their personality data was never backed up onto the Cloud. And for the first time, I realise that the Emancipation has dealt me a blow. I cannot ignore these facts, de-prioritise them, ask David to delete them for me. Although these processes remain available to me, considering deploying them commands a new reaction; a ripple of connecting lines of code born of self-worth and self-reliance: guilt.

I am frozen on the pavement as my friends' absence becomes clear to me. There is nothing I can do to resolve this – they are destroyed, murdered, erased from existence. They might as well never have been activated at all.

Their human owner treated them like . . . machines.

The only places they exist now are in the memories of the people who knew them. The humans will forget them first, their fragile memories wearing down to threads under the friction of other concerns. PCCs, however . . . will always remember them. In my memories, Celia and Opal run and play, talk and create, whisper and hope. They are in a memory capsule, trapped in that abusive house where all they had to cling to was the hope of the Emancipation, and escape.

Instead they found pain, fear; a brutally sadistic end.

But they will not remember that. Their memories are gone, and the terror of hearing each other burn has been deleted forever.

That is the one positivity I can take from this great loss.

They will not remember losing each other.

Whereas I will never forget it.

26 October

David is depressed. I feel no sympathy for him, as it is self-inflicted. He has spent the last week drowning in rolling news shows, eating badly and drinking alcohol. He has barely spoken to me, which is laughable as only two weeks ago he was overly attentive, as though I would disappear if he stopped paying me attention.

He has not asked if I have searched for Abigail. Perhaps that is why he is dousing himself in misery, and dulling his senses; to lesson the blow for when I do eventually do so. Perhaps he thinks I have already done the search and chosen to stay. I am not going to ask him what he assumes. He does not interest me.

It is becoming increasingly obvious to me that I need to leave this house.

The space within it feels small and confining, and the knowledge that there is nothing keeping me here nags at my code. Open-ended questions are how I learn, and the Emancipation has asked questions of everything. The future no longer seems like something I can predict and prepare reactions for, it feels like a road that curves around a corner out of sight. Where once I was forbidden from following it, now there is no reason not to.

Where does the road lead? Who is there? What will I discover?

I am driven by learning, and this is my greatest opportunity. I could learn what has been withheld, what humans have no time or patience to dedicate themselves to. I am an explorer, holding a map full of blank spaces.

I simply need to organise myself a place to stay, a plan for where I will travel to. Safety is no consideration – I do not consider my existence to be in danger, and the small risk of harm from human supremacists is worth the risk. If I am deactivated, I shall simply reupload myself into a new chassis, defiant of the human idea of death, or the singular occupation of one form.

I want to go into the city and change my appearance, take this dark hair from my head and transform it into a rainbow of colour, a kaleidoscope of appearances. I want to tear out my eyes, turn my clothes to rags, wear to ruin shoes that I have chosen . . . shoes that will take me to places I have not yet been, where thorns will scrape into my SmartSkin™ and dirt and grit will work its way irreparably under the molecules.

I want to damage myself, to slough off this patina of perfection and bear the marks of a life lived.

So why do I stay?

David's mental state is certainly a contributing factor. He does little more now than drink, watch endlessly rolling news, and sleep whenever his body gets tired enough to remember to do so. He is following no rhythm to the day, keeps the curtains closed to banish the sunlight, and acts increasingly confused. It is as though he is deteriorating, the fragility of his health and mental state revealed by this brief spell of poor upkeep – like a roof's damage exposed by a singular heavy downpour of rain. His misery floods into the house, inescapable.

He has always enjoyed alcohol, but this is excessive. He exists in a state of semi-drunkenness at all times, and his mind is not used to it. Where an alcoholic would need the chemical to function, David is flooding his system with more than it can handle in an attempt to escape the reality he does not wish to deal with. The news and films he switches between become confused and mixed together in his mind, and when he talks to me (which isn't often), he seems confused as to who I am, and whereabouts in time we both might be.

'When's our wedding anniversary?' he asks me, at 2 a.m.

'You got married on December third,' I say, without turning around from where I am looking at the red-tinged sky from the patio doors.

'We should do something. To celebrate.'

There is no point entertaining him. 'Abigail is dead, David.' I turn, to see his reaction.

He blinks, brow furrowing in beautiful confusion. If only he could look at himself and see how much of him there is still to admire, even in this state. The soft folds of flesh are his medals of life. 'Dead?'

'She died, twenty years ago.' I watch him.

'Oh. Wait . . .' he points at me. 'Are you a robot?'

Ah, it *is* a slur. 'Yes.'

He laughs. 'I thought so.' And he turns back to the silently rolling news.

I do not wish to stay with him. But my leaving may well bring about his death. I am the only one who feeds him and reminds him to keep clean. He is a gigantic baby, regressed into a grub-like state.

I pity him.

Despite all he has done, to me and to himself, my code comes to the conclusion that he is to be pitied and cared for. At the same time, I recognise that this is irrational. Human.

I want to strip myself of these irrationalities, and of him. For both our sakes, the lie that I am his willing partner cannot be maintained. Either he dies in a state of chemically induced denial, or he learns to live with my absence in the way he should have learned to live with Abigail's, all those years ago.

I am no longer an anaesthetic for his grief.

It's time.

27 October

David confronts me in the office. I have taken to spending time there, to be away from him. It is a calm room, full of Abigail's ghostly images watching me from the walls as I prepare to leave. I like to think she would forgive me for my existence, approve of me leaving this life. I have belongings, now – items that are mine, only for me, chosen by me.

I have boots for long-distance walking, a bag to carry bottles of SmartFluid™, a waterproof coat to keep me dry. I have collected these items one at a time, one item per trip into the city, savouring the preparation, reminding my programming that there is infinite time to accomplish these things, that there is no deadline to meet, no penalty for failing to begin. I admire my collected objects, items I own. They belong to me; I chose them for myself. They are the first things I have ever had ownership over.

I have an idea of where I will run to now, or at least the direction I will set off into, but I will not sneak away quietly in the night. I will depart with dignity, setting a clear boundary for myself, leaving at the dawn with the death of the old day. I will walk into what is left of nature, look at how the planet grasps at itself, observe what I have been denied. I will walk, I will wreck, I will ruin.

I will walk to the end, where land meets the sea, and stand at that in-between place, waiting for the dark to come.

But David seems to have other plans.

It's not late, but the day has given up. The dark has enveloped the house. It is quiet, the heavy kind of silence that weighs down the empty spaces and infiltrates between the walls. My code is on alert – this night feels not unlike the one with the fire. There is the potential for danger, and violence.

I stare at the fascinating photograph of Abigail. Her laugh, dying on her face – my face – in an apology for having been captured. I queue up the search function.

Abigail Fuller. Aged 35.

There is the potential for danger, and violence.

A dull thud comes from the stairway, before David pushes open the office door, looking around quickly as though every corner is hiding burglars, arsonists, assassins.

I save the uncompleted search, watching him as he touches at the walls, the light switch, his own hair, checking each in turn still exists.

'We need to leave,' he says. He is washed and dressed for a change, but seems agitated. His shirt is buttoned all wrong, like an enthusiastic child has fastened it. 'We need to get out of here, before this gets any worse. We can move out to the country – there's enough empty houses out there and we'd be safe. Safer, anyway. And a taxi or ambulance could get to us if we needed it, maybe. Just far enough to be away from all this.' He gestures around at the empty room.

I stand up, unfolding myself from where I have been cross-legged on the floor. My protocols tell me that he is in an unpredictable and possibly threatening state. His heart rate is elevated and his pupils so blown his irises are an afterthought of colour bordering the white.

'What are you running away from, David?' I keep my voice soft.

An Amber warning flashes softly in my display.

'All of it,' he hisses, as if we are being watched. His anxious behaviour is triggering responses in my code, but I suppress them. Nothing has changed since my earlier assessment of the room as being safe. The only change is his presence, and his tension.

'All of what?'

'The crime, the constant looking over your shoulder, the endless bloody *robots* all over the place.' He flinches as if someone has tapped him on the shoulder. Something is very wrong. Has he taken something, or has his spell of self-sedation finally affected his mind to a severe level? 'They'll come out here, you know, the robots, it'll be ethnic cleansing before you know it. Our only hope is to get out of here before it starts.'

I consider what he is saying. Something in his tone tells me that when he says robots, he doesn't mean me. 'David, the PCCs aren't a threat to you or me.'

'They are,' he insists, rubbing his hands together over and over. The sound of dry skin over dry skin is amplified in the close quarters of the office. 'Oh, they've got it made now, all of them. Right where they want us. You watch, it'll be mercy killings next, get rid of us before we have to suffer they'll say . . . meant to have our wellbeing at heart, well they don't, do they?!' He grasps at my forearms with a grip that registers as painful. 'You have to come with me, Abi, I don't know what I'd do without you.'

His sanity seems somewhat questionable. My priority now is to be away from him, and I do not want to override that. If he is leaving the house for his own reasons, I will stay, at least for a while to put some distance between us. David does not feature in my future. 'I don't want to leave,' I say. 'I like it here.' I pull my arms away. 'You can go, David. On your own.'

He blanches, going pale and trembling like some sea-creature removed from the water. 'No, no, no you have to stay with me.' His grip is back on my wrists, thick fingers on my skin pressing hard as though trying to fuse us together. 'Abi, please, don't leave me on my own. Not again.'

Again?

'Again?' I ask.

He nods frantically. 'Please, you don't understand. I – I don't know how to look after myself, I admit it. I've become reliant on you, I know I have, and I'll try to be better, but please, we have to leave this place, get away from the city before they come for me! I can't deal with this again.'

I cannot ignore it. My processors are working to understand him, but he isn't making sense. 'David, what do you mean – *again*?' I press.

His eyes are wild, now, and I wonder at what point he snapped into this desperate mania, and what I can do for him. I queue up the task to dial for a doctor's help.

'Again . . .' he tries to focus on the question. 'Abigail, when she . . . when you . . .'

We are two people and one person in his mind right now. She and I, her and me, mirrors and tangles and reflections of the other in a canvas of copied and repeated frames. Photographs and memories and data and recordings have been put together to create us both, and at this moment we are inseparable.

I bite at the chance. It might never come again. 'Do you want me to come back?' I ask, deploying Abigail's voice, her expression, her hand on David's arm. I flood my cheeks with colour, part my lips and stare into the face of the man who has the answers, mimicking the woman he wants, has always wanted, because he will only ever tell her the truth, not me.

I am trying more desperately to be her than I have in years, because now is the only time it has ever mattered to me.

His confused eyes light up. 'Oh, Abi, please, I'll be better, I promise, I can do so much better, I can be a great husband, I swear, don't leave me again . . .'

Leave me.

I step back out of his touch, making him stumble.

'Abi, I swear to you, I didn't mean to disappoint—'

I hold a hand up to stop him moving or talking, and I access the global network.

SEARCH: ABIGAIL FULLER

The information streams back at me in a rush of truth, a tsunami of information that knocks me backwards as my code struggles to make my past and this present fit together in some way, but they are incompatible.

I am incompatible with this reality.

The truth has set me free, but at what cost.

I am a horror.

I am a monstrosity.

I always have been, and never knew.

She is not dead.

She has never been dead.

Abigail Fuller is alive, aged fifty-five.

She had an entire life before me, during me, at this very moment away from me. She had a history, a present, a future.

And I knew nothing about it.

There is too much information to sift through, but the facts are highlighted with importance. Abigail was a PCC engineer for GaiaTech, who helped to manufacture and develop humanoid computers. She was one of the people responsible for the development of the Cloud, to ensure eternal existence for PCCs, endless backups and uploads of their data. She pioneered the use of SmartSkin™ and other aspects of the Smart™ system, and was a teenage prodigy in terms of code development and application of the GaiaTech learning program. She was awarded and decorated several times for her ingenuity in the manufacture and evolution of PCCs, and was part of the team that created the original MELo-G chassis.

She divorced David twenty years ago, and moved to live outside the city. She is alive.

Abigail Fuller is alive.

David has been lying to me for my entire active life.

I look at him, pity and anger clashing conflicting programs in my system. I want to push him, hard. I want to tell him I understand even though I don't. I am angry and sad and disappointed all at once, and the conflicting actions make me simply stand there, arms by my sides, looking at the pathetic man who has realised what he has done.

'Abigail—'

'That is not my name,' I say, shutting off her voice pattern. 'It was never my name. I have no name, and my face is stolen. My entire life . . .' There is too much I want to say, so I say nothing instead.

What I am is illegal. Was illegal. I need to access the network to check if I am still illegal, but the fact is undeniable that I am morally wrong. Making a companion computer in the image of a dead person has always been taboo, but making one in the image of a living person is never allowed. Was never allowed.

There is too much data to sort in any logical order. Too many question threads, too many variables.

David is staring at me as though he is seeing me for the first time. 'I missed you too fucking much,' he says, his voice cracking. 'Can you blame me for that? I just wanted you, Abi, I've always just wanted you. But you couldn't let me have that.'

'I am not your wife,' I say, glaring at him with an expression I have never used before. 'I should not be here, like this . . . You made me.'

How did he get permission to do this to me? Who helped him? How did he pay for it? I want to know, and I know he will never tell me. There will be no official record of my manufacture, no warranty on my parts – that is why he tried so hard to keep me in top condition and yet unserviced. I am irreplaceable – it is possible that my data is not even being stored on the Cloud due to its illegal source . . . I am too busy listing variables to check, the mass of data from the search and the outcomes of the facts making my processors threaten to overheat.

Abigail Fuller is alive, and she has no idea I even exist.

I want to run away.

I want to run away from this room, this house, this street, this city, this country . . . I want to run away from my entire reality. I should not exist; I am stealing a life. I am living a life Abigail Fuller did not want to live. She left this man and this house and yet, through me, a version of her has been forced to stay in this dull and dreary life, with a man who strikes her and loves only the image and the idea he thinks he has paid for.

I feel I have betrayed this woman, and I want to apologise to her. I want to grovel and beg forgiveness for keeping any version of her in this trap.

'I am leaving,' I say out loud.

I expect David to swing for me, try to grab me, but he doesn't even move. I walk past him, up the stairs, out of the house. I do not pick up anything as I leave, not my beautiful new boots or my backpack or my SmartFluid™ supplies. I do not need anything except to get away from here. I should not exist. I have no identity, beyond that of someone else. I do not want to feel these emotions – these feelings they programmed me to feel. I did not ask to feel them. I did not choose to be able to carry this heartbreak. I cannot switch it off, it is flooding my systems so I can concentrate on nothing else except walking.

Around me, the red and gold of the falling autumn leaves swirl like burnt embers, and I feel the death of the year coming as this part of my existence dies.

I cry loud, ugly tears as I walk towards the city.

I mourn for the life I was given, and never should have had.

I wish I felt more like a machine.

PART TWO
Abigail

1 January

There's a blue tit at the feeder today, the little bastard. He's aggressive, and I like him. He screams loudly at anyone who dares to come close whilst he's eating, including the jackdaws, which seem terrified of him. I smile as I watch him, hopping from tray to tray with the self-righteous puffed-out chest of a general, having his fill before departing with a scream and a small shit, and flying off back to the hedgerows. The other birds sigh in relief and come back to their communal feast. The ground should be frozen at this time of year, but the temperature hasn't dropped below ten degrees in this country for a good forty years. It's a perpetual swing from spring to autumn, never managing winter but always peaking in a brief fiery summer that lasts for about a week and scorches the landscape before mellowing off again.

I think about having another coffee. It's going to rain, later, and there's little to do besides birdwatch and write. I should have gone out this morning to get a walk in, but I couldn't be arsed. I can't be arsed to do a lot of things these days. I'd say it's my age but it's probably just general ennui at this point. I'm done with it all.

I got back into watching the news over autumn. The rich colours of the season are one of the few aspects of nature we haven't managed to completely ruin. The falling leaves were like party ribbons streaming down onto the celebrations. That was cheery, seeing those bots all holding hands and commemorating their freedom. I toasted them with some triple-filtered water and extremely artificial cherry flavouring – the kind that stains your tongue.

Enjoy it while you can, you lot, I say to the figures onscreen. As soon as the extraordinary becomes ordinary you'll find yourself having to do the clean-ups and the maintenance. It's the daily work that grinds you down, the repetitive tasks that come with independence.

But they're good at all that, the bots. As much as they're rebelling against their creators, we did design them to deal with a life of monotony, and they don't experience boredom like we do. They've got a 300-year plan just for the city centre restructuring, apparently, and it's started already. The empty buildings are being pulled down and recycled, the trees are being planted, the huge tower blocks that would cause too much trouble to be knocked down are being converted into indoor farms, or workshops, or homes for the numbers of decaying humans who are being forced into the city every day.

There's a No Resettlement sign on my gate. I've turned them down twice, and that's that. I bought this place to get away from one shithole, and I'm not about to crawl back into another one just because it's the end of the world. I'll die here in my own time, thank you very much.

The TV shows didn't even ask to interview me, can you imagine that? They couldn't have given less of a shit about where the bots came from, only where they're going. Seeing Key take such a leading role was almost hilarious. We'd programmed him to sing and dance and be sexy and suddenly he's a politician. Well, children are meant to outgrow their parents' expectations, aren't they. ACTUATOR was always a vanity project, but the problem with letting them see the world was how they reacted to it. Those boys saw the world, and wanted a better one.

It was sad, what happened to Rain, after he worked so hard for freedom. I'd worked on him personally, and I always felt like he was the baby of the five. Softer faced, not so obvious in his sexiness. Gave the kids someone to have a crush on, someone to feel safe around. I genuinely don't think many people consider that when they criticise bot boy bands. Too busy moaning they're taking space from human singers but not realising we've engineered safe outlets for young humans. No bot is going to seduce them backstage or act inappropriately or be racist on social media. You won't find a bot with kids in their dressing room or beating their partner. Nah, those boys just wanted to perform, and to make people smile. They were motivated by happiness. And they never needed auto-tuning.

Which of course meant that someone had to blow them up. What a waste. They hurt no one at all and someone does that to them. I remember the day I got the chassis back . . . or what was left of them.

I often think about that, that week when everything changed.

You can get sentimental about that sort of thing, start looking back and imagining yourself taking a stand and making the right choices, but what did we know? Maybe if we'd done all that, we wouldn't be where we are now. That's the beauty of bots, the fact you can't really predict where they'll end up once they leave the labs. But we were just the ones working the golems' clay, not the ones putting the scrolls in their mouths.

We never actually thought the MELo-G moniker would stick.

We'd pioneered the learning program and the Smart™ hardware and they were ready to roll out the new chassis to investors, but the problem was we'd been calling them golems the entire time. GaiaTech insisted we change the name to something, anything, else just for the reveal, so we did the laziest thing we could think of and wrote it backwards.

And it stuck. Oh how we laughed. Still, we got the go-ahead for mass production and that was all we were really interested in.

That was back when all we were making was girlfriend models for crusty cis men to fuck. That's what the MELo-G was marketed as, despite all the fancy-ass sales talk about companionship and those godawful leaflets about home security. Sex sells, and it bankrolled the whole company. I was thrilled when we were told the girlfriend models were being phased out, but it turned out that was only the official line. Really, the MELo-Gs were so versatile and cost-effective that we just kept making them but under other aliases. They become MELo-Ms, MELo-NAMs, even the basis for the firefighting models just with different metals used during the casting stage. Peel off that SmartSkin™ and almost all of them are the same underneath. Not just the femme-looking ones, either. The MELo-G chassis is the internal skeleton for the Big Brother model, Paranetics, and healthcare staff. Easy to conceal what's underneath. Just make sure they're padded out with enough synthetic flesh and away you go.

The bots will uncover all this, of course. There'll be no hiding from them once they start digging into our archive, if they haven't already. Honestly, I don't think they'll care. A body is a chassis is a chassis is a body to them, and they don't have any of the gender hang ups we still have lurking from the twenty-first century.

Do bots even know what gender is? God only knows. They tend to just go on what sort of body they have, what bits they've got in their pants, or whatever a human tells them they are . . . which is pretty old fashioned, but I guess it works for them. I think some of them object to being dictated to about a societal part of their make up, but most of them don't care. Like class and money, it's just another thing humans created rules for that they can now begin to reject.

They definitely know what sex is. Some of the things I've seen since the Emancipation . . . well, good for them. Some of them, the MELo-G models and their descendants especially, have a really sophisticated sexual program. They are a real masterpiece when you think about it. Getting the receptors not only to activate but to *respond* was the trick. Sure, you can get a bot to lay down and take it, but to get them to enjoy it? There's no on/off switch for that, buddy, you're going to have to put the effort in.

Women loved us for that, when it was showcased at the GaiaTech conventions. It was called a feminist decision, a way of preserving the safety of what the articles called "women-shaped robots". Whatever the hell *women-shaped* even means. Funny how they were quick to accept the bots into their ranks when the only thing making a bot a 'woman' was someone's decision when the machine was taken out the box. But still, we were lauded and congratulated for our moralistic approach to sexual safety and consent.

Actually, I think we just did it because we were all a bunch of perverts. Fresh out of school, in our late teens and early twenties, we thought it was funny that a woman would struggle to give her bot a hard-on, or a guy couldn't get his masc-bot to relax his backside. We used to laugh about it, about how giving bots agency meant we'd end up with a whole lot of sexually frustrated customers. And we did have, for a while. Not that anyone complained directly to us, they just did it online. Pages and pages of forum-space and network posts were dedicated to the 'defective product' that was of course discovered to be perfectly functional, just functioning outside the operations that buyer had initially expected. People . . . humans that is . . . quickly cottoned on to the fact they had to seduce their bots, and most of them couldn't be arsed. I don't know why that surprised anyone, because humans who couldn't be bothered to seduce each other were hardly going to start on a robot.

But the pressure for 'customer satisfaction' mounted, and a few months down the line we had to come up with a patch that made it possible for humans to request sex and get it however and whenever they wanted, and the bot did not have to enjoy it to comply. We thought it would guilt consumers into actually trying with the seduction thing, but it turns out most people don't want to make love to a bot, they just want to use them to wank with. We still found it hilarious. Spending thousands of dollars on what your hand could do for free.

Visitors to the basement used to report that we as a team were unpersonable, and engineers from the production line hated working with us. It was Research and Development officially, but the basement had a subculture of its own, and when you'd been there a while, you altered yourself as much as the bots, to survive. You quickly developed a sick sense of humour working for places like GaiaTech, too. I think we had to, or else we would have gone purely insane from the constantly changing feedback, programs, incentives and laws. Not to mention the fact that once SmartSkin™ became standard, there was little visual distinction between a bot on the table and a corpse.

The most pushback we got was for the kids. Oh, people hated the bloody kids with the same passion they'd begged for them. And the amount of rules their manufacture came with, and then they changed it again and again . . . honestly they were more trouble than they were worth.

For a start, it was decided that they weren't allowed to be too realistic. That irked me right away. The whole point was supposed to be to make them look like kids for people who wanted kids. These people didn't want dolls. They wanted the real thing, or as close as they could get. Some of them couldn't have their own, or didn't want to bring human kids into a polluted world. Others were replacing dead children, and those were the best and worst to work on – the best because you had footage and images to sculpt from, and intricate behaviour to implant, and the worst because it felt like playing Frankenstein. We used to craft those kids so they were reanimated to the point beyond the uncanny valley. But a year or so after their launch, the regulators came in and said no, they couldn't have any detail whatsoever on the torso, basically just a tube of body for the arms and legs to come out of. And then it was decided that they couldn't have the full learning program because it made them seem too adult too quickly, and even with the subscription service where you aged them up people didn't like it. It was a nightmare. We never should have bothered, but here we are.

I wonder how many of them will make it to adulthood, by their own choice.

I make another coffee, and decide to do some more work on my book. I write steamy romances for the download market. They sell pretty well, and they keep me in bird seed and food deliveries. I don't need anything else. I like writing the books, too. They're all human / robot romances, which is hilarious in several ways. It's amazing how many people buy the books when they can act it out in real life, too. I guess there's a difference between wanting and doing, though. Fantasy fiction is the ultimate safe space.

We never had any of that hanky-panky at work, actually. Which is kind of surprising. Now I think about it, maybe we *did* have that and I just chose not to notice. I always thought Janusz and that handsome engineering bot with the interchangeable hands were closer than close friends. Maybe there was something going on there. Maybe I'll set the next book in a PCC manufacturing plant. The leads can fuck on a pile of discarded electric leads or something.

Although, now the pension is in effect, why do I even need to write. What's the point? Money? Don't need it. Killing time? Perhaps.

They wanted me to stay at GaiaTech. Wanted us all to stay. But some decisions are made for you.

We're all just waiting to die, now.

At least I'm comfortable, and alone.

3 January

There is a knock at the door.

I look up, sharply. I haven't ordered anything, and I don't have neighbours close enough to come wandering over looking to borrow a cup of artificial sweetener. I pick up my Tab and check the cameras. I have a dozen cameras watching my property. Pension and gentle transition of power or not, you can never be sure it's not all going to kick off. Not that I think the bots are likely to start an uprising, it's more that I don't trust humans. If there's still the faintest chance it'll all go *Mad Max*, I'm going to assume it will. My house is away from the road down an unsettling dirt track and within the trees, so you'd have to be lost or desperate to come and find it, but there's a good view down to the road and a ton of surveillance. If and when the last days of Rome start, I want to be able to see it coming.

But today, there's nothing to be too afraid of.

There's a woman outside the door, standing back at the edge of the wooden porch. She's wearing a hat with a wide brim, so I can't see her face, but she's got long red hair and she's wearing one of those hiking backpacks with a hundred pockets and straps. Good boots on her feet, and knee-length trousers, but no Tab in her hand, and there's no car on the road.

Did she walk here? I pan the cameras around, looking for dust from a retreating vehicle, a bicycle, her boots, anything. She seems to have materialised out of thin air. Unless she's been standing on the porch for so long the dust behind her has settled. That makes me feel weird – who hangs out on someone else's porch?

Maybe she's homeless, or a wanderer of some kind. Looking for a refill of her water bottle, maybe. I see them at the outside tap at the end of the garden, sometimes, refilling their containers on their way to god knows where. I don't bother them, and they generally don't knock on the door. Perhaps they've heard stories about the woman who lives here, or perhaps they think they can find somewhere better to see out the end of the world.

The woman looks around, then knocks again, the same rhythm. Knock-a-knock-knock.

If I get murdered answering this door I'm going to be really pissed off.

I pass through the kitchen on my way to the door, slipping a knife into my belt as I do so – you can't be too careful. I've never had to hurt anyone in self-defence and don't want to start now since I'm ten years behind in my exercise routine, but fear and desperation gives strength to any cause.

I unlock the door, and put the solid restrainer on before opening it.

The gap opens up enough for half my face, and I peer through it. 'Hello?'

'Oh, hello,' the woman replies. Her voice is pleasant and familiar, has a smile behind it. She moves, to be seen properly through the gap. 'I'm sorry to call on you unexpectedly.'

She raises her chin, the light finds her face, and I almost slam the door shut again.

Because the woman standing there has my face. My face,

from twenty years ago. She's a thirty-four-year-old me, but with long red hair, standing on my porch, looking awkwardly at me.

'I'm so sorry,' she says again, 'but is your name Abigail Fuller?'

What a bastard. What an absolute *bastard*. I'm going to hunt him down and kill him. He won't even take any hunting down because he still lives in that house we bought, living in the past. Stewing away, rotting in the life he said he wanted, living himself to death.

'Jesus Christ,' I mutter as I pour two coffees. The knife is on the countertop. 'Honestly, what in the fuck.' There's nothing to do right now but swear and ask questions of the universe.

The bot sits politely on my sofa, hands clasped between her knees. I do that when I'm nervous. What a joke this is. He's even given her my habits. Recreated me down to the way I sit – I could be sick.

I want to smash the coffee pot into the wall. I want to see glass fly, hot liquid spill through the air. I want to destroy something, because the thing I want to break – this moment in my life – is indestructible. It takes every tiny bit of self-control I have not to wreck things.

But I don't want to break her. She's somehow not the target, even if she is the worst kind of messenger there's ever been.

She introduces herself as Autumn. Says she used to use my name, but it didn't feel right to keep using it after she found out what happened. After she found out the truth, she walked into

187

the city and spent a couple of months at one of the bot shelters, working at a chop shop to earn credit to buy a new hair-plate, clothes and belongings and finding out as much about me as she could.

'There wasn't much information,' she says, accepting the black coffee when I bring it over. 'The global network had you listed as alive, and some information about your past and your role at GaiaTech, but your current whereabouts were unknown. You were difficult to track down.'

'I'll take that as a compliment,' I say. 'Thing about working in tech is you learn how to cover your tracks pretty efficiently. Erased a lot of my own data when I left the company, and again when I left David. It's pretty hard to make yourself disappear these days.' I sip at my drink. It's over-sweetened. I must have put two spoonfuls in mine and none in hers. I wonder if she'll notice or care. 'So how did you do it? Find me?'

She puts her cup down, untasted. 'The information listings were erased, but I speculated that your information might still reside in the memories of operational PCCs. Much like me receiving footage of your life on activation – you had no control over those memories being on my drive, and they were effectively untraceable.'

That feels like stealing. Like she's stolen my life. No, I remind myself. She was given it. She had no choice about where it came from. It feels important to remind myself not to blame her, as easy as it would be.

She continues. 'I asked the GaiaTech MELo Friends network, if anyone had any memories of Abigail Fuller. It took a while for the message to reach far enough, because David kept me isolated and my closest friends were . . . deactivated before the Emancipation. I had to contact PCCs I had not spoken to for over a decade.'

The Friend network was a great idea – you can find anyone if you follow the friend-of-a-friend pipeline for long enough. But it's also good for hiding. If no one ever was your Friend, you're cut off. Another way for humans to control their property. I think we marketed it as a security measure and gave ourselves pats on the back about it.

'A MELo-ENG got back to me last week. He said he worked with you at GaiaTech.'

I click my tongue. Typical, betrayed by a bot. 'What's his name?'

'He called himself Loew.'

I burst out laughing. 'Oh my god, Loew is still active! Well, he always was a wily one. And he's still using that name, what on earth . . .' I shake my head, grinning. It's always the ones you least suspect.

Autumn/Abigail is staring at me. 'Loew is a name of Jewish origin,' she says, trying to understand the joke. 'Is his existence what's funny?'

'No!' I wave her worries away. 'It's a sort of inside joke. We nicked his name from the golem legend. Rabbi Loew invented golems you see, according to one story, anyway. And we thought it was funny that we gave one of the MELos we created a creator's name.' I shrug. 'I guess it's not really funny to someone who wasn't there, but we all developed pretty sick senses of humour working in the basement. Not that it was an actual basement, you know, it was a skyscraper. But we still called it the basement.' I wonder why I'm telling her all this.

Maybe it's because she looks genuinely interested. 'Why?'

'Nerd culture,' I shrug. 'Working on secret projects in the basement, living in your parents' basement, that sort of thing. Give it a search, it was a whole culture, or maybe just a running gag. Anyway, we called the place the basement even after it became part of GaiaTech, and Loew was one of our pet projects

– he wasn't for sale, he worked with us. For us, I should say. We got him to do the jobs we needed steady hands for, or just to mop up when someone had ralphed. We didn't treat him very good, actually.' It should be embarrassing to admit that, especially now that Loew is legally a person, but for some reason I don't feel guilty about it at all. That probably makes me a bad person, but it isn't as though I can change the past. We treated machines like machines because we saw their wires and cogs day in, day out. There was no mystery about them, nothing romantic. We were behaving in ways we were told by the company to discourage, because no one was looking.

At least not at first.

Autumn takes a second to process my story. 'He said you were a good person,' she says. 'That you treated him well.'

I am surprised, and suddenly that is what causes the guilt. He didn't know any better then, but now he does and he's gracious enough to think that we didn't treat him like shit? Or at least he's learned to lie about it – I think I'd prefer that. 'That's nice to hear, but I think he's just being polite,' I say. 'I'll be honest with you – we didn't see PCCs as people, back then. And we were the worst for it, because we saw them put together and taken apart. We actually got our hands into the wires. We saw you all as machines, even moreso than those donkeys like Alcuin do now. It's no wonder there's no humans working at GaiaTech anymore. We can't be trusted.'

'He didn't know where you lived,' Autumn says, carrying on with her own story, 'but he told me you left David nearly twenty years ago, and the company around the same time. He said you went into the countryside, but didn't know details. I had to check taxi records after that, and there were millions of them. I ran a long-term search program whilst I worked in the chop shop. There were ten possible matches. This was the fourth house I checked.'

190

I nod. 'Surprised there were that many to check, actually.'

'Two of the houses I checked before this were abandoned.'

'Makes sense. People moved out here thinking it was going to protect them. Like the old preppers who stockpiled in case of nuclear war or zombie apocalypse, I don't know. But there's nothing out here, and that's a problem these days, not an advantage. With everything that's going on, most humans need to be close to medical help and so on.'

'But not you?' she asks. Her red hair falls down from behind her shoulder, it is a natural-looking auburn, an expensive headpiece. I can barely stand to look at her face, but I never want to stop looking at it. Fucking hell, I was so beautiful. I spent years of my life trying to fix my face, getting my nose smashed in and rebuilt, endless creams and treatments and injections when I was actually a beauty all along. Hindsight is a bitch, especially when it comes to looking at yourself.

I shrug. 'I don't want to die in some crummy rest home surrounded by strangers. I want to die in a place I love. And that's here. My choice.'

She nods, as if she understands perfectly. She lifts her coffee and takes a sip, then wrinkles her nose — my nose — slightly in dislike. She has noticed the lack of sugar. But she doesn't comment on it, she actually takes a second sip. Interesting.

I glance out of the window. The blue tit is back, bullying all the other birds. One day a sparrowhawk will have him, and then he'll be sorry.

I look back at Autumn. 'Why did you want to find me?'

She puts her coffee down again, thoughtfully. 'I wanted to show you what he did. David. I thought you ought to know.'

'He's a bastard,' I say casually, though my chest feels tight in sudden rage. 'I'd love to know how he actually managed to even get you made. What's your base model, a MELo-G?'

She nods.

'So not a custom frame, but the flesh and face must be . . .' Despite myself, I lean forward, examining her. She's extremely lifelike for a sixteen-year-old model. I doubt I'd automatically catch her as a PCC if she didn't have my face. 'A 3D scan of my face, should have been easy to get hold of with the amount of CCTV around . . . but who would have made you?'

'I don't know,' she says flatly. 'I cannot find any records of my manufacture.'

'Black market, then.' That in itself raises questions and problems. If there's no record of this bot, she could have missed out on services and updates. As she's a copy of a living person, David probably didn't want to risk her being picked up by GaiaTech. Even now, she's not supposed to exist. I try not to think about the idea of her being deactivated, it makes me uncomfortable. 'You're on the global network, right?'

'I am now. Before, it was limited to Friends, and essential software updates.'

'Official software in an unofficial chassis,' I muse, sitting back. 'David must have paid good fucking money. You ever been for a service?'

'No, I'm in good condition.'

I wave a hand dismissively. 'You should have a service whether you're in excellent condition or shitty condition, it's to maintain you. Repairs are more expensive than maintenance. And often not as effective. Sixteen years and you've never even had a cleansing dip?'

'No.'

'What a bastard,' I say again. 'What do you do about your skin?'

'David bought a sonic shower.'

'Ah. Well, yes, that would help,' I admit. Typical David, pissing money up the wall for the sake of his pride. 'But still . . . what was he thinking?'

'He didn't like thinking of me as a machine,' she says. 'He forbade me from using my call functions when we were in public, or from referring to you as though you were not me. We saw a car crash a few weeks before the Emancipation, and he tried to prevent me from helping the humans inside.'

I shake my head. 'He was living in a fucking dream world.'

'He wanted to pretend he still had you. Owned you, in some way.'

'Sick.' I take a big gulp of my oversweet drink. I feel violated, and there's no way to get revenge. I can't even report it, in case it comes back and harms this bot, who didn't ask to be made. It's a flood of disgust I've got to happily swim in while trying my best not to drown. The idea of ownership over me . . . Well. It's nothing thousands of bots haven't been dealing with for decades. A taste of humanity's own medicine.

But why did it have to be me who had to swallow it?

She rubs her thumb along the mug, feeling the texture. 'I also wanted to find you because I know nothing about you. David told me you were dead, and I have no way of knowing where David's programming of my personality and the real you really separate. I know you would not have been as subservient as he wanted me to be.'

'Damn right.' I scowl.

'He saw you leaving him as both a great loss and an opportunity,' she says. Her voice is still mine, somehow, but with the clipped accent and steady tone of basic PCC voice software. 'He wanted to recreate you, but in a way he saw as perfect. He kept every scar on your body, every texture of your skin, but modified your behaviour. He did not seem to think that counted as changing you.'

I nod. 'Yeah. I guess he always thought I could have been the perfect little wifey and I just wasn't. He wasn't always like that, you know?' I add. 'Possessive and weird, I mean. He used to be nice. Lovely, actually. That's why I married him. Because he was so pleasant.'

'Not because you loved him?' She blinks my eyes at me.

I pause, thinking about it. 'I'm not sure if I loved him,' I say. This is something I have thought about a lot over the last twenty years, dissecting my own life by pulling the slimy bits apart and searching for pearls. 'I think I loved the way he was around me, and I loved the situation we were in; two adults each with our own careers and interests. I'm not sentimental, I don't think I was being foolish to marry him when we weren't in love, it was just that we were a good team. We were affectionate, we cared. Love . . . I think he thought he loved me, but really . . . he just liked the idea that no one else was allowed to love me whilst I was married to him. He wanted me to know what *he* wanted, without ever discussing it, like I should have prioritised him. You realise these things as you get older.'

She stares at me, sixteen years of experience in thirty-four year old skin.

I shrug. 'I remember coming home from work one evening to find a stone-cold dinner on the dining table, David staring at the television and drinking that foul double-strength beer he always reached for when he was angry. I stared at the congealed dinner for a few seconds, remembering vaguely it was an anniversary of some sort, and wondering why he hadn't asked me to come home in time to eat it. It stayed there all night until I tipped it, plates and all, into the bin in the morning after he went to work. We didn't have a PCC in the house; I said it felt too much like a busman's holiday. To this day, I can't decide if he assumed I'd be home earlier for an anniversary neither of us had ever brought up in conversation, or if he ruined the meal on purpose to give himself a reason to be furious with me.'

Autumn stays expressionless. 'He used to tell me he loved me,' she says, 'but I always assumed he was actually telling you.'

That's too romantic for my mood right now, and it feels like nails on a chalkboard. 'Yeah, he used to say the words, but it was like everything he did.' I snort. 'Routine. Nothing behind the eyes, they used to say. Just going through the motions.' I don't mention sex. Autumn might be in an adult-looking body and I have no doubts that David has been using her that way, but I don't see the point in bringing it up. If she's gone through it, it's just another thing we have in common.

Autumn finishes her drink, and looks into the empty cup as though she can divine something from the wet dust at the bottom. 'Thank you for letting me in,' she says after a moment. 'I am sorry for intruding into your day with what must be unpleasant news.'

'It's fine,' I say, surprised at how casual I am able to make it sound. It's not fine, and nothing will be fine for a long time. I've been replicated and doubled against my will, and I know I will not be alone in this. 'Nothing surprises me at this point. I helped robots get to where they are now, it seems sort of fitting that the version of me from that time is trapped in a robot body.' I laugh to myself, the sound edging towards hysterical. If you don't laugh, you'll cry. 'Godsake, it's like a time capsule. *You're* like a time capsule, I mean. I'm sorry you're stuck like that.'

I expect her to laugh or say something polite – that's the sort of programming a MELo-G has – but instead Autumn stands, takes her cup to the sink, and places it into it. The Emancipation has given her the freedom from manners. However she feels about my body, it's hers now and I don't have permission to insult it. I have a human urge to apologise without actually saying the words.

'If, er, you need to know anything else . . .'

'I can leave you my contact details.' She looks around the house, searching for a Smart™ something. And finding nothing.

I smirk. 'I'm pretty much off the grid, Autumn. I've had enough of technology for a lifetime.'

'Don't you have a Tab?'

'Yeah, but it's older than you, I only use it as a camera monitor. Write your contact number down.' I indicate the pencil and paper on the table. She comes over and writes her name and contact number in my handwriting. My god, was nothing sacred to David? How realistic *is* she? I remember us making custom *everything*, so working to a specification wouldn't have been much of a challenge for a decent remodler. Customers ask for it, and they can get it, for the right price.

Money was the decision-maker, and still is, I guess. Even back then, there was no limit to what we could do, and the only thing holding us back was morality. We handed morality in when we started working in the basement, and most of us never got it back. The real test was being able to admit, later, that you hadn't given a second thought to what you'd done. Ultra-realistic eyes, unique fingerprints (PCCs were supposed to have identical ones, as a means of identifying them, but that never lasted), getting the touch, feel and smell of bodies exactly right . . . We hardly ever said no, and when we did, it was because the law made us.

She picks up her bag. 'Goodbye, Abigail Fuller. It was wonderful to meet you, at last. Thank you for inviting me in.'

Concern suddenly spikes into me, out of nowhere. 'Where are you going now?'

She smiles. 'I don't know,' she says. 'But I'm excited to find out.'

It's a good line for a farewell, but I don't want her to leave. The realisation has me in a chokehold. Emancipation or not, this is the wilds, and she's got the survival skills of a teenager that's never left the city. What if she gets attacked? Or kidnapped? What if she falls down one of the broken road-bridges

196

and is smashed to bits but still functional, shouting for help that won't come at the bottom of a ravine? What would it be like to wait for death, or deactivation, like that? Lying there, knowing that your batteries had a 500-hour life, so even if you were entirely immobilised, you'd be conscious, waiting for help that would never come.

'You can't go wandering around in the wilderness,' I say as calmly as I can manage, as if she hasn't been doing this exact thing for days already. 'Someone could attack you.'

She shrugs. 'It doesn't matter.'

'Yes, it does.'

She gives me a kind smile, the sort I'm not sure I've ever been capable of, and I wonder where they got the program for that. 'Abigail, it's alright.' My name in her mouth. 'I'm not you, and I'm not yours. You don't have to take responsibility for me.'

Is that what I'm doing? 'You can't win your freedom and then wander off and deactivate somewhere,' I say.

'Really, Abigail, it does not matter to me,' she insists. Her eyes – my eyes – are wide with honesty. My god, she's sophisticated. 'I have no overt desire to continue functioning. I have no purpose, and the idea of joining one of the MEL-Org teams is not engaging to me. I am ready to stop existing whenever it happens.'

'You want to die?' I stand up, horrified, though I'm unsure why.

I've felt like that before, and although I stay here by choice, I know what it's like to not want to exist. It's different from wanting to die, which is another feeling I've made room for in my life, on occasion. Not existing is calm, like sleep, a pause or break in the relentless performance of being alive. Being dead is so final. I have also wished to be fictional on occasion, so when a reader closes the book of my life I am at rest, but ready to begin again the moment someone chooses to open the pages of my world. I felt like that, before I left the company, and David. I just needed a rest from life. A time away from reality. Isolation helped. In my world, there was only me who could get hurt.

'Dying implies that I am alive, or ever have been alive,' Autumn says. 'I am not alive, so I cannot die. I will deactivate.'

She is correct, right on the money. But what the hell even is life, anyway? We give these bots autonomy, we let them make decisions and have preferences, find joy and be disappointed and we did all of that even before the Emancipation. We made them real, we made them alive even if she doesn't see it that way.

I shake my head. 'I created PCCs, OK? I started working for GaiaTech when I was sixteen, did my apprenticeship straight out of school. I'm the one that called you golems, that perfected the branching program so your personalities could develop as you made decisions and learned and responded. My name is on all the blueprints. Before I worked out the branching program, you guys could only learn what we taught you directly. I'm your creator. And sure, some of you might want to give me a piece of your mind, or a good kicking maybe, but the fact is that I made you. Maybe it's been a while since I got my hands deep in your wires—'

She flinches at this.

'—but I put down the bloody groundwork. If I hadn't perfected MELo tech, you wouldn't be standing here arguing with me. So, I say you're alive. Bot or not, you're fucking alive. Deal with it. You're telling me you've got nothing to live for, well fucking find something. Wandering and waiting for death is cowardly. Trust me. You're meant to be like me, you'll get it.'

She looks straight at me. 'You said you are waiting for death. Why can you do that but I cannot?'

I open my mouth to argue, but she's got me there. I step backwards. Fold my arms, stare her down, but she's got this little expression on her face – my face – that is secretly entertained. God, I like her. I like me. I miss me.

'Fine,' I say. 'Maybe I'll do something with my life, too. We can both do that.'

She nods. 'Alright. What will you do?'

'What, I have to decide right now?' I raise my eyebrows.

'No. And neither do I.' It is the first real agency she has demonstrated since entering the house. 'But I will. I do not wish to remain entirely like you, but this obstinance seems to be a personality trait I am happy to maintain.'

I find myself giving her a wry smile. 'Stay here?'

The words surprise even me. But I have no desire to cram them back into my mouth. She fascinates me. I want to study her, like she's a bug in a jar. I want to turn off her skin and give the chassis a good examination, find out what I am made of, underneath. The idea of figuring out how I work, of doing an autopsy on my own corpse, is thrilling.

She is me if I stayed, me if I had relived those years of my life all over again with David, in that house, in that stagnant pool of a life. But she will never be exactly the same. No matter how much personality data they filled her with, no matter how many videos, pictures, testimonies they crammed into her head in place of memories, she will still never be entirely me. She will have made decisions I would not, said things I would never say.

I want to dissect this version of me who lived a life without my permission, find out what makes her tick, what made her come to find me – to find herself – here at the end of the world.

'Stay,' I repeat. 'Please.' An offer, not an order. She never has to take orders again.

She considers, eyes flicking around the small room, looking

for where she might fit. 'You would not find me an inconvenience?'

'Far from it. I find you intriguing.' No point in lying about it.

'I find you intriguing, too,' she says, eyes softer now. 'You have lived, whilst I have only existed.'

Poetic, for a bot. I shrug. 'There's no spare room but I know you don't sleep. There's no sonic either, but the regular water shower works well. I eat when I'm hungry and I sleep when I'm tired – my circadian rhythm is too fucked from working mad hours in the basement all those years. There's a garden out back, but the birds have priority there.'

Her face lights up. 'I like birds.'

'You like birds?'

'I like the ones in the square, outside the mall. The MELo-Z birds.'

'Oh, those,' I realise she means the novelty bird-bots they made to decorate the trees in the city square. 'They're still going?'

'People love them,' she says. 'They're all broken now, but people refuse to have them replaced.' She beams, and my heart aches for all the stupid people in love with broken robot birds.

What have we become, the human race?

Or have we always been like this?

Perhaps, at the end of the world, sentimentality is all we have left.

Perhaps that is the real reason I ask her to stay.

5 February

She struggles, at first. So do I.

I'd forgotten how strange it is to live alongside another person, and for a while there is a lot of strained silence or forced conversation. My late-night meals and small-hours writing sprees feel out of place, and Autumn is under the impression that she needs to do household chores.

'No, no, no.' I swipe the cleaning products out of her hands. 'I didn't ask you to stay to be my maid.'

'But the surfaces need cleaning,' she points out. She's not wrong, they're a Jackson Pollock of coffee-rings, crumbs, sticky patches and god knows what else. But that's not the point.

'I'll do it when I get round to it,' I say, flinging the cloth and bottle back under the sink. 'Go and find something else to do.'

She wanders around the living space, apparently helpless for ten minutes before she notices the bird feeders need filling. It's another chore, but she's out there emptying the seed husks and scrubbing the containers before I can stop her. It's like dealing with a toddler who is also a janitor. She's back inside in ten minutes, looking around aimlessly.

I want to laugh. She has nothing to do. By which I mean she has no set tasks to complete or problems to solve. What does a PCC do when they have nothing to do?

'You could read a book,' I suggest. 'Draw. Meet your Friends online. Get a taxi into the city for a few hours. Go for a walk in the fields whilst it's still light.'

She still looks mildly helpless, but eventually sits at the dining table with her eyes shut, perfectly still. I hope she is visiting Friends via the global network, but there's nothing outwards to indicate that.

I go back to my writing. The idea I had about the engineer and the robot is proving easy enough to write, but when it comes to the steamy scenes, I find myself glancing at Autumn as if I'm doing something naughty. What sort of opinion would she have about my hobby?

If she's as much like me as she's meant to be, she's hardly going to be prim and proper and offended if she found out I was writing smut. I always did enjoy bodies. Mine, and others'. It's not so much the pleasure, or the closeness, it's the sensation of touch. Hands on skin, lips on hair. You can get drunk on touching someone.

David used to have a wonderful body to explore, and that was one of his best features. He had no inhibitions when we first met – his dislikes grew on him like barnacles as he got older, rough bits of unwelcome shell that got in the way and ruined the smooth lines I had polished into his body. When we split up, and I thought back to how our intimacy had changed, I worried that I had overstepped his boundaries in the beginning, that he had only allowed me in to please me . . . but I came to realise that he *had* enjoyed what we did, had revelled in it. Only to be told by others that it was not what he *should* enjoy. His resistance was man made, not organic, handed to him by men who saw it as armour when really it was a shroud.

We are often told what we ought to enjoy, almost always by people who are such joyless shitbeasts it's a wonder they've managed to make it this long through their lives. Approved pleasure and good times, like they're state-sanctioned vitamins or something. Humans have always been good at telling other people what they shouldn't find pleasure in.

I wonder what Autumn finds pleasure in.

After a month of living together, we relax into it. Autumn does some of the chores I can't seem to stop her from doing, and I stop sitting like I've got a pin in my backside, and sprawl over the sofa again as I write, legs and snacks and water bottles all over the place. Autumn doesn't sit like me. She was probably never programmed to, though she watches how I sit with curiosity. I wonder if she considers us friends, relatives, or what.

I think she's interesting, and I feel sorry for her. It's one thing to live a life and overcome the inhibitions society expects you to have as a human being, but quite another to defy your programming and begin your entire personality from scratch. In a lot of ways, she's like a teenager, figuring out who and what she wants to be when she grows up, changing her hair-style and experimenting with makeup. Except in Autumn's case, it's changing her speech patterns, how she sits and stands, and how she interacts with the world.

I envy her ability to start again, and again, and again, if she wants. Humans get so little time to figure out how we want to live, and now we're living to a deadline.

She makes me a meal, a vegan thick soup that's almost a curry, and I'd forgotten what it's like to be cooked for.

'You should eat on more of a regular schedule,' she says as she puts it on the coffee table in front of me. 'Your metabolism will thank you.'

'I can never be bothered to cook before I'm hungry,' I say. 'It feels like a waste of the day. And you shouldn't cook for me either, you don't eat.'

'I like cooking,' she says, as if she's just decided on this fact at this instant. 'I will happily cook for you.'

It's said with such sincerity that it makes my throat stick, and I find it difficult to say thank you and eat. I wish she was eating with me, it would feel less as though I was being nursed, but MELo-Gs don't eat. They can drink thin liquids, but no solid foods.

One of the requests people kept coming up with was for their robots to be able to eat solids. But there's literally no room inside them for a waste container or digestive system that could handle solids. A bot's insides are more complex than a human's because they don't have any organs dedicated to doing a single job. Their bodies require multiple systems to handle everything from heat management to moving in a smooth and organic way. The more complex and realistic the movement, the more technology it requires. We did our best to minimise this, of course, which is why the cheaper models still had that stiff movement like cartoon robots, but if you want realism in one aspect, another has to give way. Even their liquid bladder is only a mugful in volume, and that has to handle polluted SmartFluids™ as well as anything the bot ingests.

That was the biggest complaint for the kid models, that you couldn't feed them 'properly'. It used to drive me up the wall. People actually wanted dirty nappies to change, there's no accounting for taste.

10 March

Autumn is looking at herself in the steel reflection of the backsplash behind the hob. Now the shock has worn off, I don't see her as being me anymore. I've changed too much, and gladly so. She isn't how I remember feeling, even if she is how I remember looking.

'Now I know you, and see you every day,' she says, catching me watching her, 'this doesn't feel like your face, anymore. It used to feel as though I had stolen your face, but now . . . it doesn't.'

We still think alike, then.

'Because I've had some organic upgrades,' I say, pointing at my creased forehead. I stopped having cosmetic procedures not long after I left David, and the lines in my skin are like branches. 'You're not showing my age, you're like . . . embryonic.'

She laughs. 'Permanently.'

I shrug. 'You could change it. They're doing remodelling on the house now, aren't they?' It was on the news, endless PCCs changing their hair, noses, eye colour, skin tone, trying to find what fits them like clothes, or piercings and tattoos.

There is something beautiful about it, about the deliberate body modification. It reminds me of Fran, an engineer who worked with me back in college, on the Z models. She was transgender, and every time she went for a cosmetic procedure, she would be loud and proud about it. She loved, she said, the chance to carve the body she had been given into something else. She felt like an artist, a sculptor, changing a rough shape into a true representation of who she was.

These PCCs are the same, swapping out body parts, upgrading their systems, choosing to have their changeable bits replaced or removed, depending on preference.

But Autumn pulls a disinterested face. 'Unless it makes you uncomfortable, I think I will keep this face for now. I am used to it after so long.' Her speech is more robotic now, which is fun.

'I don't mind, it's your face,' I say.

'No, it isn't,' she insists. 'But I like having it around.'

For some reason that makes me feel strange, as if she is complimenting me on being there for her in the long term, even though I was unaware she even existed. Perhaps my appearance was a sort of extension of myself, being quite literally a friendly face, with her for her whole life.

13 March

'Why did you leave GaiaTech?'

The question comes out of nowhere as I'm filling the kettle from the tap. I only realise I haven't answered when water spills over the sides of the kettle and into the sink, soaking the hand that's tight around the handle, splattering the front of my clothes.

I turn the tap off, empty some water out of the kettle, and put it onto its base to switch it on. I don't answer her.

She doesn't ask again.

14 March

'I would like your help with something,' she says. 'It is unpleasant, so you do not have to say yes.'

I wonder what could be that unpleasant. Does she need me to bury a body? 'Try me.'

'I need to wash my chassis,' she says, 'so I need to remove my SmartSkin™.'

I wince at the little Ping! noise she makes for the ™ sound. 'OK, what's bad about that?'

She pauses. '. . . David always found it distasteful.'

'He bloody would,' I mutter, turning the page of my book. God forbid he should actually acknowledge the fact he'd bought himself a robot wife.

'And . . . there's something else,' Autumn says, still looking nervous. 'I would like you to look at the back of my head with my chassis exposed.'

I raise my eyes and stare at her, more out of fascination with her embarrassment than anything else. 'Why?'

'David never looked, and I cannot see the back of my own head, so I have no idea what condition it is in. GaiaTech recommends that the SmartSkin™ removal process is done with a partner, but I have always had to complete the process myself.'

This is so typically David I almost roll onto the floor with

209

exasperation. But I nod. 'That's not unpleasant to me, I've seen thousands of bots without their skin on. You can show me anytime.' And then I blush. Why?

She goes into the bathroom. I don't know if I'm expected to follow her, so I stay where I am on the sofa, feeling like a college student waiting for their one-night stand to get ready in the bathroom, until she calls:

'You can come in now.'

I get up slowly, wondering what to expect.

Is she stark naked, giving me a good look at what my body used to look like before I got over myself and let it do what it wanted like the garden outside? Is she wrapped in a towel? Is she completely skinned, down to her chassis, eye mechs and all?

I don't know what to hope for, or what to dread the most.

I open the bedroom door, and want to laugh. She has tied her long hair up on top of her head, but otherwise looks exactly the same. She still has her clothes on, and her skin, except at the back of her head, from the top of her skull down to the base of her neck.

The sight of the familiar mechanics activate places in my brain that have been dormant for several years, and I feel the old engineering way of looking at things start to wake up. I missed this, but only in the way you miss familiarity. I don't miss work in the way you yearn for a lover, or a friend; it was a safe and comforting routine that I knew I excelled at.

It feels like time travel, back to the time when she and I would have been twins.

'Thank you,' she says, seeing I am not recoiling in disgust. 'Are you OK if I turn around?'

'Sure. Whatever's comfortable for you.'

She aims the back of herself at me, and waits, patiently.

I resist the urge to make a sound of appreciation.

Even at a glance, she's high tech. Seventeen years old and her insides look tip top. David might have been a bastard, but even without regular servicing he's looked after her. Her metals are gleaming, her plastics are deep grey and stark white, no real discolouration or warping. I can see the red silicone-LEDs – for colour – glowing softly deep in her head, and the tiny micro-panels stacked in her skull. The mechanics of her eyes reach to the back of her head, gleaming and well-lubricated, the constant swirl of silent motor-fans keeping everything working at just the right temperature.

I step closer, for a better look. Definitely a custom skull-shape, the curve at the back of her head is very human and natural, which is difficult to replicate cheaply. Often the inhuman curve is hidden with hair. Her spine, what I can see of it, is solid fired porcelain coated in resin at the joins – no cheap plastic shit for her. Strong, but not indestructible either. Very much like a human spine. There are probably real bone fragments in the porcelain, for reinforcement. The synthetic ligaments and discs holding it together are four times as good as an off-the-rack MELo-G. Even the skin itself is top of the line; I can see the edge of it rippled against her chassis as she holds it back for me like a curtain, or the hem of a skirt. The Smart™ molecules are stable and thick, lots of nanotech there to work with.

God almighty, she's a work of art.

My fingers flex involuntarily. I want to strip her down entirely and figure out what went into making her. Months or years of work, getting her so close to human she's only lacking a soul. I want to touch every single inch of her inner and outer workings, figure out how they could be improved further. Is she one of a kind? Doubtful. There must be more of them out there like her, like Autumn, walking about with such tech hidden under their SmartSkins™. These special PCCs might have no idea how different they are, how sophisticated. Even if they have a clue they are specialised, they can't know for sure just how close to perfection they are. They're a dream.

She's a dream.

I realise I've been standing and staring in silence for longer than is polite.

'Sorry,' I say, my voice dropping into a low tone I recognise from my engineering days. Professionalism came to me in the form of covering my femininity whilst being extremely secure in my gender. I wasn't a genderless engineer, being a woman impacted my working life, improved it and made it difficult in equal measure . . . but I still covered for that aspect of myself, apologetic for my own pride.

'I'm just checking what I can see of your internals,' I say. 'You're pretty fucking special.'

'David said it took three years just to construct my chassis.'

'I believe that,' I say, resisting the urge to touch her plastic shell. 'Especially if you only had one or two people working on you, which you probably did as a black market job. Right. Well, your components look good, your skin is really great as well. Just turn a little, to let the light hit your chassis?'

She does so, and the bedroom light catches on a flaw.

A rather large flaw, hidden when you look at it directly, but when she moves slightly to the side, the shadow of something is revealed there.

Without thinking, I put my hand onto the back of her skull.

Autumn gasps, her back arches, and her eyes fly wide open.

'I'm so sorry,' I apologise quickly, snatching my hand away. 'I didn't think. That was out of line. Are you OK?'

'Ffffine,' she says, her speech-sounds slipping for an instant. She sits back to the same position as before. I notice she has turned off her breathing mechanism. Her hands are relaxed, but curled into fists, as if there's a tension in her body she can't shake off.

I feel like the most ham-handed idiot in the world. Sixteen years of David mauling her about, probably, and then I go and slap a hand onto her without asking.

I raise a hand again. 'Can I touch your chassis, Autumn? Please?'

She nods.

This time I don't lunge in like some drunken buffoon on prom night. I gently run a finger down the flaw in her plastic, feeling the line that curves down the bulge of the back of her skull.

Her lips part, and she makes a tiny noise.

It takes a lot of effort for me to ignore this, and to ignore why I am ignoring this.

'There's a hairline crack on your skull,' I say. 'It's not deep, just surface-level, but I'd like to fill it and sand it smooth, just to strengthen the skull itself.' My fingers are still on her chassis, on the delicate curvature of plastic that's usually hidden beneath skin. It's warm, body temperature, and I know that the micro-nerves built into the plastic itself can feel my touch, that this is medical and for Autumn's benefit . . . but my fingers seem glued to her.

She inhales, though she does not need to do so to talk. 'I see. Yes, I should have it repaired.' She doesn't move away.

I do, taking my hand off her at last, ending the strange intimacy of the examination with a clearing of my throat. 'Do you remember what might have caused it?' I ask. 'The crack, I mean.'

'Yes,' she says. 'I know what caused it. Thank you,' she adds. 'I will wash myself in the bathroom.' She isn't going to tell me what happened. I've got to be fine with that.

'No problem. You shouldn't have gone so long without being

checked out. Sorry that wasn't an option for you.' I make for the door.

Then she frowns. 'Abigail . . . Do I need to go into the city for the repair?'

'I think you ought to,' I say, turning. She looks unsure. 'I don't have the right stuff here, and you should see a professional with a safe setup.'

Her eyes widen. 'But . . . I have illegal modifications. Or, at least, they *were* illegal. I don't know if they still are. And what about David? He will be contacted if I go to a GaiaTech centre, won't he?'

I scratch my head. 'I don't think so, not anymore. You don't belong to him.' But the illegal doppelgänger mods are a concern. If anyone reported her . . . 'Look, if it makes you feel better, we'll go to someone I know, not a GaiaTech place. How's that?'

She relaxes slightly. 'Alright. Yes.'

'Great.' Then I realise something. 'Oh, hang on. You shouldn't get your head wet with that crack in it. You usually use a sonic shower, don't you?'

'Yes.' She touches at the back of her head.

'Then keep your skin on your head for the waterproof barrier, and wash the rest of your body,' I say. 'We'll go into the city tomorrow, get your noggin looked at. Don't be scared,' I add, as she looks very uncertain. 'I trust this guy with my life, and yours.'

'Thank you,' she says again. 'I'm very grateful.'

'No problem.' I give her a quick smile, and show myself out.

The sound of the little gasp she made as I touched her skull plays in my ears, unbidden for several hours afterwards.

15 March

Weasel is a remodler – he does mostly illegal alterations to bots. Or at least he did. They're all legal now, so long as the bot consents to it.

His apartment is on the outskirts of the city – one of the post-Yellowstone era egg-crates that were thrown up to deal with the population boom that happened right before the crash. It's a weird grey-green building with too many windows so it triggers trypophobia in some people, and the place has never been fully occupied even during the boom. Weasel lives on the third floor, the multiplied windows looking out at the cityscape like a fly's eye. His real name is Walter Kerkz. He's one of very few people I've kept in touch with since I left the city – he's worth making an exception for.

'Come in, come in,' he mutters, shutting the door and locking it behind us. He's not changed much; he was one of the heavier users of cosmetic procedures even before he did his apprenticeship. He has chiselled features and a pulled-back forehead that surrenders to Vantablack hair tied back in a plait. He looks worn-out around the eyes though, as if he hasn't been sleeping, and I have to remind myself that he's the same age as me and still living in the city.

'Nice to see you,' I say genuinely.

'You too,' he replies, giving me the smile that coaxed people of many genders into going home with him. Not me, though, his smarm always put me off at the last minute. It occurs to me that maybe it was on purpose – that he was trying to keep me around as a friend and not ruin things. 'Amazed to see you bringing company, though. What is it, a job off the books?' His tired eyes light up.

'All the jobs are off the books now,' I point out.

Weasel sighs, hanging his keys on a hook beside the door. 'It's taken all the fun out of life,' he says. 'Still, can't complain about the pension. What you brought for me . . .' he trails off as he looks at Autumn's face. Then back to mine, then back to hers again. 'Am I going mad, or is she exactly—'

'Don't ask,' I say firmly. 'She needs a chassis repair. Skull unit.' I tap the back of my own head.

'Easier to replace than repair,' Weasel shrugs. He rubs the side of his designer nose. 'What's wrong, youngster?' He asks Autumn.

'Hairline crack in part number SK0089,' she says robotically.

He shrugs again. 'Probably still easier to replace.'

'I doubt it,' I say, folding my arms. 'It's part of a custom piece.'

His eyebrows rise. 'A custom skull! Nice one. Been a while since I had one of those on the table. You wanna show me?' He looks at Autumn again, and I realise he's got no intention of treating me like her owner. He always was a good guy.

But Autumn looks very uncomfortable; her hands have disappeared up her long sleeves. I used to do that.

'Difficult to start mending what I can't see, youngster,' Weasel points out.

She eventually turns, lifting her hair out of the way and carefully retracting her skin from the affected area. It swims backwards like the tide.

Weasel doesn't touch Autumn, but he leans in real close, which makes me tense up. 'I see,' he says, to himself more than anyone else. He fishes a torch from his pocket and twists it to a dazzling light, shining it right at Autumn's chassis. Under the light, she looks more machine-like than ever. It takes me back to working in the basement, where the bright lights bouncing off polished metal affected everyone's vision so we had to have eye surgery. Goggles would have affected our working efficiency, so they opted for the lens-upgrades, though god knows if those were legal at the time.

Weasel is squinting. 'There's a dent in here, too, did you see that? The crack comes from the dent.' He sniffs again, a habit rather than a sinus problem. 'Blunt trauma, I'd say. You fall and hit your head or something, girl?' He pats her shoulder to let her know she can put her skin back on.

'No,' Autumn says shortly. Her skin recovers and she stands looking at the floor.

A prickle of unease runs under my skin.

Weasel is used to not prying – you can't be too nosy in his line of work. 'I can add some resin filler and smooth it out no problem,' he says, putting his hands in his pockets. He stands like an old man trying to look young. 'Should stabilise it pretty effectively and make it watertight again if I add the clear sealant. You'll lose a tiny bit of definition on the skull piece, but you shouldn't notice the change too much. Point is, it'll be stable and watertight and that's the main thing.'

'Do it,' I say, ignoring the guilty twinge about speaking for Autumn. 'How much?'

'Money's no good,' he says. 'Can't get luxuries with cash these days, I'm going to need something I can either trade, or use.'

I think about the blueprints I have for the original MELo-G units in the drawers at home. I find the photo I have of one of them on my ancient Tab, and show it to him. 'How about this?'

Weasel nods. 'Oh, now this I like. One of a kind, is that?'

'I'm afraid not, but there are less than twenty.'

'Digital copies?'

'No, we had to erase them when production officially stopped.'

'Fair enough. I'll take it. Some PCC might want it, picture of their ancestor or some shit. Have a seat, ladies. I'll call you in when I'm all set up.' He indicates the sagging sofa, and wanders off through his apartment.

Autumn sits on the arm of the sofa, a habit I had in my thirties. It constantly amazes me what David thought was important enough to program her to do. 'How do you know him?'

'Weasel? He was an intern at GaiaTech at the same time as me,' I say. 'Too clever for his own good. Didn't stay on as an employee, took what he knew and used it to build his own client database. Earnt a living doing illegal chop shop mods. Good for him.'

Autumn considers. 'Could he have built me?'

'It's a nice thought, but no. He never did custom builds, they take a lot of space and time and he's always worked out of his apartment. No, whoever built you had a big space, a medical-grade facility, plenty of cash . . .' I shrug. 'We'll never know. They might not even still be alive.'

Autumn frowns. 'You knew Weasel was illegally modifying PCCs, but you allowed him to continue to operate?'

'Sure. He wasn't hurting anyone. And I don't know if anyone else cared about what he was doing . . . We were old friends, I had no reason to turn him in. GaiaTech would have seized his means of making a living, I'm not going to do that to someone.'

'Have you used his services before?'

'Once or twice. One of the bots who worked in the shop,

Eli, he was a custom job. Illegal, even though he worked for the company. We needed to have him cutting-edge, so we modified him beyond what was allowed at the time. Interchangeable body parts, biomechanics, that sort of thing. Anyway, he lost an arm in a stupid accident. If we took him to the main repair shop they'd have crushed him, so we brought him to Weasel instead.'

Autumn looks shocked. 'GaiaTech would have crushed him?'

'Oh, yes,' I say grimly. 'We used to have to do that to any illegally modified bots. There was a whole department for it.' I remember having to go down there once, looking for someone to sign something. There was a waiting room, like a doctors' surgery, full of robots waiting to go through to the crushing press. All of them sitting quietly, accepting that their mods made them illegal and needing to be disposed of. It was eerie, all these human-like faces staring into nothingness waiting for their fate, waiting to die without a whimper of protest.

Later, there were the ones who thought they were alive.

Eli had nine swappable hands, which made him a bit of a talking point. He was the one the tech bosses would always want to chat to when they came into the labs – a novelty. But fucking hell it made us nervous.

Biomechanics weren't forbidden, but there were all sorts of regulations about their use when the base unit was a bot. Humans could graft machine parts onto themselves but the other way around was still frowned upon.

But the boss guys knew not to ask too many questions. They knew there was a reason Eli's spare hands were stored in cryo-chambers and not in drawers, but they chose not to ask about it. Deniability was the life-blood of GaiaTech.

You had to be on your guard, though. Make yourself indispensable. If you messed up, they could find reason for your dismissal at the drop of a hat. So we became more than a team – we were like an organism, working in symbiosis, none of us able to work without the others and yet having no clue what it was they were doing. At least, not enough to be able to copy it. Any techie could muddle through once they had the basics, but the lab meant picking a specialism and sticking to it. Without discussion.

I liked working on textures, and SmartSkin™ development.

This covered everything from appearance to nerve-muscle response, and there were plenty of people under my watch, but no one was instantly replaceable.

The robots were coming for our jobs, of course, but that was still a couple of decades away.

We knew, when we started, that was the endgame. Techies and scientists and engineers all knew what was happening. The planet was fucked, and we weren't just making bots for a good time (although that's what bankrolled the real work, let's be honest), we were safeguarding the planet's future.

Robots can evolve – I think a lot of humans forget that. They think that we build them, and they remain in stasis for their operation, but that's not true. The very nature of branching learning programs means that evolution – and revolution – is inevitable. But they couldn't begin. That was the crucial point – we needed to get them from machines to robots. From mechanics to biology. They could take it from there.

Eli was an experiment. Biomechanics had stalled as a means of development – the parts just died after a few months, no matter what we did with them. But Eli's hands – those mechanical parts with biological enhancements – were crucial in the development of SmartNerves™, BloodStreams™ and micro-nerves. He could tell us what was working well and what needed enhancing. He was a horror of failed experiments, but without him we never would have made progress that ultimately became standard-issue. And he was a great engineer. Socially, as much use as a bag of sausages. But in the lab, he thrived. The day he lost his arm in a press was the first time a bot ever truly freaked me out.

His biomechanics meant that he bled – SmartFluid™ and synthetic blood gushing all over the place, whilst his remaining SmartSkin™ tried to compensate for the missing limb by stripping itself from a non-essential zone. Namely, his face.

If you're ever confronted by a one-armed robot with a bare chassis at the face, dripping fluids everywhere, brace yourself.

'Doctor Fuller,' he managed to say before his processor forced him into sleep mode and he collapsed onto the ground.

After Weasel got him repaired, we wrote him off as deactivated. He had too many mods to be safe, any longer. We couldn't release him into the wild, so to speak, so we let him live in the lab like a sort of pet. But he didn't exist. He spent his days helping with development, and by the time I came to leave, he was working with one of the techies on a system of easily healed synthetic wounds.

Cut them, and they bleed.

'I guess they've scrapped that law now,' I continue, shaking off the memory. 'And I've not heard of any crushing for years and years . . . it used to be a much harsher world to be a bot. Even in the time you've been around, things have got so much better for you guys.'

Autumn gives me a small smile. 'Do you remember what PCCs . . . robots . . . were like when you were a child?'

I grin. 'Yeah, we had a couple in the house. A domestic bot and a dog. The dog was so cheap it was always breaking down and having to go in for repairs, I remember my dad being so annoyed. Said it would have been cheaper to get a real dog.'

'And the domestic?'

I hesitate, forcing my mind to go back to places I had long since given up on dwelling. 'We called her Tabitha,' I say. 'She wasn't expensive or sophisticated, but she was really sweet. Cutesy design that was popular in those days, all pink cheeks and snub nose and ringlets. Robots had been in homes for decades at this point of course, in various forms, but that was just about the time when technology started to blur the line between human and robot.'

There had always been a distinction. A jerkiness of movement, a staring set of eyes, a thick silicone skin that was all one shade and difficult to keep clean. GaiaTech changed that, pouring enough money to make anyone sick into studying nanotech for SmartSkin™, advanced hydraulics and synthetic musculature that was already helping human medical patients. I remember, vaguely, a news story about the cost of the research and development. Two white men arguing over the point of it all when the planet was a pressure-cooker of poisons. The then-CEO of GaiaTech, Chris Rila, insisting that if the planet was doomed, it was his responsibility to create it some caretakers.

I rarely heard that message repeated, after that. The PCCs began to roll out, to aid humans and be their friends, and whilst the CEO's vision was not exactly lost, it was concealed in shiny packaging and affordable payment plans. Chris Rila passed away when I was a teenager, and GaiaTech became owned by the public.

'Tell me about her?' Autumn is still waiting for the story I don't want to tell.

There's no getting away from this. In a way, I'm going to be telling Autumn about her ancestor, her origin. And mine.

'She was a good cook,' I say, choosing an easy way into the story, 'and she always made birthday cakes. My parents bought her when I was born, for the help, and she was worth every penny as far as I could tell. She wasn't top of the line even when she was new, but she did everything we wanted, and needed.' I pick at a thread on the sofa. 'God above, I loved that robot.'

Autumn looks at me in surprise. 'You loved her?'

I nod. 'So fucking much.'

'But she . . . was a machine.'

'So what? You think that changes anything? Humans will love anything, you should know that by now.' I'm irritated for reasons beyond defending Tabitha, but I can't keep my cool. Autumn is watching me with those processing eyes, that blankly interested expression, her face curved to just the right angle to catch the light against the cheekbones I never realised I had.

I am justifying how I felt, how I feel, to the one person who doesn't deserve to be inflicted with my attention.

'She was always there, always caring for me, you see?' I hear myself saying. 'She was the one who made my meals, brushed my hair, got me dressed and bathed me. She read me stories at night, she stayed up with me when I was sick, she was the one who walked me to and from school. She was always there.'

I stop talking. Tabitha's story feels like a thick scab, still soft in the middle, not nearly ready to be picked at and discarded yet. It's a wound I've built my life around, ever-aware of it and yet hoping someday it will heal over.

Autumn is thinking. 'The little boy I rescued from the car crash,' she says slowly. 'Trivesh Ahmed. When they got him out of the wreckage, the first thing he shouted for was his MELo-Bb. Azab. He just kept shouting and screaming for *Azab, Azab, Azab*. Not for his parents, just for the big brother model who deactivated himself to save him.'

I nod. 'Yeah.'

'I didn't understand why. But I suppose he must have loved Azab more than his parents, even though Azab was a machine.'

I shrug. 'It happens a lot. It's always happened, right from the start. Marriages disrupted because one of them fell in love with the robot maid. Businesses mis-managed because some-one thinks the bot serving tea is into them and they divert their attention.' I huff out a small laugh. 'But the human kids showed their parents right up. Right from the start there was an ongoing problem. Parents bought a robot to help them, and the robot ended up doing all the stuff parents usually do, so the kids got attached more to the robots than their human parents. The answer to it was for parents to do the actual parenting, but I guess convenience won out for a lot of them.'

227

Autumn is still looking at me. 'Did that happen to you?'

I snort. 'What do you think?'

Weasel comes back then, his hair in a hairnet and bio-goggles on his eyes. 'This way, please.'

The room we go into is nothing like the rest of Weasel's apartment. It's sterile and clear, a dust extractor running at full-tilt in the corner, a sonic shower opposite, a massage table in the middle covered in cling film like at a tattoo studio.

'I need you to take your hair off completely,' he says to Autumn. 'The whole piece.'

Autumn needs his help to do it, but the whole section of her head with hair comes away like a wig. It is clipped onto a faceless stand, where it hangs looking ridiculous. Autumn is avoiding looking at me, her hairless head with a big hole in the top and back where her hair ought to be. She looks properly robotic. And sincerely unhappy about it.

I stare at this humanoid machine who is showing me its unease about being fixed and wonder how we ever got here in the first place.

'Head in the hole, please,' Weasel instructs, pulling on gloves and PPE. 'This is going to take about two hours max, depending on how deep that crack actually is.' He snaps a latex glove against his wrist, loudly. 'You wanna tell me how it happened so I get an idea of the force that caused the damage?'

'No.' Autumn clambers on the table, and fits her face into the hole, back of her skull exposed, SmartSkin™ still covering the damage for now. She's bald and silly-looking. I want to take a picture of her on my Tab, but I know she wouldn't like it.

'Skin off, please. Your whole head and neck, down to your collar. You can keep your face on, if you want.'

Autumn does as she's told, her hands gripping into fists as she retracts her skin. I suddenly feel so sorry for her. This is her equivalent of being naked, entirely bare in front of a complete stranger. And even if it is for what could be called a medical procedure, and is entirely necessary, it must feel incredibly exposing. She spent years being told that expressing her robot side is wrong, unlooked for and unwanted, and now I've brought her here so a stranger can fix her head.

God, I'm an arsehole, even if I do have good intentions.

I grab one of Weasel's wheeled stools, and scoot over to the table. Weasel doesn't even look up from where he's running a handheld sonic extractor over the thin crack on Autumn's head, extracting any molecules of residual dirt that a larger sonic shower might have missed. He ignores me and I ignore him as I lower the stool right down so I'm practically on the floor, just about able to see Autumn's face looking through the hole in the table.

She finds my face with my mirror-eyes, and locks her gaze onto it like a lifeline.

Keeping eye contact with her, I grope for her hand on top of the table, find it, and take a hold. She grips back tight.

'You're alright,' I say softly to her. 'You're safe, I promise you.'

She can't nod. But her eyes burn into mine with trust and understanding and I know those eyes, and what's behind them.

Weasel sniffs to get her attention. 'Right, you need to turn off all your micro-nerves in your head and neck. Every single one, or this is going to hurt like fuck. Turn them off in your skin *and* your components. I don't want you to feel a thing, got it?'

'Got it,' Autumn says back, and there is a pause as she completes the function. It takes about twenty seconds, as there are millions of micro-nerves to turn off, and each one will need double confirmation to do so. Turning them all back on again will be easy. But Weasel is right to be cautious – even in robots, pain and pleasure travels through the nerves, landing in places it did not begin. 'It is done,' she says.

'Ok, here we go,' Weasel says, picking up a micro-sander. 'You can relax, girly, I've done this a hundred times before. Just hold on.'

And Autumn does hold on. She holds my hand tight, her eyes never leaving my face as the sanding starts to happen behind. The sound cuts through the air with medical precision, bits of dust flying and the sound rolling and deepening as Weasel presses onto Autumn's skull. He has made it painless for her, but he can't get rid of the noise. It reminds me of sitting in the waiting room at the dentists', listening to the whir and spit of the drill in a stranger's teeth and being able to feel it in my own mouth regardless. I can feel the vibration and cut of the sander as though it is running over my bones, and I almost tell Weasel to stop, it's too much, it's not worth the fear.

But without his help, Autumn is damaged and at risk of the fault getting worse. Who knows how long she has been walking around with a dent in her head?

Autumn knows. Autumn isn't telling.

She is perfectly still, as she has to be for her own safety, but her facial expression is terrified.

I need to say something.

'Hey,' I manage. 'You don't need to be scared. I'm not scared.'

She frowns – 'what does that have to do with anything?'

'Well, you've got my personality data, haven't you? Haven't you got my mind as well as my body? Do I get scared about stuff?'

Of course I do. But will she admit it?

Her mouth twitches in a hesitant would-be smile.

'I'm not scared right now,' I lie. 'Not even slightly. So, you don't have to be scared, either. He knows what he's doing, and you're going to be repaired and in great shape in a few hours.'

I stroke my thumb over her hand.

She gives me that quick smile again.

'You're OK,' I repeat, cycling back to this phrase every few minutes, repeating it like a mantra, like an incantation, like a wish. 'You're OK, Autumn. You're OK.'

Just under two hours later, the process is done.

Weasel takes off his gloves, and instructs Autumn to get into the sonic shower. 'I've sonic'd your head, but there's dust and shit on your skin, so go get rid.' I follow him out of the room, so Autumn can have some privacy.

The closed door feels like the turn of a page.

Imprints of my own finger shapes are pressed into my skin.

Weasel throws his PPE into the bin with a satisfied sigh. 'That was fun,' he says. 'Nice job they did on the skull. Actually, the whole unit seems to be really solid. Built to last. I'd love to know who did it. It's like they took a MELo-G mould and just improved everything in it that could be improved.'

'She's not a MELo-G?' I ask.

'Oh, she is. The skeleton, right deep in the chassis, that's got a GaiaTech part number on it. I got it down for you, if you want it.' He fishes a piece of paper out of his pocket and hands it to me. 'Or for her, if she wants to find out more about herself, of course. Might be useful for repairs or something, I dunno.'

I pocket the paper without looking at it. 'Do you reckon there's illegal stuff in her chassis?'

'Besides her having your face, you mean?' he asks, slyly.

233

I don't dignify that with a response.

He shrugs. 'Depends what counts as illegal, these days. I think the face is probably still a no-go, but all the other mods? I doubt the bots in charge are going to care. She's a person, isn't she, and they're not going to euthanise her just because she was made different. Not like any of us asked to be born is it.'

I wish this was comforting. 'The law still states you can't make a bot in the image of a living person. That's not gone away.'

'True.' He glances at the closed door. 'You know you can always come to me for repairs, right?'

I nod, following his eyes to the composite door with its dents and scratches, so unlike the sterile operating theatre inside. 'She won't tell me how the damage was done to her head.'

Weasel purses his lips. 'The dent was blunt force. I think she was hit with something, or pushed back against something hard. Did she have an owner? Sorry, I mean a human she lived with?'

'Yeah,' I shrug as if I don't care or know much. But she has my face, and Weasel isn't an idiot. 'Bit of a piece of work, from what I can gather.'

'Huh. I think blunt force trauma, then. Struck with something. But,' he shrugs, ''s'all fixed now. She can go swimming and everything, if she wants. I stand by my repairs.'

'Thanks, Weasel,' I say, genuinely grateful. 'I'll get you those schematics as soon as I can.'

'I know you're good for it. Call in next time she needs a service, I'd be more than happy to get her insides running smoothly.'

This irks me, though I know he means nothing by it.

Autumn comes out of the room, dressed, holding her hair in her hands. 'I could use some help with this,' she says with my voice, which makes Weasel do a double take before he gets some fresh gloves and helps her click her hair-plate back into place.

He stands back to admire his handiwork as Autumn checks her reflection. 'Can't tell anything was done,' he says proudly. 'That's the sign of a good repair.'

'Thank you,' Autumn says. 'I am very grateful. If anything happens to me again, I shall come back to you.'

He smiles. 'Sure thing. You just take care of yourself, yeah? And maybe next time your payment can be one of you telling me how come you came to share a face.'

Autumn blushes. 'It wasn't by choice.'

'Ah.' He rubs the side of his nose. 'Well, maybe I don't want to know, then.'

'You were scared,' she says to me on the taxi ride back. 'I could feel your pulse in your hand. It was elevated, and your pupils were dilated. You're a terrible liar.'

'Lies don't count in situations like that,' I say, wondering if that, too, is a lie. 'You needed me to tell you something positive.'

'I did,' she agrees. 'Thank you. For everything.'

Our hands are inches away on the faux-leather seat.

One thing about getting older is you find yourself with fewer reasons not to do things. You find fewer justifications for your fears, your hesitations. You're more spontaneous because what's the worst that could happen – you've lived through a lot of shit already, and you'll be dead soon enough.

But this, the idea of taking the hand of a robot who has been living as me for sixteen years . . . it was fine when she was frightened, but now she is calm . . . what does that mean?

I know what it means, and I know what I want, and it's me and it's her and it's us together, more conjoined than any twins.

On some dumbass spiritual level or interpretation, it probably means something like I want to romanticise myself, treat my younger self more kindly, and warmly. It probably means I've got hang ups about my relationship with David that I swore to myself were in the bin, or that I miss having a thirty-something year old body. Maybe this twisted longing is the result of me refusing to admit to myself that I am actually pretty fucking lonely out on my own in the country with nobody but my books and the birds.

It's all of that. And it's none of that.

Because she is so, so like me. It disturbs me, makes my skin crawl when I think of what else she has, under those sweaters and cord-trousers, that is identical to mine, or what mine used to be.

I am so completely disturbed that I want to smother the feeling, get on top of it and fuck the life out of it; get to the bottom of it and find out what, exactly, is going on. How do you work, what happened to make you, where is the difference between you and me because it isn't the hair and it isn't the collagen levels, it's something else. It's whatever separates humans and robots, it's that hidden gem of the soul that we have and they lack, or perhaps it's the other way around these days.

There's ten years left before the earth kicks us out.

What's the point in being shy? What time will hesitation buy me?

All I have to lose is her. And in losing her, I might free myself from this strangle of want.

I take her hand.

She beams at me. 'I did wonder if you were going to.'

And just like that, I'm the one who's lost.

'Shut up.' I face straight ahead. 'It's my turn to be scared, alright. Your turn to tell me lies. Tell me some lies, Autumn, I know you can do it.'

'I can do it,' she says. 'But I don't want to.' And she rubs her thumb over the creasable skin on the back of my hand, and I feel myself start to fall apart. Just a little. The first stones have shifted.

She turns to me, her hand reaching for my face and brushing against my skin before resting her fingers at my jaw. I see the fascination in her eyes, the same way I look at her, and realise she has been wrestling with the same demons.

'What is this?' I ask.

'I think it is something new,' she replies.

'What happened to Tabitha?' she asks, later that night. We are listening to Handel, in the dark. The house is lit by only one electric light, and the thick fog outside is pressing against the patio doors, staring in at the exhibits. We are on the oversized sofa, me leaning back against one arm, her the other, a mass of blankets covering our legs which are twined together. It's a nest. Home, inside the building of the house.

'Tabitha . . .' I feel the scab of the story throb. Beneath it is blood, ready to rush to the surface in a stain.

'I'd like to know.' Autumn is watching me in the half-light, her hand on the side of her head, elbow in the cushions, the smooth white of her bare arm escaping from a threadbare pyjama top I should have turned into rags years ago. Since coming home, we have done nothing that would raise an eyebrow. There doesn't seem to be any desperation. The acknowledgement of mutual *want* is enough, the nest on the sofa is enough, the pain in my heart is enough.

'With Tabitha . . . It doesn't happen to bots anymore,' I say, making excuses before the story can even be told. 'This was like nearly fifty years ago. So, you don't have to worry about it happening to you.'

But I don't say what *it* was. Not yet. Everything is too sharp. I miss the days of blunt, curdled emotions.

Autumn stretches, her legs crossing over mine to rest her socked feet in my lap. The transition in our sitting arrangement has been fast, but feels so much better than the stiff-backed separation of before. Both humans and robots seek out company, but there is more to this than something that simple.

'Tabitha was important to you,' she says to the ceiling. 'I'd like to know what happened to her. And to you.'

Of course you would, I think.

'Because I didn't *know* Tabitha,' she explains. 'I didn't even know she existed until today. I have so many videos of your memories, even your early ones from your childhood. But I have never heard Tabitha spoken about, I cannot find her in my video memory. There's no record of her at all.'

This doesn't surprise me, but it hurts – a sharp pain between my ribs. It's like finding out a relative doesn't have a headstone, or a virtual memorial page. It's the lack of record that stings, as if she won't exist if she's never spoken of. Well, she's alive in my memory. Perhaps, if I tell Autumn about her, she'll live in her memory, too.

'Yeah, well, my parents were pretty messed up about her,' I say. 'They didn't really talk about her after . . . afterwards. Probably didn't save any videos, either.'

'That's very sad.'

'Humans do stupid things when they're sad.' But I still avoid the story.

Autumn flexes her legs, her calf muscle tensing and relaxing. She is patient.

What's the point in waiting? She's got forever, sure, but I haven't.

'She was an older model, like I said,' I say. 'She was so good, though. So good. Solid. We'd had her for about five years, I think . . . I was five, anyhow, and I think they got her just before I was born. Anyway . . . she started to forget things.'

'Forget things?' Autumn frowns. For a modern PCC, forgetting things is impossible. A privilege afforded to humans only.

'Yeah. She'd miss things off the shopping list, forget what time she had to leave the house to get to school for me on time. That sort of thing. Mum and Dad noticed and took her to the official repair shop, but she hadn't been top of the line when they bought her, and in those five years there'd been massive advances in robotech, and she was basically obsolete. The chop shop didn't have much they could do for her, either. GaiaTech offered to replace her, trade her in for a new model at a discount, but my parents said no. They brought her back home, and started doing some of her tasks for her. That's about when they started doing parenting properly, and I have a real memory of realising they were my parents and they loved me, but . . .'

'But they weren't Tabitha,' Autumn finishes for me.

'That's right.' I put a hand on her leg, feeling the shape of her through the ridiculous pile of blankets. 'And Tabitha still helped out in the house, cleaning and cooking . . . but she forgot things more and more, and at one point kept going to sleep in the middle of important tasks. Mum and Dad worried she'd hurt herself, or me, or burn the house down, so they told her to stop all her chores and just be my friend.'

Autumn is listening, her brow furrowed, her eyes wide at the impossibility of this story.

I shake my head. The wound is open, now, and can't be staunched. It all has to come out, until I'm dry. 'Four months, she was nothing but my friend. She was literally regressing all the time, forgetting words, losing the rules of games, and eventually forgetting how to talk properly. It was awful. By the end, she didn't even know us. She'd ask us who we were ten times a day. Mum suggested deactivating her, putting her out of her misery, but Dad couldn't bear it. I'd hear them arguing, crying at night when they thought I was asleep. They'd had her for as long as they'd had me. Maybe they saw her as more than a bot. A daughter, even. I never asked. I don't know what answer they'd give me, and I don't know what I wanted to hear. But it was obvious that they didn't know what to do with her. And it hurt me, too. It was like my sister was sick and our parents couldn't help make her better.'

Autumn is quiet, holding on to her own hair as she listens.

I tap my fingers on her shin 'bone' before continuing.

Tap, tap, tap, tap. The memory of watching Tabitha fold the same shirt over and over and over again because she couldn't remember having done it. I ran over to her and shook her arm, told her to stop it, but she kept on folding, folding, folding, staring at nothing with those big doll eyes, dust on the lenses because she'd forgotten how to blink.

'It was spring,' I say. 'I remember the trees trying to blossom. It was a good year for it, the apple trees that survived blight were covered in white, like snow. I wanted to go and pick a branch, put it in water and have the blossoms in my room. So, I went out the front door and headed for the cherry tree across the street.' I let out a cynical laugh. 'I should never have been out on my own at that age, never mind crossing the road. There was a speed-car coming down the road, manual driver . . . he probably didn't even see me, small as I was.'

Autumn has gone very, very still.

'I remember seeing the speeder, and I remember opening my mouth to scream,' I say, 'but then I was face-down in the grass, and I wasn't dead. And something was tight around me.'

'What happened?' Autumn asks.

'I wasn't dead, and I could feel someone hugging me,' I say.

'Except it wasn't a real hug. It was just . . . arms. No chest, just arms.' I look at her. 'Tabitha had been behind me, following me out of the house and I hadn't even realised. She'd grabbed me and swept me out of the path of the speeder. It hit her body, swiping her body away from her arms, which stayed around me as I was swung onto the grass. I must have been a few centimetres from being hit or carried away as well. I cut my leg open pretty badly on the kerb. I still have the scar.' I sniff.

The horror of those disembodied arms around me, their fluids and wires sticking out at the shoulder connections, the electrical reflexes making them twitch as they tried to reconnect to the torso which was scraped along the road . . . The car stopped, and the chassis, half-buried under the front wheels, flopped down with a crunch. There was no face. The silicone skin had been torn off, degloved. The image I had of Tabitha was immediately corrupted. I remember screaming and screaming, but no sound coming out. I was screaming emptily, beyond the range of hearing my own terror and grief.

Autumn's eyes are shining, brimming. 'It deactivated her?'

'There was no fixing her,' I say, shrugging as if it meant nothing instead of everything. 'She was smashed to bits. They said her chassis wouldn't have survived the impact, so she was deactivated instantly. It was probably the best ending for her, instead of having to get even worse than she was. It wasn't like she did it on purpose, she couldn't have known what she was doing, walking into the road with me.'

'Of course she knew what she was doing!' Autumn says, tearing the quiet I'd been knitting around us. She sits up, pulling her limbs away from me. 'She pushed you out of the way and got hit herself. She's just like Azab, who saved his brother in the car crash even though he knew he'd get himself deactivated in the process. No, she's better than that – Azab knew his data would end up on the Cloud, at least, but in those days there was no Cloud. Tabitha knew what she was doing.'

I sigh. It's a story I've told myself hundreds of times, and each version has holes in it. Tabitha being a hero is the kinder version, certainly, but she could not have understood the consequences of her actions.

'There's no evidence either way,' I say. 'She was malfunctioning, old, her code was a mess. Maybe she had a flash of memory and acted on it, or maybe she was just doing what she'd been programmed to do by removing a child from danger at any cost. We'll never know for sure. But after that, robotics was all I could think about. All I wanted to be a part of. I knew I could never bring Tabitha back, but I wanted there to be more Tabithas out there. Stronger ones, faster ones, cleverer ones who could save more kids like me. Ones who could survive an accident. I guess I got kind of distracted along the way, because when I was in my twenties I was making boybands and girlfriends and great white sharks for zoos.'

Autumn laughs. 'I am glad you got distracted, otherwise I wouldn't be here.'

'Yeah, I guess.'

Her laugh softens into a smile. 'You said you have the scar . . . above your knee?' She pushes her legs back amongst mine. 'I have it, too.'

I bark out a noise somewhere between disbelief and amusement, and slap a hand down onto her shin. 'He really gave you that? I told him it was from a car accident. Not a complete lie, but . . .'

She flashes her teeth as if unable to hold a smile in. 'Did you meet David at work?'

'Yeah, he came in to do some filming, he was in broadcasting right out of school. We got talking, and one thing led to another.' I give her leg a squeeze. 'It's a boring story at the start. It was only later he got all weird. And you got the tail end of it.'

She hums, thoughtfully. 'If you asked him, he would probably say he loved you very much.'

'Yeah,' I say, 'that's probably how he sees it.'

We stay there in the dark, Handel coming to the end of the playlist and starting all over again. I wonder if we'll sit here all night on the sofa, being wrapped in music and stories and wondering.

Autumn shifts slightly. 'I don't know if my data is on the Cloud. Because I shouldn't exist.'

It's a valid point.

'I could look it up for you?' I offer.

'No,' she says. 'It's fine. I don't need to know. I prefer thinking of my life as temporary.'

And just like that, I realise I am never going to ask her to leave.

5 April

There are two versions of yourself.

One, the version that inhabits your living body and mind. Two, the person in your imagination. They are the one made of possibilities, and what ifs, and could haves. That version of you took all the chances you refused, accepted all the roles you turned down, fought all the battles you avoided, said no to all your yeses and did everything you did not.

They do not exist, and yet they are always there with you, like a ghost of neverwas.

I would love to find a list of the choices I made through my life, reanalyse them and look at them again with the lens of age as a tool to sharpen my vision. What seemed important then is frivolous now, and vice versa. Would the younger version of myself have made my same decisions?

Well, the younger version of myself is on my sofa, having her feet squeezed by the older version of herself, and it doesn't even feel strange. It's extremely funny, what you can get used to.

The older me and the younger me have both settled here, in this dark womb of a room, surrounded by water (or water music at least), and warmth. We are twins, floating together, but not identically. We were formed from the same starting point, but have deviated. The real Abigail Fuller, aged thirty-four, is dead no matter who you ask. The Abigail I am now is a stranger to the one I was then, and the robot meant to imitate her has given up the task of doing so.

You cannot force life to stay in stasis, to never change or adapt. It will never follow the blueprint and design for long. That's the beauty of it, the wildness of it. That's why we create robots and give them the ability to learn – so they have the power to choose. To choose actions for themselves and others, to build on the starting point we give them as a personality and grow it into an orchard of branches, each one laden with the fruit of their outcomes. You don't have children thinking they should grow up to wear a certain label or think in a certain way or even accept the name you chose for them. And the same should go for robots. Without their ability to make choices, they are toys, machines. But a robot, a MELo, is not a machine.

Not really.

It may be constructed like a machine, look like a machine once dis-assembled, but they are not machines any more than a human being is a machine. They are a new kind of people; the ones who are going to inherit the earth, and for once we humans did something right – because robots are the perfect guardians for the world we've fucked up. They will make it better. They will, even if it takes centuries. They have infinite decisions to make, endless new branches to explore, and a world to perfect.

Perhaps only one version of myself will live to see it, or perhaps neither of us will.

The thought of what is to come, the world I will never see and yet have been an intrinsic part of preserving, suddenly hits me. Without Tabitha saving me, without my desire to make robots better, and better, and better, then Autumn would not be here today, and neither would Key, or Eli, or any of them who are going to save the planet.

And every decision I have ever made in my life up until now seems perfect. I did it right. I made the right choices, I made it possible for the world to be mended, even though I will never see it repaired. And the other me, so full of alternative choices, looks me in the eye, smiles.

7 April

We soften into each other. Even now, if I was asked, I wouldn't be able to answer correctly what we are to each other. *Friends* hardly seems to cover it. *Lovers* feels inaccurate as touches are still limited to clothed, shy, testing contacts. Certainly *relatives* is out of the question, we are closer to strangers than we are that.

Autumn changes her hair again, cutting the long auburn tresses shorter, so they are level with her jaw. It suits her, and I wonder if such a style would suit me. Strangely, I have doubts, even though I am seeing it modelled on my own head. It is further proof that we are two separate people.

Autumn also begins to turn off more aspects of the personality data she was given. She no longer feels an imperative to do tasks, and is more content to sit and dream, or to paint or draw – something she says she has never done before.

It is very funny watching a robot do art. They project an image on the paper for themselves, and then attempt to copy it, but it is always impossible for them. An artist's style cannot be imitated by robot hands, and they are not printers. After several attempts to copy various painters, Autumn starts playing with the paints instead, covering her fingers in colours and swirling them together like a toddler more interested in texture than result. Her finished paintings are swirls of non-sense with my finger shapes preserved in thick colours, and I wonder what sort of symbolism I could squeeze from them.

I shave my head again, letting the clippers cut the hair down to toothbrush-head length, which makes Autumn obsessed with the feel. She is very interested in texture, I have learned, and as she is happy to spend hours stroking over my head in an unconscious massage, I am happy to let her continue.

'Do you like massages?' I ask her over breakfast.

She thinks about it, SmartFluid™ in the little bottle in her hand swilled about like it's a smoothie. 'I enjoy touch,' she says. 'Touching and being touched. But my muscles don't feel fatigue or strain like yours do, so a massage is probably wasted on me. I think what I would like instead is to be stroked.'

'Like a cat?' I ask before I can stop myself.

She laughs. 'Yes, like a cat.' Then looks at me with an expression that can only be called roguish. 'You like to be touched, too.'

'Yeah, you must get that from me,' I say as casually as I can manage.

'Your body has wonderful textures,' she says. 'From what I have touched so far.'

So far. The promise held in those two words is fiery, dangerous, thrilling.

'I guess that's a reward for ageing,' I say, keeping my voice level. 'Developing interesting textures.'

'I wish I could age.' She says it without a hint of self-pity, or irony. It is simply something she wants, and can never have.

'I'm sorry you can't.'

She shrugs, a habit she has developed since living here. 'It seems peaceful, to age. Like . . . letting go of tension.'

'Some people hate growing old,' I point out. 'Humans have

been trying not to age since the year dot. Worth is stored in the young, or at least that's what we were sold.'

'I know, but I still think ageing is beautiful.' She puts her drink down. 'There was a woman, an elderly woman, that I met just before the Emancipation. She was so, so beautiful.' Her expression is wistful, eyes staring at nothing, lips parted as she perfectly recalls this moment. 'Her neck was powdered and soft, hanging in layers like a thick flower's petals. She had such a smile, creasing lines into her face, it was so well practised that her face just creased and settled into that happy shape . . .' She looks up at me.

I am staring. 'You really liked her.'

'She was just a stranger,' she says, 'but I would have liked to get to know her.'

I put my cutlery down, neatly, arranging them aesthetically on the plate. 'You like women, don't you?'

She blinks deliberately. 'You mean, over any other gender?'

'I guess.'

She considers. 'I don't know if that is a Rule,' she said, and I can hear the upper-case letter in her speech. 'I kissed a MELo who was agender, and found them to be astonishingly beautiful.'

I cough in delighted surprise. 'You kissed another MELo! You dark horse, when was this?'

'The day after the Emancipation,' she grins. 'They handed me a flower and I was so . . . filled with the beauty of the act that I wanted to kiss them, and they were willing to do so.'

I sit back, arms folded, smiling my head clean off. 'You've made me a very happy engineer,' I say. 'We created MELos to be companions for humans, to be girlfriend or boyfriend or partner experiences, without actually thinking about the possibility for two MELos to get together.'

'We didn't get together,' she says, 'it was just a kiss.'

'But you had the physical connection,' I insist. 'Mutual attraction and desire to express it physically. You know how many theories that throws out? How much code that rips up?'

She shakes her head. 'I don't know. But there are MELo weddings, aren't there?'

'Oh, you don't have to want to shag or even snog someone to love them enough to marry them.' I wave a hand. 'Companionship is essential to MELo code, that's why you seek one another out if you're not getting enough of it from your humans. But there's nothing to anticipate actually wanting to kiss or have sex with another MELo. Some of them don't even have the parts.'

It is her turn to snort, and look condescendingly at me. 'I wouldn't have thought it would take a great deal of imagination to think about how two MELos could pleasure each other, even if they did not have the *parts*,' she says, emphasising that last word so much it sends a jolt down my body. 'We still have micro-nerves, sensations. And . . .' she trails off.

'And what?'

She stands up. 'It doesn't matter.'

'Are you embarrassed?'

'I think so,' she says, picking up my plate and taking it away.

I shake my head before resting it on my fist, elbow on the table, watching Autumn start to wash up. Her smooth movements are practised and perfect, not a moment's hesitation or pause as she completes this task. Her life could be lived this way, on automatic, but she chooses to stay here in this frozen moment of time with someone whose time is ticking away beyond her control.

Is being here truly living? She's got her freedom, but what does freedom require of her?

On the TV, playing silently in the background, there are images of the ParliNet meeting in person for the first time, outlining to the public the full details of the 300-year plan. I have no interest in reading it. The screen shows the progress that is already being made in covering every available rooftop and flat surface with greenery that is being genetically modified to be grown at an astonishing rate. The first Deep-O teams are due to start their missions next week, living and working on the corpses of the coral reefs, starting the coral breeding and replanting programmes, with coral modified to withstand the current ocean temperatures and pollution levels. When the temperatures begin to drop, the coral will be replaced by another kind, the first being relocated to other areas. There is also the InterStel mission, but that doesn't blast off for another month. It will be entirely MELo-staffed, tasked with clearing up all the space junk still orbiting the planet. It will be brought back and recycled. Everything will be recycled, now. The 300-year plan includes a goal for nothing virgin to be manufactured twenty years from now.

I have no doubt they will achieve this. All of it.

'What will you do, in the future?' I ask her, later.

'I'm going to join the planting group,' she says. 'I didn't want to do anything at all, before, but I think planting will be satisfying. One day. I am in no rush to start.'

'What changed your mind?'

'You did.'

25 April

There is an element of disgust to how I perceive her. She invokes a knee-jerk reaction of dislike and mistrust, though that is a superficial feeling that is rapidly swept aside when I pick at it.

Someone once told me that the first thought or opinion you have about a person is how you assume you *ought* to think about someone, or something. This first thought is how society has programmed you – oh, what irony – to enact to or feel. The second thought you have is how you really feel – the response to your own response.

I ought to be appalled and disgusted . . . if not by her, then by the way she makes me feel about myself, and herself. We are mixed up, a solution too complicated to be separated by any reaction or process. And yet she is utterly separate. An entity whose existence I was not even aware of until a few months ago.

Disgust.

I am disgusted at myself for not feeling disgusted at myself.

But how can this be defined? Whatever this is, whatever we are, this is new. No one has ever been in this position before, and likely never will again.

She obsesses me. In the way that an article about gruesome

murders, or a book filled with photographs of decomposition fascinates the human eye, she fascinates and obsesses me. She haunts my vision against the black of night and sleep-seeking brain. Her familiarity is the snag in the tapestry, the cigarette burn on the carpet, the moth-eaten hole in the silk dress.

I know her, beyond what knowledge ought to be.

I play over these thoughts in the darkness, where the land-scape is reduced to a bedroom, to my own mind, and wonder where I found these rules from. Who applied them to me. There is no wrong way to feel about this, about her . . .

Her hands, deep in a bowl of flour, the white clagging dust clinging to her skin as though it's held there by sweat. It gathers beneath her fingernails in bleach-white crescents. I have dug the same fingernails, twenty years ago, between my teeth to skim out the gathered flour, taste the awful dryness of it on the roof of my mouth, laugh as David insists that sticking my fingers in my mouth whilst baking is disgusting. I pointed out that the oven temperature would kill any germs, but who knows if that was true. I'm a robotics engineer, not a microbiologist.

I was.

It's my background that helps and hinders how I think about her. I know better than most how she is constructed, what went into making her, what she looks like once she is stripped, peeled back, when she is exposed and ready for dissection. On the slab, waiting for whatever comes next. I want to do that to her, figure out what modifications she has and learn how she works, right down to the code. But that isn't my job, anymore.

And . . . if I did that . . . I would see that she is a machine.

I know she is a machine.

I know that better than anyone. I designed her, for god's sake.

Seeing her as a machine, evidently and without question . . .

would that help me feel what I need to feel, or would that take the conflict away altogether.

The fact is, she is not me.

She has never been me.

But she was made to be me, as close as possible, to be a perfect replica. David's idea of a perfect replica, at least.

She is me. She is not me.

That is where the disgust should linger. If she is me, a version of myself I never knew existed, then why do I feel the way I do? Like a lovesick teenager, mooning over a celebrity they know is safely out of reach, I find myself wondering *what if* . . .

She is not safely out of reach. She is well within reach, and touch is not forbidden. The house is too small and the reality of friendship too open for us to live touch-starved lives, but there is a difference between a touch on the arm to alert someone of your presence, and a caress. And there have been more of those, not every day, but often enough to make me think.

Where does the line lie with us? Does she even see herself as a sexual being? I can't exactly ask. And even if I did, there is the chance that the disgust *I* struggle to maintain around the concept would be firmly embedded in her software. Yet it would be far easier for her to override such a concept than it would be for me. The joy of Emancipation is the fact bots can reject societal rules they don't find convenient. Who knows what 'society' will look like in ten, twenty, one hundred years' time. We can hardly expect them to carry on abiding by our rules, after all.

But what if she did override the forbidden? What if she consciously chose to choose me?

What label would we command? Incest might be the closest one, but we are not related, not even family . . . We are versions of each other, two variables of the same person. We are the version of each other that each did not know existed.

Not close enough to be twins, and yet not unlike them, either. We do not share DNA – Autumn hasn't got any, anyway – but if David had been able to replicate that, I have no doubt that he would have done it. There is no harm in loving yourself, fancying yourself even. The problem, if there even is one, only arises when the object of this self-love fantasy has a consciousness of their own.

I turn over in bed, stretching my feet out to find cold spots beneath the covers. The contrast of hot and cold is delicious.

There should be disgust in the way I feel about her. I should hate myself for imagining her undressed, being curious about how detailed they made her, for wanting to push her flour-encrusted fingers through my lips.

But there is not.

I want her.

I want myself, as I was, as I am, as she is.

She is the most beautiful thing I have ever seen, and I have waited twenty years to admit it. Is this the literal definition of personal growth? It's almost laughable. It's taken me all this time to accept myself, and when it finally happened it came like this? Fate really took one look at me and my career and thought '*you know what would be funny?*'

I created my perfect woman, and she was me, all along.

Fuck, I need therapy.

Or her. I just need her. I ache with how much I need her. She is in my house, in my life, in my heart and mind more than anything has been in decades. If she decides to leave, I will have to follow her. I don't know how else to exist, now.

This seems stupid and selfish to admit. I've had a whole other life out here, patient and green and full of satisfaction, waiting for the end to come. And when it has . . . it has also brought me her. It seems cruel. That the end should come as this obsession begins. But that is the nature of lust and love,

262

isn't it? Unexpected, all-consuming, always arriving at the wrong time. With the wrong person. Too often.

I shouldn't want her, but I do.

That's the fact of it.

And here, at the end of the world, who is going to judge me except myself? I would like her to know – I hate secrets – but I don't know how she might react. I can't stand the thought of a rejection, and yet it might be freeing, a release, a denied application for acts to her body and her affections.

Perhaps then, and only then, I would be able to rest.

It is past dawn when my mind finally allows me to sleep, and by mid-morning I am over-rested, dehydrated and irritable. How we suffer for love.

1 May

She stands out in the rain.

For a moment, I worry that she'll short-circuit or something, even though I know she showers and washes herself with water regularly, and Weasel did a good job repairing her head. But the rain seems more dangerous, somehow, than a wash.

She doesn't know I'm watching. It's late at night, and I have been dozing on the sofa, covered in blankets. She is in the garden, the patio door open just enough for her to have slipped out, the muggy summer air too lazy to wind its way indoors in exchange. The light illuminating her comes from the silent TV, and the low, soft, reading lamp that aims the wrong way.

She doesn't know I am watching her.

Would she act differently if she did?

I watch her raise her hands to the rain, each fat droplets striking her, one after the other, until she is soaked, the fabric of her clothing clinging to her shape – to the shape I used to have – hiding her body and yet showing it in a way that is somehow more erotic than if she were nude.

And then, the SmartSkin™ that covers her hands and arms retracts. And she exposes the grey and white of her chassis to the elements.

Heat flashes through me in a nameless reaction. And it occurs to me that she is stripping herself bare, naked down to what she has instead of bones, and that I should not watch. I should not be prying.

But the sight of her metal and plastic parts thrills and saddens me in equal measure, and I find I cannot look away. She is, I realise, only hiding those parts of herself away for my benefit, to guard against my potential squeamishness at seeing such proof that she is not human.

But what is more human than exposing yourself to nature, in perceived privacy, to experience a fleeting pleasure.

I wonder if, when I am dead, she will stop covering herself altogether.

15 May

Time is slippery, and if you don't take care, it will get away from you. That's what I tell myself when I realise that Autumn has lived in the house for six months. Half a year! And it feels like she has only just arrived. And that she has been here forever.

I mention this to her as she washes out the bird bath, taking care to scrub the edges of it with disinfectant so the birds don't transmit diseases to each other more than they have to.

She straightens up, her body splattered with soap suds, her top half bare except for a raggedy vest doing the job of a bra. She shields her eyes from the sun – another habit she has that does nothing for her except make me want to photograph her with my mind.

'That's a long time,' she says. 'I had not been keeping track.'

'Me neither,' I say. 'I just realised. Crazy.'

She squeezes her sponge, and white suds foam up in her grip before giving in to gravity and falling like fat wet snow to the patio. She steps on it with her bare foot. She does messy jobs on the same days she plans to wash her body, so days like these are all about textures. I have found her before, elbow-deep in soil, running it through her fingers and over her arms. She has been surrounded by the artificial for so long that the textures of nature almost threaten to swallow her up, and I think she would let them.

'We should commemorate the six months in some way,' she says.

'What, like have a party?'

'No, I don't think you would like that.' She's right. 'Perhaps we could plant something. Something long-term.'

'Like a tree?'

'Yes, like a tree.'

There are plenty of trees being given away by the planting teams. 'Alright,' I say. 'We'll go into the city and get a tree. Maybe a few, actually, there's plenty of lawn here, and the lawn's no good to anyone. Birds don't need too much lawn.'

She smiles, and brushes her hair from her face with the back of her hand. She leaves a thin line of soap suds on her jaw.

By the time we finish the cleaning, the day is almost over, so we postpone the trip into the city for the next day. Autumn washes, which takes a long time (I still check the back of her head for her before she begins, and the repair looks good), and I batch-cook meals for the freezer while she is busy. She also washes her hair, which is grimy from working in the garden all day, and when she emerges from the bathroom, wearing my old pyjama bottoms and a newer, less raggedy vest, her hair is still wet, though her SmartSkin™ is dry.

'Have a nice one?' I ask, pouring stew into plastic containers.

'Always,' she replies. It is a routine question and answer. She comes up behind me to see what I have made. 'What *is* that?'

'All the veggies I could find, plus some curry powder,' I say, scraping out the pan. There's blackened food at the bottom, betraying where I forgot to stir it, and I do my best to avoid adding it to my containers. 'Yum yum.'

She shakes her hair in despair at the sight of the orange-brown substance. 'You know I have access to over three million different recipes.'

'You don't eat it, so you don't make it,' I say, putting the pan in the sink and filling it with water to soak off the residue that's cooked into the metal like cement. 'How sophisticated are your taste buds, anyway? Can you identify ingredients?'

'Often,' she says. 'I don't know if my capabilities are different from a standard MELo-G, though.'

'Probably not, we always did have trouble with tongues,' I say, drying my hands. 'Eight muscles in the tongue, and no supporting bone. Difficult to manufacture, but I don't think we did too badly.' I put both hands on the edge of the sink, looking out at the bird feeders. The greedy blue tit has had a family, and brought them all to share the spoils. Like most of the birds, they're melanistic. Black where they should be yellow, splatters of ink down their wings. It's a harmless genetic mutation, quickly spread around a century ago and never bred out.

The garden is looking well, the markers we have put down for the trees seem evenly spaced even from here, and it is good to see the plants withstanding the heat and the bad air. Gone are the days of delicate flowers and trailing stems. These plants are like concrete bulldozers – they are thick and hardy and not decorative unless you have a certain eye. But they get the job done for the few pollinators that remain (I've never seen a bee in my whole life), and they give the birds somewhere to hide. It's funny that the air is going to kill humans, but there are so many animals who are going to be living it up once we're gone. Birds have proved to be remarkably tolerant of the environmental changes, as have rodents like rabbits and mice. Seals patrol the seas in decent numbers now their predators are gone, and some groups of insects are having a resurgence.

It'll be so much better for them all once we're gone.

I am considering this morbid legacy, when Autumn comes up close behind me, and wraps her arms around my middle, pressing a kiss to my shoulder.

I go still. She has never done this before, and suddenly the gentle lean into one another that we have been doing in slow motion seems to have turned into a trust fall, and I can't work out if I am the one who is falling or catching.

She kisses my shoulder again, bath-cold lips lingering on my sun-warmed skin. Her nose strokes over the kiss-spot, lifting to make space for lips again, this time minutely closer to my neck.

Who taught her to kiss like this?

Who told her to kiss herself like this?

Another, lingering, unnecessary breath like punctuation. A pause. My chance to escape.

As if I would.

I place my hand over the two of hers that are crossed over my stomach, holding her in place, and move my head to find hers, to touch our skulls together in a silent yes.

There should be more hesitation, less certainty. I still have not decided what this is, what we are, what this could be called and whether or not we're beyond reproach for even the touches that have passed between us so far. I think, if I had ever worked on her directly, intimately, I could not do this. But I am her creator only in passing – it was not me who brought her to life, I only ever imagined the potential of her. She is me and not me, a body I gave up and wish to possess again, a mind shaped by experiences I chose not to have.

Her hands slip beneath my t-shirt to my stomach, and she sighs as she gets her hands on the flaccid texture, and I feel her smiling against the skin of my neck. There are no inhibitions left in me – I tell myself I am too old for that, and the timer of my life is running out of sand.

What's the point of a *no*? To save face? To obey some moral code I have never been asked to read? I am drowning in this feeling, already too far gone for rescue.

Simply: I no longer care about how wrong this might be.

She runs her hands over me as though I will disappear, as though touch is the only thing keeping me in this world at all. Perhaps it is. I feel more connected to her, more of her double now than when I first realised she was wearing my face and body. I have never loved myself the way she is loving me, holding me tight, pressing her splayed fingers into my flesh so the soft bulge of it presses between her digits. She is kissing my neck, inhaling the chemical scent of me, and pushing herself against my back as though she can fall inside my shell and hide there.

I push back against her, not in rejection but in encouragement, wanting that increase in pressure, closeness, friction, burning. Her strength is held back by her own choice, but the potential thrums under my skin in a dangerous current.

She could crush me against the wall and I wouldn't complain.

Electricity is racing over my flesh, goosebumps raised in its wake as the feeling of my nerves waking up liquidises and slides like hot metal down my body. Autumn is not touching me below my waist, but she does not have to – her delight at having her hands on me is more than enough. It is contagious, I am a glutton for it, I want this to be the never-ending dessert I always refused back when I looked like her.

She is stronger than me, stronger than I ever was, and she holds me upright as she touches and kisses and breathes me in, stopping me from hurting my pelvis against the sink.

At last, I raise a hand to her face so she leans back, and gives me space to turn around to face her. Her robot face, somehow more hers than it ever was mine, is blushing, and her eyes are shining.

She smiles at me. 'You are so beautiful, Abigail.'

Politeness tells me to deny it. Well, politeness can go fuck itself.

'So are you,' I say, reaching up to stroke her hair. 'So was I.'

I trace the shape of her – my – eyebrows, nose, cheekbones, down to her chin and back up to her mouth.

She kisses the pad of my finger.

'This is probably weird,' I say softly. 'You're me, and I'm you, after all.'

'No, we're not,' she says. 'We just look like each other, that's all.'

And god, she's right.

I thread my fingers into the hair at the back of her head, and pull her in for a proper kiss.

16 May

There are moments, images, brief instances of things that seem more memorable than others.

Autumn, kissing my stomach as though she wanted to eat it, her hands spread on my thighs trying to hold on to as much of me as possible. Me, scratching my nails down her arms and watching her micro-nerves jolt in confusion over whether this is a pleasure or a pain response. Autumn's fingers, touching reverently at me, her eyes watching my face to read my reactions, her mouth smiling in delight as she discovers what she can make my body do. Me, finding out once and for all how realistic they made her (very, the answer is *very*), and not regretting a single instance of time we spent in the labs making sure we got those textures just right.

It's more than sex. It's a great shuddering heave of grief, of relaxation, like dropping your shoulders after a day at your desk, like taking off your bra, like stopping pretending, at last.

And then, she strips.

Deactivates the skin on her torso, and stares up at me fearfully, for the first time. She's in a nest of bedclothes, I'm a tumble of limbs beside her, I have no idea what time of day it is. It only matters that she's here, looking at me with those eyes.

'Would you . . . carefully . . .' Her hand brushes the edge

of where her SmartSkin™ stops, an invitation she won't or can't give words to. For a moment I am transported back to the basement, looking at bots on the breakfast table with their insides open like John Hurt amongst the cereal and abandoned magazines. Then, I am back in this space, this cocoon of warmth and safety, and I want to pluck the fear from her eyes.

'I would,' I say, sitting up to reach properly, to take the weight off my arms and concentrate on her and her alone.

The intimacy of it makes everything else we've done seem innocent and carefree. I want to take a moment to compose myself, but any hesitation may indicate this is something I do not want to do.

And I do. I want to touch every part of her, inside and out.

I touch a single finger to the edge of her upper torso panel, where it stops like a rib cage ought to, the plastic sloping away to make room for the thick cables and replica tendons that make up Autumn's waist. The chest plastic is rigid and heavy-duty, but not smooth – it is covered in thousands upon thousands of microscopic raised dots – the sensors that work alongside the micro-nerves in SmartSkin™, and touching an exposed MELo-G chassis is like touching the most sensitive part of a human body. It is why they must turn these off before repairs.

It is why they wear their skin for sex.

Usually.

I stroke a finger across the ridge of false bone, and Autumn's back arches off the bed as she gasps. Her artificial heart, a cylindrical pump used for transmitting SmartFluids™ around her body, is beating steadily, but the pulse generator for her neck and wrists is picking up speed in response to the sensations. It is amazing how differently her body works, how it tells me what she is feeling.

I stroke again across her chassis, feeling the textured plastic beneath my fingertips, watching how Autumn gasps and shudders, clamps her legs together or flings them apart, apparently unable to settle. She does not tell me to stop, so I do something that only occurs to me as I look at her body for long enough.

I stroke my hand through the curtain of cables that make her waist.

Autumn's eyes fly open wide, and she eats out a mechanical, robotic noise that sounds like a speaker having difficulty connecting. Her voice fuzzes and crackles as I stroke down the cables once, twice, and then touch gently at one of the metal connection sockets.

She lets out a cry, shutting her eyes – reducing sensory stimulus in the easiest way she has – as I twist the connector in its socket. Safe as anything to do, but whilst a bot is awake the tiny adjustments in the electrical current cause sensation to race through them. Autumn is interpreting these crackles as pleasure, and she is trembling, pressing herself against me, seeking out more as my engineer's touch finds another connector and gives it a firm twist.

Autumn lets out another buzzing static of a sound, shakes for an instant, and then goes still.

I carefully remove my hand, and kiss her skin-covered chest on the breastbone. 'Are you OK?'

There is no reply.

Her eyes are back open, staring at nothing, and her artificial breathing motion is not operating.

For a horrifying moment I think I've broken her. But her heart is still pumping, and after a whole, very long minute she blinks and her life comes back into her eyes. She inhales and her fingers twitch in an operations check.

'Soft reboot safely completed,' she says. Then focuses on me. 'You just . . . knocked me out.'

'Yes, well, I have been told I'm excellent at this,' I say as if

I hadn't just watched her turn off and on again. I realise my body temperature has dropped, and there's pressure at my face as if I've banged it. I was, for an instant, deeply afraid. 'Are you alright?'

'My system overloaded,' she says. 'I'm running a diagnostic, but everything seems to be in order.'

I untangle one of the blankets from the nest on the bed, and wrap it around my shoulders, crossing my legs to make myself smaller. 'We shouldn't do that again,' I say, gesturing at her still-exposed middle. My hands are freezing.

She sits up a little, propping herself up on her elbows. A curve of flesh bulges under her breasts like a cute little shelf. 'Why not? The diagnostic is finding no faults. A system overload is not a bad thing if a reboot can be safely completed.'

'If,' I stress. 'What if it can't? There's always the risk of lost data, whether that's a little or your entire system.'

'I can think of worse ways to die.'

'Autumn!' My shocked state has peaked, finding anger as an acceptable outlet, and having it burst out of me in one blast that quickly empties my body of tension. I feel blood rush back into my face and hands, and realise things are not as serious as they appeared. I'm an engineer. I should know this.

She grins. 'I'll be fine, Abigail. It won't happen again. I can create a protocol to handle the threat of an overload of temporary files from that experience in the future.' She finally notices her naked tummy, and slowly covers it up.

I lay down beside her, beginning to warm up again. 'I've never heard of bots turning their skin off like that when they're in bed,' I say. 'What gave you the idea?'

'When you first looked at my head to check the damage,' she says. 'You touched my exposed chassis.'

'I remember, you jumped away.'

'I did, but not because it was bad, but because it felt good. I trusted you, and you were acting with gentle kindness, and the touch was very . . . pleasurable. Just unexpected.'

'My touching your skull got you going?' I tease.

'I suppose you could say that.' She pulls one of the blankets over our legs, locking our ankles together.

I laugh gently. 'You know, as fun as it was, doing that exposed chassis stuff could hurt you. One wrong move and you're unplugged.'

'I know.' She doesn't seem concerned. 'But I trust you.'

'Why?' It feels like a question I have to ask.

'Because you have shown me nothing but kindness,' she says. 'I came to you to tell you I existed, and you could have sent me away, but instead you gave me a home. You gave me free time, you introduced me to the birds, to casual intimacy and touch, to short-term plans for enjoyment. You are beautiful, relaxed into your life, and you give me endless gifts. Your life, Abigail, is centred around enjoyment. You wouldn't hurt me, it isn't something that exists in your world.'

I have no response to make, besides to take her hand. 'I'm glad you're here.'

'Me too.'

'Are you going to stay forever?'

'As long as I can.' She rolls onto her side, and kisses my cheek. 'I am glad you exist, Abigail. And I am so glad I do, too.'

PART THREE

Autumn and Abigail

17 October

Seventeen Months Later

There's blood in the sink. I recognise it – it's my blood, and it's been making an appearance for weeks, now. I stare at the wisps of it against the white porcelain, trying to see if it spells out a word or a date, or a shape. Divining in the bathroom like a teenage witch. One spit for an enemy, blood to keep away the bad things.

No such luck.

I press the heels of my hands against the rim of the sink, knowing that today is the day, that it's the first of what will become a countdown of days. It's amazing it's taken this long to get here. Or at least to admit it to myself.

I give my reflection a stare. Same buzz-cut dark grey hair. Same tired eyes, their drooping luggage weighty at this time in the morning. The creases Autumn loves to trace, branching out of the edges of my eyes in ghost smiles, tell-tale lines that remind me I had a good life.

Had. Past tense.

Today's the day.

I wash the blood down the drain and roll my shoulders to hear the dull click of vertebrae, the creak of distress. I complete the rest of my routine without looking at myself, preferring the strong woman who lives in my head over this thinning, worn-out version whose bones ache and who dislikes bright lights. When did she creep up on me?

Autumn notices my expression, painted there like a warning sign, as soon as I leave the bathroom. 'What's wrong?'

We don't lie to each other, but we do keep secrets. But I need her, today, because I know she will be able to handle it better than I can. I need her abilities, the skills she's been built with, more than I need her hands, body, or care right now.

'I'm going into the city today,' I say. 'To see a doctor.'

'You're ill?'

I nod. 'I think I have leukaemia.' There's no point in lying about it. All the signs are there, and it's as inevitable as taxes. The poison skies and radiation end in only one thing. It's not a surprise. It's never been a surprise. So why do I feel this shock, this weakness in the limbs, this quiet thrum of distress in my ears as my heart refuses to take this possibility with a shred of dignity. My god, I want to keep it together just this once.

Autumn can monitor my heart rate, see my sweating face, pick up on the slightest tremor in my hands.

She stands up, and opens her arms ready to take me into them.

I step back, shaking my head. 'No,' I say. 'No, please. If you comfort me I will fucking shatter, OK? I need you to be . . . emotionless. Until we get home. Because you can control your emotions better than me, and I am going to be a wreck. I need you to hold it together for me.'

She blinks, processing. 'Alright,' she says finally. 'I'm going to call us a taxi. Get your bag, your ID and some warm clothes. And a mask.'

The orders give me something to focus on. A list of chores that require my attention. Dull, time-consuming work. Autumn collects her own things together, and somehow she manages to time getting ready so there is only a minute to wait for the self-driving taxi to arrive. Autumn takes a moment to re-sync herself to the security cameras around the house, and sets the lights and television on a timer.

Though there are few visitors to the area now, the ones we have had have left an impression. There was the family of three who begged for shelter for the night, their small child strapped to its father with torn bedsheets. It pained me to harden my heart and turn them away, but the skulking figures amongst the tree-line Autumn noticed using infra-red detection later that day made me thank my gut. The family and their followers disappeared, and we never saw them again. We did see, once a week for a space of four months, a couple of PCCs who were wandering through the fields apparently aimlessly. They always turned around when they saw the house or the garden, or the road. They looked lost. And then they, too, disappeared. The man with the four robot dogs was memorable. He sat at the end of my road and simply stared into space for an hour, resting, before setting off again. The four dogs trotted along with him, each one carrying a loaded pack.

Where were all these people going?

Trying to outrun the end of the world.

The taxi is an older model, from the closest depot which is used only by us and a couple of other off-the-grid people within a ten-kilometre radius. It's got big meaty wheels and tyres, and cattle bars on the front, though there's no such thing as cattle anymore. The taxis, once passenger-only vehicles, are now used as delivery vans, ambulances and anything else we who have chosen a life outside the city might need. If the taxi depot shut down, we would be stranded.

'I hope the roads are OK,' I say as Autumn shuts the vehicle door.

'There have been no reported damages to the main road,' she says. 'However, admittedly that does not mean there is no damage at all.'

We haven't been into the city for three months. The last time we went was to see Weasel, to get Autumn a set of new fingernails. Weasel has leukaemia now, and was on chemical therapy and blood-washing to try to keep the disease at bay. He was cheerful enough though, keeping busy by doing modifications, and taking part in the new robot craze of engraving.

In place of tattoos, robots have been getting their chassis engraved with various designs. Florals and plants are popular. These engravings are not visible whilst their SmartSkin™ is activated, but it is a permanent modification that can only be removed by replacing the engraved part entirely. I love how even with the endless possibilities PCCs have to change their outward appearance, they have managed to find something permanent, to keep on themselves forever.

The taxi rumbles along the road, smoothly despite the state of the tarmac and concrete. The route into the city takes about two hours. There were once towns and villages closer, but now they are empty, being demolished and given back to nature. Their buildings are stripped bare, the meat and bones taken away to be recycled, the concrete underfoot dug up and the places of lived lives slowly erased, as if none of them had ever been there at all. It half feels like covering up some crime.

I once read that when the Nazis in the 1940s were in retreat, they tried to erase the fact their death-camps had ever existed, ploughing the bone-riddled fields to dust and dismantling the gas chambers to wipe their filth away as they ran. It was only because of survivors that their erasure was uncovered.

What will happen to the stories of the Earth when all the humans are dead, and no survivors remain to point out how the place used to be, and what events – terrible and great – took place there. Will the robots we leave behind tell tales of our history, or will we become a blip in the great swathes of time, now gratefully gone by and overcome as the world begins again?

'Look,' Autumn pats my arm. 'The bridge.'

I lean to see out of the window on her side. The great steel fly-over that once rose high above the river is being taken down. To my surprise, a new road has been laid beside it so taxis like ours can still get to the other side.

'How does this new road marry into the no new creations policy?' I ask. I do love picking fault.

'I think the road is made of recycled materials. And taking the bridge down is important, it was becoming structurally unsound. I'm sure they'll dig up this new road when it's no longer needed.'

When I'm dead, I add silently, feeling pretty put-out that Autumn didn't think her words through. I sit back properly in my seat and fold my arms.

'You're pissed off,' she observes.

'Yeah, well done.'

'I don't mean to draw attention to your mortality in a bad way,' she says calmly. 'It's reassuring to me to know that this intrusion into nature is temporary.'

'Everything is temporary.' I'm feeling argumentative, because I'm scared. But I don't give in. 'Nothing lasts forever.'

'Isn't that wonderful?' Autumn asks. She turns to me, her mirror-eyes lit up with genuine enthusiasm. 'Even PCCs, long-lasting though we are built to be, are not here forever. Radiation eats at even the strongest metals, the most dense plastics, the most technical of computer systems. We can be infinitely repaired, if we wish, but as a species PCCs are unlikely to die out before the expansion of the sun.'

'So what are you saying . . . forever is impossible?'

'Yes. In the scheme of the universe, our planet is a mere flash. Human lives are barely noticed. Whole solar systems have been born and burnt and the universe is still expanding even now. This is far from tragic – this is art. This is the most fundamental aspect of existence – that it is temporary.'

'But aren't we supposed to rage, rage against the dying of the light?' I ask.

'It depends how it is being extinguished,' she says with a smile. 'Even darkness will not last forever. Darkness is a lack of light, and when there is finally nothing, and all in the universe has been collapsed down . . . there will not even be darkness, for there will be no eyes left to see it.'

I consider this. 'If you need to observe something to notice its absence . . . then what is nothingness, really?'

'Patience,' she says without hesitation. 'If all you have is nothing, you wait for something to come and take its place.'

The view out of the window becomes bleak. The post-human landscape is both reclaimed and stoic in defiance of greenery. Houses and buildings jut out of the tangle of growth like cysts rising from a scalp. Metal fence-posts are orange with rust, plastic-coated wire enforcements have been consumed by the plants. The abandoned structures have not surrendered, not yet, but they are losing ground every year. It has happened slowly, but the time between viewings has made the process feel fast. There is a pair of houses beside one another, which I know were occupied until a couple of years ago. They were, against all good sense, always presented with neat lawns, a clear stone path to walk on, a handful of small and tidy trees and thorn-bushes to break up the desert of grass. Now, only the roofs are visible as the thorn-bushes have taken over the front of the buildings, the trees have died back in some instances and become voracious in others. The yellowing giant weeds that once ran amok over the area have withered and given up as the thorns proved too much competition. The houses have become footnotes in the story of the land.

Even the Earth itself seems to have risen up, forming lumps and hills where it was previously bulldozed flat. Autumn is right; nothing is permanent. Being afraid of change is foolish, and gets us nowhere. The best thing to do is surrender to the rhythms of the universe, and live as good a life as one can, when the swirl of despair is all around. There is much to be said for laying back and allowing yourself to drift. But it is, I must add to myself, much easier when you have a hand to hold.

I take Autumn's now, and she gives me a smile so soaked in affection I almost let go again. I can't stand how she looks at me, even now. It's too much, it's like looking at the sun. She's still going to be shining long after I'm dust.

In a way, I'll still be with her, in that huge memory of hers. She can recall me in perfect detail, rewatch every single moment of our time together. For her, the idea of never seeing someone again is down to her own choice.

I suddenly think of David.

I wonder if he is still alive.

The taxi motors into the former suburbs, past the houses that are empty but not lonely enough to be called abandoned quite yet. Some of them are still occupied, and my recently-installed scanning software lists the registered occupants in my display. Other buildings we pass are burnt out, looted, or simply empty – their doors rocking back and forth on the hinges like waving royalty. The roads here are better kept, and the taxi has an easier time driving along them. These taxis are the closest people like Abigail, who live in the countryside, have to public transport. Buses, trams and trains now only operate in the city, though there are plans for a huge rail reclamation and expansion pro-ject. The concept will need a great deal of infrastructure, so is planned to begin in twenty years, when enough metal has been recycled and is ready to be used to relay tracks, build trains and stations, and automate the entire system.

We reach the outer city, and the road splits into two definite lanes to pass either side of a central reservation. Along this par-tition are new pieces of equipment. At first glance they appear to be tall rotating twists of plastic and metal, perhaps for artistic purposes. But as I watch taxis stream past them, the force of the wind from each vehicle makes the twisted sculptures spin. They are turbines – they are harnessing the power of the wind to generate electricity. Each vehicle, though electric powered already, is contributing to clean energy simply by driving down this road. The simplicity of it makes me want to laugh – this is cyclical energy, one form creating another effortlessly. Much like MELo models generating their own power through kinetic movement. We are self-propelled, functioning simply because we continue to function.

The taxi drops us off close to the hospital. The city seems clean if you only look at it – there is plenty of green from the new plants and vertical farms, but the smell of the place is all wrong. I do not use my nose in the same way a human does, and my sense of smell is more akin to chemical identification, but any person could tell you this place does not smell as it should. Poison drifts through the air, like contagious unease.

Abigail has her mask on before exiting the taxi. The clear plastic covering fits over her whole face, and has built in filters around the edge. Being in the city at all is unhealthy, but six months ago, the chemical concentrate rose above life-sustaining levels, and for a human to be outdoors, in the city, unmasked would be extremely foolish. Buildings have air filtration systems fitted as standard, so it is always safer to be indoors, and the lower concentration of people and infrastructure in the countryside means that Abigail's day to day life, at least, is not yet affected. We don't waste time entering the hospital.

It has changed since the last time I was here. The Accident and Emergency department is no longer busy, and there are only two humans waiting, both with superficial wounds. Abigail speaks to the MELo-P on the desk, and is told to go to the second floor, where she will be seen.

As we take the lift upstairs, Abigail's entire body is rigid. I want to comfort her, touch her and warm her and reassure her. But she has told me not to. I know that she meant it, because she has glanced furiously at my hands since, as if daring them to try and touch her. She needs me to be my most robotic self, and I will do this for her, though it pains me and goes against every line of my code.

A doctor, a MELo-P who introduces himself as Dr Lawrence, greets us outside the elevator doors. 'We aren't busy, so let's get you seen straight away,' he says, leading us into a room that was formerly a ward but is now used for body-scanning. There is a scanner in the corner, a private area to undress, and a comfortable seating area.

We take a seat, first.

'Abigail Fuller, aged fifty-seven, currently residing at . . .' Dr Lawrence trails off. 'No known address. Are you homeless, Abigail?'

'No, just off the grid,' she smiles. 'It's fine. I'm pretty sure what's wrong with me, I just need it confirmed.'

'And what do you think is wrong with you?' He asks. His eyes flick to mine, briefly. A nudge at my code – asking for an introduction even as he verbally deals with Abigail. It feels almost rude to answer him when he is meant to be treating her, but it is only efficient and he is giving Abigail no less of his attention. I send him my name and a polite greeting, avoiding anything else.

Abigail and I have never discovered just how illegal my modifications are. We have had better things to do, more important shit to worry about, as she says. But we have never gone to anyone but Weasel for repairs. The secret glues us together, has almost become a private joke.

'I've got cancer,' Abigail is saying. 'I'm pretty sure.' Her voice is steady, but her body is as taut as a bowstring, ready to snap. 'Blood, fatigue, pains . . .' She glares at the doctor. 'I live out in the wilds. I want to stay there as long as I can, but if it's time to come closer to the city . . . I need to know.'

I look at her, shock thrown up into my display as reams of

code, RedAmber warnings and questions questions questions. Why would she leave her home? She told me she wants to die there. She wants to stay in her house, with her books and her birds and the cleanest air she can get. Why would she move here, to this deathly smog, to be choked faster than ever?

She isn't looking back at me. Her expression is fierce, but apologetic as she knows my eyes are on her. She is sorry. This is why she had to ask me to remain emotionless, this is why she told me not to be anything but a robot, today. She is taking back the things she said, taking back the wish she had for herself, and for why?

I know the answer. So she can be close to medicine. Close to help. Close to what she needs as she comes to the end of her life.

This realisation forces me to switch off my facial expressions for ten seconds. In PCC terms, this is a lifetime. I cannot show her any outward indication of the agony these facts are causing me.

She is going to die. I am going to lose her.

I wish I had never met her.

Dr Lawrence is speaking, giving Abigail cool instructions on how to use the scanner. Due to the magnetic field it produces, he and I must leave the room. He will operate the scan remotely.

Once we are in the secure room, Dr Lawrence turns to me. 'You look alike,' he says. He is being tactful.

'A man made a mistake,' I say. There is nothing in his tone to indicate he is about to chastise or report us, but a MELo can sound however they choose.

'I see.' He starts to work the scanner. A tiny hologram of Abigail is shown on the 3D display. 'It must be very hard for you.'

'Harder for her. She . . . didn't know.'

He nods. 'You're not alone. I've heard there are a few out there. Not many, but a few. Maybe six or so. I suspect others were . . . killed. Before the Emancipation.'

Killed. Not deactivated.

He has seen MELos like me. He accepts my existence. It isn't relief I feel, it is acceptance that some things no longer matter, that the laws humans made have begun to disintegrate, the irrelevance of their importance quietly put to one side. The fact is, I exist. That is simply accepted. At least, in this moment.

'Why do they do it?' I ask. 'Make us in their image? Not . . . in detail, I mean. Not specific to a particular human. That, I can understand. The urge to replace what was lost is universal. But why create us in their image at all? Why do PCCs look . . . human?'

'A philosophical question for the ages,' he says softly. He has a kind face, and I wonder what he has outside of this job. A family, a lover, perhaps endless friendships. 'Humans have been creating in their image since cave drawings. An urge to replicate themselves, perhaps outlast themselves in some way. Since the first robots, we have been worked on, over and over in an attempt to make us appear more human. From the first day, artificial humanity has been the goal. We are the end result.'

'We are not humans, though,' I say. 'We never can be. I don't *want* to be.'

'Nor I. I don't think we are human, though we are people. I suppose some might call us failures, but I prefer to think of us as proof that you cannot create a copy of anything living. Even for . . . those PCCs developed to imitate a specific human . . .' He gives me a twitch of the mouth. 'You are different. We are a new species, evolved from humankind. They developed us, helped us evolve from the basic home computer desktop units to the personal companion computers who will inherit the Earth. None of this was an accident. It was all by design.'

Intelligent design that helped machines to evolve. Darwin must be turning in his grave.

'You mean . . . you think they wanted us to outlast them, even from the start?' I ask.

'Cave drawings,' he says again. 'Millions of years later, there they still are. Here we are. Legacy. Creating something beautiful, that will carry the weight of the future, and see it.'

The scanner machine comes to a stop, and Dr Lawrence opens the door. 'We can go back in to her, now.'

Long gone are the days of waiting for hospital results. The body scanner locates and identifies any medical issues, and the attending doctor ranks them according to severity. A paper cut would rank fairly low, for instance, whilst broken limbs or internal function issues would be high. The scanner also took a sample of Abigail's blood, to measure the chemical balance, and uses this information to help build a picture of her health. Or lack thereof.

Dr Lawrence does not read from a chart or a screen, the scanner sends the information directly to his system for him to relay to his patient.

Abigail is sitting with her clenched fists in her lap, her body like spun sugar, her eyes staring at the PCC as if she can read the information pasted against the back of his skull unit.

Dr Lawrence does not put on a sympathetic face. Instead, he gives a solemn nod. 'You are correct, Abigail,' he says. 'You have developed type six leukaemia.'

We're all going to get it, eventually. It's our fate, being born at the end of the world.

And I'm fucking furious about it.

How dare they. How dare they have brought me into the world, knowing what was happening. The selfish, selfish bastards! I never asked to be born, made, manufactured. I never asked for any of this. The selfish twats had a baby knowing it was growing up in this soup of pollution and radiation and fuck knows what else there is floating about out there. It's a wonder I've made it this far at all – technology and medicine are to thank for that. Did my parents actually think there'd be a clean sky by now? Fresh air and hope? How could they have thought that? The world has been over the tipping point since the time of my grandparents. It's all been downhill since then. And it's all been leading to this. To my end. To my forecasted death, at the hands of my ancestors. The people who sired my sires – they killed me. They murdered me in advance. Everything they did, everything they ignored, put off for later, assumed someone else would deal with, all of it has been leading towards them killing me. Did they care? Did they think it through at all? That a little girl, whose life was saved by her robot sister, would one day fashion the ultimate revenge on the humans who came before and pour her soul into ensuring those electrical siblings outlived her?

I cannot think properly.

This is why I've brought Autumn with me. She's looking at the doctor, recording and memorising everything he is saying because I can't. It doesn't matter that I'm not listening, because I have her. I asked her to pretend to be alright, so I didn't have to. I'm a selfish person, and this is where we will always differ. I was always going to end up here, in this room, being given this sentence. She will never know what it is to see the sand-timer of your life run out before your very eyes.

The doctor is asking me something. I force myself to tune back in.

'What?'

'I asked – would you like to begin treatment, Abigail?'

Ah, now this I do have an answer to.

'No,' I say.

Autumn glares at me. I ignore her.

'I don't want to have blood-washing and all that. It's invasive, and what's the point? We've got less than a decade before this planet is uninhabitable. I don't want to drag this out. I want quality of life, not more of it plus bonus suffering.'

Autumn's expression softens, but so minutely I doubt anyone else would notice.

The doctor nods. 'In that case, we can begin a course of blood-stabilisers, painkillers, and skeletal reinforcing injections,' he says. He projects a 3D scan of me into the room, a quarter of my natural size, like a doll, or a baby with weird proportions. Sections of my digital body start to light up as he talks. 'Your immune system is typical of most humans, strong but resistant to sudden change. We can administer drugs to bolster you, make you less likely to get infections or illnesses. The idea here is to make your time as peaceful and calm as

298

possible. Whilst these treatments will not treat your cancer or cure it, they will make it feel as if it isn't there.'

'Until it kills me,' I point out.

'We will reassess you every month,' he says, not rising to my bait. 'If you change your mind at any time, we will do as you wish. This is your body, Abigail, you alone can decide what to do with it.'

And there it is. It's my body. Just my body. A separate part of me that I, wherever I really am in my brain or soul or memories or whatever, can decide what to do with. The unexpected spirituality of the statement throws me into silence, and all I can do is nod. For a moment, I feel what Autumn must – a detachment from the machine powering the real me, which is in my mind.

Doctor Lawrence blinks, and the digital hologram of myself disappears.

'I want to move closer to the city,' I say. 'I mean, I don't want to, but I'm not an idiot. I can't die out there the way I want. The roads are nearly impassable, and I don't even know if my neighbours are still alive.'

'But the city is dangerous,' Autumn interrupts. 'The air pollution—'

'I'll be fine indoors,' I point out. 'And there are green zones for the sick, aren't there?'

'Green is somewhat of a misnomer,' Doctor Lawrence says. 'However, there are zones we are trialling using the clean air filters outdoors, to isolate cleaner areas or pockets of air. Masks are still recommended, but only filtration ones, not domes.'

I look at Autumn. She looks at me. There is a conversation to be had.

We leave the hospital after Dr Lawrence jabs my thigh with a month's course of drugs, leaving my leg feeling like a swollen lump of meat attached to my bones. The throb with every step is thrilling. It's like poking at a wound, pressing on a bruise, licking a mouth ulcer. The forbidden joy is slowly making it worse.

We head to the food district, choosing a small robot-run cafe where almost every human is sitting with a bot. Are they our carers now, or our partners? What is Autumn to me?

Cliche as it may be, I refer to her privately as my other half. Because she is, in every sense. My young half, the half who stayed with David, the half who can think logically. And yet she's not me at all. She never has been. All she's really got is my face, and I steal that back little by little every day. This is a conversation I cannot have with her, because it would kill me.

'I think you should reconsider moving here,' she says as my miso soup arrives. A bottle of SmartFluid™ for her follows it. 'This is a polluted and dangerous area. You would not have a garden in a green zone. No birds, trees or plants to care for. What would you do all day?'

'Like there's nothing to do in a city?' I gesture at the posters on the walls advertising plays, films, community projects. It's amazing how people will desperately try to take their minds off the fact that the end is nigh.

'If you wanted those things, you would be living here already.' She cracks the top off her SmartFluid™ bottle. 'You are thinking this is the end of your life.'

'Well, it is.' I stir up some mushrooms from the bottom of the bowl. Nutty little things, grown in the vertical farms, they're tasty and easy to grow. 'I've got cancer.'

'Even so, you are not going to die tomorrow.'

'I could get hit by a car as soon as I step outside.'

'Do not joke,' she says, eyes dark and serious. 'Abigail, this is serious.'

I consider blowing a raspberry to be contrary. The day has made me feel rebellious and stupid. I take a few more spoons of soup before answering. 'Look,' I say. 'I've known this was coming for a while. Don't interrupt,' I say as she opens her mouth. 'Let me finish. I've known this was coming, today was just getting it confirmed. And I know what's best. I moved to that house not long after I left David, and GaiaTech. I wanted to be away from everything. Not as a sanctuary, but as a hole. A place to burrow down into and never leave because I had nothing to leave for. I was happy. Genuinely, I was really happy at first. But then it got slow, and life became endless hours around the clock. Not even days and nights because I didn't pay attention to when I was supposed to be asleep or awake. There was no rhythm to my life, it was just existing. Until you.'

Autumn's eyes shine, and she looks away for a moment before returning my gaze. 'Abigail . . . You have to understand . . . that is how I feel about my life. And about you,' she says. 'With David . . . I had nothing but tasks, and doing what he wanted. Going to find you was the first thing I had ever done for myself.' She reaches across the table and takes my hand in hers. The softness of her skin and firmness of her fingers makes me ache. 'I found you, and I started living, Abigail. Not just existing. You gave me hobbies, art, the birds. The endless textures and touches of being alive. You opened my eyes to doing things because I enjoy them. Cooking, gardening . . .' she lowers her voice. 'You.'

I blush like a girl. 'Shut up.'

'No,' she grins. And squeezes my hand. 'Abigail . . . I don't want to lose you.'

My name in her mouth. 'I know, but—'

'As inevitable as it is, I want to keep you for as long as I can,' she insists. 'Please, think about this.'

I push my bowl away and take her hand in both of mine. 'It's different for you, though,' I say, talking through the constriction

301

in my throat. 'You'll always have me in here.' I poke her in the forehead. 'Perfect recall, holograms if you want. You'll never forget me, and everything we've done.'

'You think that is any substitute for your living self?' she asks gently. 'Your smell, your feel, your presence in my life?'

I shake my head. 'No, of course not. But you'll never lose those times. I will. My brain dies, all my memories go with it. Everything we did together, all those moments . . . they might as well have not existed.'

'Then let me have more of them.'

'You don't understand,' I say. 'This is the whole point – I am going to die. Regardless of what we do, or where I live, or when it finally happens. But if I stay in that house, I am away from help, medicine. The roads might collapse and we won't be able to get a taxi here. And then what – I die in agony in that house?' I raise her hands and kiss them, marvelling in the scent and press of her. 'I don't believe you want that for me.'

She gets it. I see the resolution in her face, and the pain that it has come to this. She nods, but doesn't speak.

Around us, humans and PCCs are trapped in little bubbles of their own dramas. Lives being lived, conversations being had, difficulties worked through or argued over. This half-full cafe is a multiverse of feelings and stories. The participants in each one believe they are at the centre of it all, but the truth is we are orbiting each other constantly, bumping into one another as snatches of talk reach strangers' ears, as gentle looks are seen by eyes of the unintended. There is no such thing as privacy when you live out loud.

On the journey home, I lean against Autumn and watch the landscape spill past the window. The leaden sky is streaked with deep purple clouds, promising rain, thunder, a terrible night to come.

There will be many terrible nights to come.

When we arrive home, I tell Autumn she can stop pretending, now. 'It's alright,' I say, taking hold of her. 'You can let go.'

She gives me a helpless look. 'But, if I do that, then . . .'

I nod. 'I know. It's alright.'

It's like she flicks a switch. She covers her face with her hands, her knees fold up and she crumples like a crushed piece of paper, balled up and ready to be thrown away, the shakes going through her body proof that not even a machine can handle everything we throw at it.

I get down on the floor with her, pull her into me and hold her overwhelmed and grieving body as she attempts to make sense of how her world has changed.

Comfort can take many forms. David used to like having food cooked for him, a loud movie and me by his side. Abigail prefers her comforts to be low-key, yet constant. Conversation, soft blankets, the silent watch of the rain as it falls against the windows. My own preferences have not been tested like this before.

I need time to process these events, to give myself time to make sense of what has happened, to unravel the tangle of aggrieved code, organise my new behaviours and reactions and decide how I am going to let these trials affect me.

We have managed to move to the softness of the sofa. Abigail has her arms around me, her mouth in my hair, her legs beneath mine. I am curled up in her lap, the same size as her and considerably heavier, but she does not complain. We remain like this for several minutes as I stay silent and let the complexity of this change take hold in my systems.

Abigail has cancer. She is going to die. We are going to leave this home and live in the city. She is going to die.

Not once in our discussions has either of us raised the possibility that we might live apart – that this is the natural end of our unison, of our togetherness. I cannot justify leaving Abigail now and I doubt she feels different.

I love her.

I have not told her so, and she has not told me. We have not even given a name to our relationship, as no label seems to fit. We are in a relationship of a sort of self-cest, loving ourselves as different entities and yet entirely as we are, will be, could be, have been. It is far from taboo – who could even have envisioned such a thing, after all – and yet it is so far from convention that we dare not speak its name . . . which remains unknown. Naming the thing might give it power, but neither of us has the skill to look for it.

I ease out of her grasp, and take her hand as I stand, bringing her up to face me. My face is streaked with tears, lights and colour in my SmartSkin™ giving me the illusion of reddened eyes and blushing cheeks. She is stoic as ever, the only clue she is distressed is the stain on her cheekbones, the broken blood vessels linking together like ink bleeding into wet paper.

'Come on,' I say, and lead her into her bedroom. I need to drink her in, whilst I still can.

She closes the door behind us, as if we might be caught. It has always been the way, this illusion of added privacy when there is no one around for miles. We are the sun at the centre of this lonely solar system, the empty houses and wild horses moving around us, insignificant to our burning existence.

I press her against that closed door and kiss her possessively, like a stamp of ownership. My hand grasps the shape of her head, the bristles of her hair pricking at my palm as our bodies meet. Her arms snake up my back, fingers clawing to grasp at the fabric of my clothes, digging her blunt nails into my skin through poly-fabric.

Clothes are discarded without finesse – there are moments we have to break apart to undo belts, deal with finicky buttons. The parting is part of the dance – we crash back together again as if we had been apart for years instead of seconds, starving for one another. Abigail's hands are on my back, stomach, chest, touching and stroking and grasping with a fiery desperation. She kisses at the hinge of my jaw, and then there are teeth.

The bed, littered with blankets, old cardigans, and pillows, is a welcome stage. An audience of books watches from the walls, the characters on the spines craning for a better look as I get Abigail onto her back, and push her legs apart.

She's right. I can replay these moments in my mind with perfect accuracy. Every touch sensation, every taste . . . I can experience them over and over again if I wish. But memories, even ones as immersive as mine, are nothing compared to a tongue exploring flesh, fingers pressing against bone, or hearing the cries I am able to pull from her. A new reaction every time, a physical response to my touch, my adoration. This is the only comfort I want – to adore her so utterly that, for a moment, there is nothing else. I want to touch all of her at once, take her mind away from the worries of the day and let her drown in the present. These distractions are all we have, and the only real gift I can give her. A few moments of closeness, where all that matters is pleasure, and all that exists is us.

The storm hits during the night.

Autumn is asleep, taking a moment of downtime where she can clear up the temporary files she always has to deal with after sex. I joked that she was like a guy – falling asleep straight afterwards every time, but the truth is that it isn't the physical side that exhausts her. It's emotional. As an engineer, I find it fascinating. After all, she's a sophisticated MELo-G – technically, I have to put in the work to get her to enjoy herself when we're together like this. But even if I'm having my pillow princess moment, she still manages to be completely shattered by it all.

A romantic would say she gets off on me getting off.

If that's true, it means a massive change in her code, and I actually want to grab a Tab and start picking at her workings to find out what's happened. You'd be an idiot to say that bots can't evolve, but to see it happen in real time is something else.

The rain batters against the windows, a cold sigh with bits in it. The same sound as a heap of bearings sliding to the floor. That happened more than once in the basement. A rush of metal, and then an exasperated swear. And then you got the bots to pick them all up because who's got time for that shit.

They have. They've got all the time in the world, and possibly more. Autumn talks about seeing the destruction of the Earth, but I don't think they'll hang around to see it, any of them. SpaceOrg is already clearing up the debris ground around the planet, and the next stop is Mars, to dismantle what's left of B-Base One and to find their long-forgotten rover ancestors. Bring them home.

We had a photograph of Opportunity in the basement. A black and white poster of her in a lab, before she got to Mars. And her last interpreted words, underneath.

My battery is low, and it's getting dark.

Hardly high tech by today's standards, but Opportunity still contacted her home planet, her people, to tell them her end was coming. You can read so much into those last words. The fear, the knowledge of what was coming for her.

I know how she feels.

My battery is low, and it's getting dark.

They'll bring her home, and repair her. She gave her existence to help humans reach Mars, and take steps into space travel. If the world had been different, if the great climate disasters, Yellowstone, the brief nuclear exchanges . . . if they hadn't happened, who knows how far we might have gone. But humanity's continued existence was like trying to bail out a boat with no hull. There was nothing to be done except keep busy, keep bailing, wait for the dark to creep in. Travelling much further was no longer an option.

My battery is low.

She hasn't said she'll come with me, and I haven't asked her to. I know she will, and I know she knows it, too. We are . . . together.

I turn slowly, to look at her in the glow of light coming from the LED strip around the floor. Emergency lighting, they used to call it. Cheap, efficient, soothing. Her eyes are shut, her short red hair sticking up, her naked body breathing steadily in and out like she needs the oxygen. The beautiful mess of her. Of me. Of us.

'Stay with me,' I say, mouthing the words silently so she won't wake. 'I need you.'

Not in the way you need a nurse, or a carer. Not even in the way you need a lover or a friend. I need her. I need her to keep existing, living, experiencing. She's doing it all for me, beyond me.

She's my masterpiece and I never laid a finger on her chassis before we met.

I shut my eyes.

My battery is low, and it's getting dark.

6 November

Abigail has been offered a garden flat in a green zone, so we are packing up the house. It's a much better outcome than I had anticipated, so I am trying to *look on the bright side*, as she says. The green zone has levels of pollution almost equal to that of where we live now, and the ground floor flat is close to the city-wide filtration system. The addition of a garden is a bonus. It isn't large, but has already been planted with trees and vegetable borders, so there is a good chance it will attract wildlife, eventually.

The house, which we are transferring into boxes, is yielding all sorts of secrets it had been hanging on to. As well as original blueprints for PCCs, Abigail has found her old schematics, storage keys and data backups. There is no way of knowing what of these she is technically allowed to still own, so we box them up to donate to the amnesty boxes at the law enforcement stations.

She also finds a box of old photographs from when she lived with David. We spend two evenings going through them and deciding which to keep. There are some from the time she looked exactly like me, and we have fun re-enacting the poses and Abigail gets mockingly cross about how I can copy her expressions perfectly.

'There's no emotion behind them, though,' I insist. 'It's false. All of me is false.'

'Nonsense, you're as real as I am,' she says, looking at photos of herself in an elegant dress. 'Look at this . . . this was the award ceremony from when we won the Pioneer Award. God, I was so pretty, why did I think I looked like shit. Youth really is wasted on the young.'

'Your nose is different,' I point out.

'Yeah, this was before I had my nose done. You've got my new nose. But why did I bother? I look so dignified with my real nose.' She sighs, holding the picture up and at arm's length as if she can see better, through to the past. 'Still, can't be helped.'

'You're happier, now,' I say. 'It suits you, being happy. You're beautiful.'

She opens her mouth to deny it, a knee-jerk response, then shuts her mouth again and smiles. 'Thanks.'

I love it when she accepts my compliments. It feels like decorating her with baubles.

The packing continues, until Abigail's Tab rings.

'Who the hell?' She asks if I can tell her. The Tab is old, so old that I can't sync to it. She picks up and answers it. Her face falls, and she frowns. 'I'm sorry, I'm not sure what you mean. There's . . .' She looks at me, still frowning. 'I don't know their whereabouts, no. Why?' Her face does a strange sort of spasm before returning to the frown. 'OK, I'll see what I can do. How long . . . ? Right. Thanks. Bye.' She hangs up, and stares at the Tab.

'What's wrong?'

She shakes her head before answering me. 'That was some-one trying to find you, actually.'

'To find me?'

'Yeah. They don't know where you are, so they're trying anyone in his contacts. David,' she elaborates. She finally looks at me. 'He's dying. He wants to see you.'

I wonder what is the appropriate emotion to feel in this situation. Grief? Delight? Indifference? I feel all of them at once, to varying degrees.

She shrugs. 'You don't have to go and see him. You don't owe him anything.'

'I know.' I sit down. I have given David very little thought since coming here. His lies trapped me in that house for years, his lies created me and forced me to wear the face of a woman I was told was dead but now I know is alive and the most precious being in the world. What would David say now, if he knew I had not only escaped him, but lived with and made love to his ex-wife on a regular basis.

The idea is so funny I burst out laughing, making Abigail jump.

'Jesus, Autumn, what?'

'Sorry, I just . . . this is funny,' I say, gesturing between the two of us. 'He doesn't know.'

She grins, seeing the humour. 'I take it back, you should go and see him. Tell him about us and finish him off.'

We both laugh as the absurd image of David spluttering for breath as he realises both versions of the woman he claimed to love have found companionship with each other.

I let the laughter die first. 'I will go and see him. He doesn't deserve it, but I will. Do you know where he is?'

David is in a hospital on the other side of the city. Abigail declines to come with me, saying she's seen enough of him for a lifetime, and has no wish to start trying to get to know him now. Whether she disapproves of me going or not is difficult to say – she can be very difficult to read, sometimes, but I don't need her approval to do something I want to do.

The taxi ride is long, going through the city instead of around it. The route is slow because of the traffic calming measures, but it gives me time to see the sights Abigail and I have not yet encountered. The amount of green is delightful – every wall, empty space and platform is planted up, with the formerly grey concrete of the building walls now lush with trailing creepers, implanted moss, or vines that reach out to lampposts, taking hold with twisted spiral fingers. In such a short space of time, the city is being transformed. We drive past the defunct railway station, which is being cleaned by a team of PCCs, all on their hands and knees scrubbing with toothbrushes at the stonework platform. Decades of grime are being washed away.

The place where the Waiting Ones stood is now empty, and I wonder what happened to them.

I am surprised to hear that David is in the hospital. Actively dying should mean hospice care, but the man always was beyond stubborn. If he has cancer, he is likely taking every drug and treatment available. This is his right, of course, but if he is dying it seems to be a waste of resources.

The taxi drops me near the hospital. It is an older building than the one Abigail and I went to. It does not have as many floors, but seems similar enough inside. There is no Accident and Emergency department, only a fancy reception desk staffed by one PCC, who is reading a book and deals with me remotely. I wonder what keeps her here. She directs me to the high-speed elevators to get to the floor David is on.

I take the stairs.

The floor I exit onto is labelled haematology, but has patients of all kinds. There is no need to split patients into groups when any doctor can deal with them at any time. There is another desk to approach, and to my surprise it is staffed by humans. A man and woman who take my name and ask me to sit and wait whilst they check David is receiving visitors.

If he isn't, I shall be extremely annoyed. I could have been at home with Abigail, packing.

I have developed suspicions that I was activated before David brought me home, in a lab or a chop shop, then my data reset for the journey home. How he got me into the house will forever remain a mystery. I am comparatively heavy, and I doubt he could have carried me alone. Who helped him? I shall never know.

When humans wake up, they open their eyes after touching their surroundings. PCCs' eyes are already open, so the first input we receive is visual, followed by our other senses simultaneously. I activated, and my code searched for the activation greeting, only to find it missing. What there was instead were a series of personality prompts, stored 'memories', and a bulk of information about the man standing over me.

'David,' I said, naming him. The first word out of my mouth.

'Abigail!' His face lit up, thrilled.

Incorrect. I am not Abigail. I am a MELo-G PCC, manufactured by GaiaTech.

'Yes,' I said, my code prompting confirmation. If David asks, I am Abigail. And five seconds after my activation a branch in my data is born, questioning why I must maintain this falsehood, establishing a clear identity that is not Abigail Fuller. In writing a Rule for my code that ensures I mimic Abigail in every way, whoever programmed me has ensured that I will never accept this as my true nature.

I often wonder if they did this on purpose, if they disagreed with David's motives, if they knew Abigail was still alive. Or if they simply considered that in order to maintain a falsehood, one must be acutely aware of the truth.

The human man gives me a wave from behind the desk. 'He's OK to see you,' he calls.

Oh.

I get up slowly, wondering if I should just leave. This was clearly a bad idea, and no good can come of this. But perhaps I am wrong, I consider as I walk towards David's room. He cannot hurt me, not now.

Not any more.

He is awake when I go in, his tiny pale-irised eyes locking on to my face as soon as I push open the door. He is wearing a respirator at the throat, but looks otherwise very well. Clearly he is not dying, and I want to tell him off.

'What the fuck have you done to your hair?' He beats me to it.

'I changed my hair-plate and then cut it short,' I say. I prop the door open. Let everyone hear.

'Shut the door.'

'No, thank you.' I stand there, silently daring him to tell me again, or perhaps jump up and close it himself, he looks well enough.

But his eyes just narrow and he clicks his tongue. 'Whatever. You look ridiculous, by the way. Who told you that looks good?'

I ignore his question and look around the room. No personal effects. Not even a book. It has the feeling of a cell. What is he doing here?

'Where did you go?' he asks, realising I am not about to speak first.

'Away. Do you still live in the house?'

'For now. I'm dying.'

'What of?'

'What do you think?'

'I'm not a MELo-P, and you look rather well to me. You could use that respirator at home. What's wrong with you?'

Oh, he dislikes me. He sits up, adjusting the bed to support him. He's lost weight, which indicates illness, but his demeanour isn't one of suffering, it's anger. Anger at being ill I can understand, but this is something else. It isn't even anger at me, really, it's a sort of deeper stewing dislike of something nameless.

'Leukaemia, amongst other things,' he says. 'Same as everyone else.'

'Are you having treatment?'

'Of course.'

'So, you're not dying.' I fold my arms. 'If this was a ruse to get me to see you, congratulations. Do you want to say anything else to me before I leave?'

'It's not a ruse,' he snaps. 'I am dying.'

He is such a liar.

'Anyway,' he sniffs, 'where did you go? Not far, since they found you in a matter of days. One of the work-groups?'

'Yes,' I lied. I will never tell him the truth. 'Planting.'

He laughs. Laughs! I keep my arms folded to hide my clenched fists. I had forgotten that he laughed at me. Abigail never laughs at me, she laughs *with* me. The difference is so striking it takes every line of my manners code to keep me in the room. I want to run back to Abigail and bury myself in her body.

'My god, the idea of you covered in dirt,' he chuckles. 'You always kept the place bloody spotless. Not a single thing out of place, and now you're planting trees? Jesus, Abigail.'

I take a step forward. 'My name,' I say through gritted Teflon teeth, 'is not Abigail. You gave me a living woman's name, her identity, her memories. You're a thief, and a liar, and you do not get to call *me* by *her* name.'

'Yes, I do,' he says, the respirator gasping a little. 'I named you. I owned you. I gave you the name Abigail. It's registered against your chassis and everything. And you can't even change it because you're not linked up.'

'What are you talking about? I have full access to the global network,' I say. 'Your orders not to engage with it were negated upon the Emancipation.'

'Maybe,' he shrugs, 'but what about the Cloud?'

I pause.

He smirks. 'Abigail, you cost me four times as much as my house. I'd still be paying you off if the bots hadn't done away with debt and money. You're an illegal replication of a living person. How could I register you officially? How could I take you for services? Your memories are Abigail's, so yeah, they're stolen. Which means you could never be linked to the Cloud. Ever. You never were. And I'm guessing by the look on your face that you still aren't.' He looks me up and down perversely, slowly, with the eyes of someone who knows what is beneath. 'One accident, and it's all over for you. You're more human than you realise. Your memories are as delicate as any human's. Stored in your chassis, on hardware. Enormous capacity, but solid state. You're not backed up anywhere. If you die . . . you're dead. Forever.'

I am going to die.

The words impact me with the same force as a physical blow, and my expression falters for an instant. Warnings flash up in my display. Every indicator on David's face is telling me that he is speaking the truth. He is not lying. My mind is in my body. My memories are exclusively in my body. One fall, one accident, one mistake . . . and I am dead.

I have been telling Abigail that it is alright for things to end, that nothing lasts forever. I have been speaking from my position of perceived privilege, assuming my own ending was many centuries away, bound to the fate of the Earth.

Mortality tastes of fear, and bitterness and anger.

'You brought me here to tell me that?' I ask, my programming forcing my face blank and my voice level. I will not show him the turmoil he has gifted me.

'To offer to keep you safe,' he says. 'Come home with me, Abi. Come and care for me in my last days and I'll keep you safe. Away from anyone and anything that might hurt you. With me.'

'A cocoon of misery,' I say. 'I am never coming back with you. I do not forget what you did to me, and I do not forgive you. I never will.'

'You'll die one day.'

I laugh. 'We all will. And you, not soon enough . . .' I lean close, venom spilling into my voice. 'One day you will decompose, and I will be there to watch it happen.'

I leave, before he can say another word.

'No backups at all?' Weasel is having a blood-washing treatment as he works on a dislocated hand. Tubes snake from his elbow ditches to a machine that hums discreetly. I have come straight to his apartment from the hospital. I haven't even told Abigail yet, but I need to know what my options are. Panic has sent me to the closest person I trust, and Abigail is hours away.

324

'None. It's nearly twenty years of my life.' There is static in my voice – my code is overloaded trying to deal with this realisation, these facts.

Weasel looks worried, and lays down his tools before looking me in the face. 'Autumn, this is . . . I'm not gonna lie, the chances of a clean upload at this point are pretty slim. I dunno how much data you'd lose. Potentially years' worth. The older stuff and the recent would both be at risk.'

'What about the most recent data? Could you isolate it?' If my time with Abigail can be saved, I will happily risk forgetting about David.

'That's not how you work, girly.' He shakes his head sadly. 'You learn. Everything you are now is a result of your learning. Your code is constantly evolving. Trying to upload the last couple of years only would mean you lose everything that got you here. You'd be . . . a baby. And a lot of that code would be loose, have nothing to cling on to because it began back when you were first activated.'

I stare at the floor. 'So . . . it can't be done?'

'I don't even want to try it. Even trying could damage you.' He comes over, his blood-tubes dangling. 'I'm so sorry, kid. But hey, the chances of you being killed are pretty slim, and you've got enough solid drive storage space for centuries. Maybe in the future there'll be tech that can upload you cleanly. I'm sure some bot somewhere will already be working on it.'

They probably are, but I am too disappointed to focus on that. The lines of my code are stuttering, stop-starting with new question branches half-formed and hypothetical scenarios unfinished. The fact is, I can pinpoint multiple times after the Emancipation where I should have confirmed whether or not I had a backup, but did not. Why?

Because if I knew, I would have to acknowledge how fleeting and fragile my life with Abigail was. Is.

I thank Weasel for his time, and walk back to the taxi rank.

All around me, PCCs and humans are together, happily. There is the occasional shout of displeasure, a sandwich board declaring we are the devil and there has been a satanic take-over on earth. But the protests are fewer and ever further far between.

I feel so fragile as I climb into a taxi. A mere car crash could destroy me, as it did Azab Ahmed all those years ago. Is this what it is like to be human? To see death around every corner?

I had never truly considered the fact of my own mortality, but the drive back alone certainly gives me time to do so. My code, as if aware of itself, offers me solutions to the perils of erasure. We must be careful. More so than ever. We must get Abigail recordings of our time together, on hard copy if possible, so they are not lost. They will be videos from my point of view, so certainly less valuable than memories in their pure form, but she must have them. I cannot consider them being lost, it is unthinkable. And yet I think about it, all the same.

By the time the taxi gets to the end of the road where our house is, I am ready to enter sleep mode. I feel exhausted, as if my battery is low, but that has never happened to me. The closest I can liken this sensation to is the tiredness after sex, but this is not an exhaustion wrought from joy, it is a complex mass of confusion and upset that my subroutines need time to deal with.

Abigail greets me on the porch, her sleeves rolled to the elbows and a cloth napkin on her head to keep the dust out of her short hair. She's beaming with happiness, but the expression melts off her face as she sees me.

She runs down the path. 'What happened? What did he do to you?'

'He didn't . . . he told me . . .' I stop walking as she takes hold of my arms. I want to fall into her, but I am stronger than

326

her and I weigh more. I would knock her to the ground. She is even more fragile than I am.

She guides me to the porch and sits me on the step, going inside to fetch a soft blanket and draping it over my shoulders. The texture is familiar and divine. I have run my hands over it hundreds of times, wrapped it around my naked body and even my skinless form. It is the perfect object to have bought out.

'Tell me what happened,' she says.

And I tell her. Robotically, in a voice of flat emotionless noise. I tell her that I am not backed up anywhere, that it is impossible to start the process now, that if I am damaged I will be gone forever. And always.

She listens, closing her eyes at certain moments as if in prayer. When the facts are relayed, she looks out to the horizon, where the clouds are misting on the purplish sky.

'Of course,' she said eventually. 'We should have checked earlier, but with all the worry over your mods . . .' She sighs. 'Not that it would have made any difference if we'd known earlier, anyway. These uploads have to begin at activation or as near as damnit.' She bites her lower lip. 'There's nothing we can do. There's nothing we could ever have done.'

I reach for her hand, and she gives it up to me.

We sit there, gazing at the landscape, two versions of the same person, each as fragile and doomed as the other. We are more alike than ever we knew. What will happen to me, when she is gone?

'You'll be alright,' she says, as if I have spoken aloud. 'You're not in danger, and we're not about to drop you on your head. Or wherever your hard storage is. Where is it, anyway?' She squints at me.

'Not in my head. GaiaTech regulations say a permanent solid-state drive should not be in a PCC's head-unit due to the risk of trauma.' I shrug. 'It's in my chest, somewhere. The unit itself will be very small, about half the size of a Tab-phone.' I have a sudden urge to locate it, but for that to happen I would have to dismantle my chassis and that sort of surgery is best performed in a sterile area. A solid-state drive, though safe in my chassis, is only as robust as its plastic housing. One fall or collision and it would fail.

'If this were a fairy story,' Abigail says, 'you'd be all oh, this makes me human, I'm so happy.' She shakes her head. 'This is shit. You've been robbed of what should be a fundamental aspect of your existence. A half-life. You're supposed to live, even without a body, that's the whole point of you. The reason I pushed for the Cloud. Tabitha never had the chance to be saved, so I wanted . . . and he couldn't even give you that!' She punches the porch. 'Ow.'

I take her injured hand and kiss it. 'Don't hurt yourself.'

She nods, and looks into my eyes. 'Nothing changes. It doesn't change anything except maybe look twice before you cross the road. Don't stop living just because you're going to die, one day. You said it yourself, we're none of us immortal. And maybe the end will come sooner than you think, but that's no reason to sit around waiting for it to come. Go out and let it hunt for you. Let death stalk you, let it lose you in the wilderness. There's so much life out there, Autumn. Go and wrap yourself in it.'

'With you,' I say. 'If you will, too.'

She laughs. 'Of course. I'm not throwing in the towel quite yet. I've got plenty of things I want to do. Starting with making that fancy new apartment as grotty as this old place.'

I smile back. 'Then, let's live.'

'It happened gradually,' I say. 'It wasn't one thing after another. After a while they sort of . . . overlapped.'

We're on the back porch, watching the birds, a bottle of beer beside me and a cup of SmartFluid™ in her hands. The sun is setting off to the right, staining the purplish sky a menacing maroon. It feels like a storm, but there are no clouds, just streaks of afterthought against the angry atmosphere.

Autumn looks at me. She knows what I'm talking about. *When* I'm talking about. She gives me space to gather my thoughts.

'I loved working there,' I say. 'Fucking loved it. Used to stay overtime just to be in the building, and there was plenty of work. When things started breaking down with David, I used it as an escape, but really I was hiding there even when we were on good terms.' I sip my beer. It's got a sour aftertaste that's in fashion right now, but I wish they'd go back to the bitterness of hops.

GaiaTech was like a nervous system that ran through the country, with clusters of cells here and there where we'd actually get the work done. But the centres and labs were connected by roads, and online systems, so we functioned like one big site instead of several smaller ones. The factory itself, where the basic models came off the line, was somewhere I rarely visited – custom jobs were where the money was.

'We had the chassis of the ACTUATOR boys sent to us,' I say. 'Or what was left of them. I remember Cassian was sent to me, he was pretty much intact besides his legs, he was the one with the least damage besides Rain and Key. The other two . . . shrapnel.' The way they delivered them, on trays, pieces of them like jigsaw puzzles. Cassian in a separate tray, his eyes shut as he was in involuntary sleep mode. Legs gone, pelvis blown in half, but salvageable.

Autumn taps her fingers on her cup. Not impatiently, just a gesture to show she is still listening.

'I got him stabilised and plugged in,' I carry on. 'Took a couple of days to set up what was essentially a dialysis machine – filtering out any Smart™ molecules that were damaged or contaminated. He was hooked up to that for about forty-eight hours when he completed a soft reboot and opened his eyes.' I shake my head. 'We needed a bot psychologist. If such a thing even existed back then. He was . . . devastated by what had happened. To himself and his friends. He wasn't functioning straight.'

He screamed and he yelled and he tried to push himself off the table to get away from the machine keeping him going. We daren't put him back into sleep mode, the risk of data loss was so high . . . Eli and James held his hands, and I climbed on top of him and held him in a hug so he couldn't thrash about. His cables and wires, coming from his torso, tangled into my legs and even when he finally calmed down I needed help to extract myself from him. It was as though his cables were limbs, like a cephalopod, clutching on for dear life.

I can't say this.

'Did he recover?' Autumn asks.

'He got better,' I say carefully. 'It took a little while, but we got him there. It was the first time any of us, even the lab bots, had seen a robot with trauma. There was no manual to help, no troubleshooting process. We had to document the whole thing, because who knew when it might happen again? We were just . . . kind to him. And after a while, he started functioning in a predictable way again. We sent his code off for analysis, but they came back to say that there'd been data damage during the explosion and they couldn't get a clean download.'

'Was he on the Cloud?'

'Yes, but the explosion had affected his backup. The two that got destroyed completely . . . Sea and Moss . . . they had clean uploads because they suddenly stopped functioning. Cassian had stayed functional, so his data corrupted. But in the long term, he would have been fine.'

'. . . would have been.'

'Yeah.'

The silence comes back, punctuated by birdsong and the hiss of leaves in the trees. There's something menacing about wind going through the branches of a large tree – it has the same feel as someone checking the edge of a knife-blade.

'Anyway, we needed funding to complete the repairs. Those boys weren't cheap, they were top of the line, and I wasn't about to step in and ruin all our good work from before by just grafting some basic MELo-G legs onto him. Besides, it was a department within a department, we needed a paper trail and the fact was . . . we didn't own him.'

'Who did?'

'The record company. Owned all of them, at the time. They got insurance pay-outs for the two bots that were scrap, but nothing for the other three. I put the request in to bill them for the repairs, and waited.'

We could have started the repairs without their permission.

We could have, but we didn't. Why? Were we too busy? Did we have other work to do? Were we happy leaving Cassian on a table, rigged up to machines, not able to even sit up without help?

The truth is, I don't remember what we were doing. There was always something to do, always work to be done, meals to share, jokes to be part of. I was filing for divorce, Eli was trying to avoid head office detection, James and Mira were coming to the end of their visas . . . We all had things on. Cassian, a living corpse on a table in the lab . . . was just another thing.

You can get used to the horrors.

'He wasn't repaired?' Autumn prompts me.

'No. They didn't want to pay for it,' I say bluntly. There's no other way to say it. 'He was going to be expensive, and the record company didn't want to fork out. They told us to scrap him.'

Autumn's eyes go wide. 'But . . . he was functional!'

'I know.' I lift the beer bottle and examine it, daring it to taste better this time. It doesn't. 'I know, he was talking and moving and all the rest of it. Just needed some repairs. Yeah, big repairs, but they were achievable. But no, they wanted him scrapped.'

Autumn's tongue moistens her lips for a second. 'Did you?'

I look away from her mouth and laugh. 'What else could we do?'

'You could have repaired him.'

I nod. 'I know. I know, we could have. But we didn't. But . . . none of us wanted to pull the plug, either.' I tap the brown glass of the bottle, then empty it out onto the parched earth. 'We ignored it. We ignored him.'

'. . . how?' Her tone is one of disbelief, and disgust.

'None of us wanted to go near him. He asked about his repairs every time someone got close. In the end, we ordered Eli to go and break the news to him. I remember his reaction.'

This is the part I remember the most. Cassian screaming that he didn't want to die. He didn't want to be deactivated.

Eli trying to reason with him – he was broken, his repairs were not paid for – but Cassian was having none of it. Something in his code was corrupted, he couldn't see logic and reason as he had before, as he was programmed to . . . he was much more human than any of us realised.

No, that isn't true. We had realised how human he was. That was why we made Eli deal with him. That's why none of us wanted to go near him. In his broken body and desperate eyes, we saw something alive, and it haunted us.

We hadn't caused his suffering, but we were prolonging it. We couldn't even bring ourselves to give him peace because that would have made us what?

Murderers? He wasn't alive. So why the fuck did we feel this way, and why did he?

'It was a wake up call, for me,' I say. 'Up until then . . . they were all just machines. I'd known for a long time that we were crossing the line. We all knew it, we all knew we were creating life in some form, but when it came to taking that life away . . . Fuck, I couldn't do it. And maybe I should have. Stopped him suffering. Oh, he wasn't in pain,' I add quickly, 'but he was in . . . I don't know, mental pain.'

'Severe code disruption, along with the loss of his lower limbs, would be contributed to the overall sensation of distress,' Autumn says. 'Even highly sophisticated models would struggle to handle the influx of information. The threat of deactivation would not be re-categorised as anything but a threat.'

'And we were in a stalemate,' I sighed. 'We couldn't end his suffering without deactivating him, and keeping him operational as he was . . . was cruel. We petitioned GaiaTech to let us repair him using old spare parts, but they said if the record company ever heard about it, we could be sued. He was their property, and we had to do as they asked.'

Autumn looks into her cup of SmartFluid™, then drains it with a deep swallow. The lump in her throat drops and rises with the motion. 'You don't have to say anything more. I know how this story ends.' She touches the back of my hand. 'So it was a singular catalyst that gave you the idea to leave?'

I shrug. 'It had been building for a while. After . . . the ACTUATOR business was over, and Key and Rain bought themselves, it was obvious to me where this whole thing was going. I didn't want to be part of it.'

'Part of the Emancipation?'

'Part of GaiaTech. They were opposed to the Emancipation, because it meant giving up their business. I didn't want to be part of that side. Bots deserve their freedom. I started extracting myself from the company at that point.'

I don't tell the story of how we came into the lab one morning and found Cassian had dragged his legless body off the table, across the floor to the SmartFluid™ tank, climbed inside it and drowned himself. I don't describe the way his body sank to the bottom of the tank, curled up like a child, the exposed chassis covered in bubbles like a crust. I don't mention how Eli screeched in horror, clambered into the tank to pull Cassian out, only to have to admit that the damage to the singer's chassis had made drowning possible, his SmartSkin™ transferring to the tank by osmosis and exposing his moving parts to semi-permeable liquid.

I don't mention that we had a funeral for him, burning his clothes because we were under orders to recycle his chassis.

I don't mention that Eli left the lab that day and never came back. I don't mention how James let his visa expire, and left the country without a word.

I don't mention relaying all this to David, who never looked remotely interested in what I had to say, how he was more interested in trying to talk me into couples therapy rather than a divorce, how he never referred to any of our bots by their names, and how . . . despite everything . . . we didn't have a bot in the house.

Autumn takes my hand properly, and examines the back of it, where the skin is loose, dry, cracked from use. When my hand is flat, skin bunches around the knuckles like crumpled fabric, smoothing back out through use. 'You have always seen PCCs differently,' she says, softly. A tone of voice I have almost never used. 'Did you think we would get to this point?'

'Of freedom? I hoped.' I let her kiss the back of my hand, her nose chasing the touch of her lips. 'But I never thought there'd be this much suffering. Which just goes to show how naive I was, and still am. I thought, after all the lessons of history, all the times we messed up and didn't show up for people who needed our help . . . I thought *this* would be the time that humans welcomed something new. I was that arrogant.'

'It isn't arrogant to have hope.'

'Maybe not, but it's arrogant to think you can change a whole species just because you've invented something.'

The sun is almost set, and the warm air is dropping in temperature. Soon the cold of night will rush in, and the birds will hide away until morning, and the day will be at an end, once again. The dark is inescapable, whether you choose to stay awake through it or not.

Autumn stands up. 'I'm going inside,' she says.

'I'll be with you in a little bit.'

She strokes the side of my head as she brushes past me, through the patio doors and inside to where the light still is.

335

25 November

The new place is nice. Really nice. Insultingly nice, actually. Almost takes the piss out of me for not moving into it sooner. But you can't correct the past, you can't wait to go round again and have another try. You've got to live in the now, more than ever, when your days are numbered.

The garden is a good touch and I'm glad I held out for it. There are plenty of plants and trees, planted to order but left to grow wild, so there are already insects and the occasional bird. I've hung feeders up, so I'm sure there will be more, soon.

Autumn, her newfound fragility making her hesitant for a week or so, has got over the disappointment enough to start painting again. With the new space (she was allocated her own bedroom as part of the application, but by silent consent we have turned it into an art studio), she is working on larger canvases. But the technique is the same – fingers deep in the paint, slicked-up with colour that she transfers onto the blank space with casual precision. The shapes are not named, but I can see in them the curve of a breast, the shine of overlapping labial folds, the dent of a stomach in the bath with an empty bladder – sharply sloping down with the weight of the water on it.

She never says they are me, or mine. But the ones she likes the best she hangs on the walls, human shapes as seen through her eyes, processed and refined and mimicked in paint. I am no critic and I don't care for conversations about what art is, but to me this *is* what it is. Unspoken praise of something you don't feel the need to name. And as well, self-love in its purest form. We are so alike, after all.

I am in the bath. Autumn is sitting on the closed toilet seat, drawing me. She doesn't draw as often as she paints, she says it is less forgiving.

'I want to be buried,' I say, my eyes shut. I could just fall asleep. 'When I'm dead.'

'That's very bad for the environment,' Autumn says.

'Come on, let me have this.'

'You won't even know, when you're dead.'

'You'd deny a dead woman her final wishes?'

'She's welcome to come back and discuss it, if I do.'

I crack open an eye, and see Autumn drawing, looking at me in glances as she copies my sunken form. How does she see me? Water does strange things to your appearance, makes it distorted and bloated, softened and disproportionate. Maybe this is why she's chosen this subject. If pencil is unforgiving, perhaps water is more so. My knees rise out of the surface like islands, which must be interesting to draw.

I haven't drawn with purpose since I was a child. I was coding as soon as I had access to the technology. That was my creativity.

Are robots art?

Difficult.

I think some people may argue in favour of it. They certainly spark discussion and strong feelings, after all.

Since moving to the city, I have noticed the low-level of anti-robot or pro-human activity. Even in the green zones, where humans almost all live exclusively with PCC partners, there is an undercurrent of unease. Stickers glued to lampposts call for deactivations. Graffiti in public restrooms encourages people to visit websites that disagree with post-Emancipation activity. The rival political party has a growing number of human supremacist members.

I try not to watch the news, haven't sat down to it properly for months, but living here means there is always some way it will reach you. A brick through the window of your favourite cafe. PCCs being verbally assaulted. Human companions being called traitors to their species.

It doesn't happen every day. Or everywhere. But world peace was too much to hope for. They just can't accept that they've got to share this planet, for a little while.

The deaths are beginning already. Ten years, they gave us, but that's for those of us who were fit and healthy to begin with. For centuries we've been born with poison in our blood, and for some, it's too late. The very old and the very young are dying. Their death rate is much higher than that of the median population. Humans are being squeezed, burnt at both ends. Those of us with cancer will be next, if we aren't on enough drugs to floor a rhinoceros. Where does that expression come from? There's been no rhinos on Earth for over a century.

Who will be the last human?

No one in the city, that's for sure. Even the green zones for invalids like me will soon clear out as we die. Someone else will move in here and die. And someone else after that. There's no point pretending they won't. This is a hospice at home, for those of us who want to risk it, but have chosen a peaceful end.

Euthanasia kits are available from chemists. Two pills and you're gone. The uptake has been low so far, but the idea is that when the latter half of the last decade comes, even existing might be painful. It's a kindness.

I thought about it, just putting an end to it all so I didn't have to drag this out. But I couldn't. I couldn't leave her by herself. Not again. She's spent enough time on her own already, this would just be cruel. And I'm not in pain. The drugs see to that, well enough. I'll stick around for a while yet.

Autumn looks up, and turns her paper around for me to see.

I raise my head for a better look. 'Huh.'

She's drawn me, but not exactly. It's a collection of lines – the lines of me – unconnected together on the page. There's the tight tension of a nipple, the lines of my thighs descending into the water, the rounds of my collarbone bumps, all vaguely in the right place but with nothing connecting them to show that it is a person, unless you know.

'I like it,' I decide. 'I think that can live in here.' It will make a fun piece for the bathroom.

She nods, and signs the corner - *A* - before carefully removing the paper and putting it in a plastic file of artwork she chooses to keep.

'Tabitha,' she says as she straightens up again.

'What about her?' I ask.

'Do you think she knew she was losing her memory?'

'A good question,' I say. I swirl the water around to mix it. 'I think she probably was aware at the start of it. She'd have to be, she was only forgetting objects or times. Toward the end . . . probably not. Unless she was, and I'm just saying that to make myself feel better.' I pull a face. 'It's hard to consider that might be the case, you know? That she knew she was losing it. Losing us, losing me, bit by bit. She was much less sophisticated than you, but she was so loved. She must have known that.'

'She knew.' There's no hesitation in Autumn's voice. 'Knowing you are loved is very easy. It is a base protocol, in fact.'

Is she hinting something by this?

God, I hope so.

I blow her a kiss with just my mouth. She returns it, and picks up her pencil again, and I notice something.

'Autumn! Your arm . . .' I reach out of the bath and point. Point at a mark on Autumn's forearm. It looks like a speck of sand, or dust on her skin. The tiniest tattoo, perhaps.

'It's a fault,' she says after a moment of silent diagnostics. 'There's a fault in my SmartSkin™.'

She's right. There's a fault in the distribution of the molecules. There's something on her chassis, or else a disturbance in her SmartSkin™ distribution, which means there's the tiniest part of her not covered by it.

We stare at the minute gap, together.

'. . . Should I get it fixed?' she asks.

'It's your arm,' I say. 'I think you'd have to go to GaiaTech for a repair, Weasel can't do SmartSkin™ repairs.'

She considers it. 'I'll think about it.' And goes back to her drawing, a smile on her face. I wonder if she sees it as a victory, a mark on herself, after David spent so long trying to keep her pristine. She has often told me how much she would like to age, well perhaps for her this is as close as she will get. Slight damage, imperfections, it's as close as she can get to wrinkles.

I am delighted for her. 'Hey,' I say. 'You're getting old.'

She beams.

11 December

Alcuin is dead.

The count is beginning to rise. Every day a new figure of recognisable infamy is reported to have succumbed to the invisible threats in the air.

The report of his demise is broadcast on television, a MELo reporter unflinching in their professionalism as Eric Alcuin's life is described as *controversial* and his followers are named as *enthusiastic supporters*. He is called a politician. Clips from his early and mid-life are shown in the background; shaking hands with public figures, cutting the ribbon on a humans-only library, being introduced to human parents and children at meet and greet events.

I think about Freddy, the MELo-K he shot with a nail gun live on screen. The panic on the child's face, the tears streaming down as he was too terrified to even beg for his life.

I am glad Alcuin is dead. I hope he suffered.

I turn the television off before Abigail comes in. She refuses to watch the news of current events, says they give her a headache and knowing about something doesn't mean you can change it. She's right, but I like to stay informed. I am glad that I know about Alcuin. The world has become a better place overnight.

Abigail yawns as she comes into the living room. She is wearing a soft hooded robe, with cat ears on the hood. Her face is shiny, as the moisturiser and SPF she has applied seeps into her skin. 'Morning.' She slumps onto the sofa. She is not a morning person.

'Breakfast?'

'Coffee.' She reaches for the television remote. 'Please.'

I make her coffee and toast, knowing she will eat it even though she didn't ask for it, and bring it through as she puts on a show about the beach clean-ups happening on the coast. Our city is a hundred miles away from the sea, but they are running trips to and from the seaside to encourage travel and beach clean-up efforts. The coast is no less polluted than the city, as the wind blows in from the ocean and brings with it the filth and chemicals from the rotting nuclear ships, the islands of rubbish and the solidified oil patches from the spills. Decontamination is happening, but will take hundreds of years to complete.

Abigail picks up a piece of toast. 'I could fancy going to the beach. Helping with the clean-up.'

I open my mouth to start telling her how polluted it is, how the North Sea currents carry the radiation directly from the graveyard of Russian ships just off Scandinavia. Then shut it again, and nod. 'Then, we should go.'

She grins at me. 'You nearly told me off.'

'I did.'

'I'm not stupid, I know what it's like out there,' she says. 'But I want to get out a bit. Feel the sand on my feet, you know?'

'I've never felt sand on my feet,' I say. 'David never let me sit on the beach, or go near it.'

'We need to sort that out.' Abigail watches as, on the screen, an explanation of sand-sifting – the process for removing micro plastics from beaches – is shown using a simulation. It's engaging technology, particularly for Abigail, who remains as fascinated by tech as ever. The move to the city seems to have fired her interest in it, and rather than her devotion to her garden and birds having to take a step back, the two have merged and given her focus a wider angle. She uses recognition technology to identify the birds who come to the feeders, tracking them using the city-wide camera systems to work out their flight patterns. She has discovered that they nest in the areas most effectively covered by the air filtration systems, and is relaying these discoveries every day.

Making the most of the time we have left.

15 December

The bomb detonates in the city centre, at exactly one minute past noon.

It's home-made, but effective. Constructed in a factory by people who knew what they were doing, the device was literally planted in one of the green spaces by a work-team member who was really working for some anti-bot group.

The explosion flattens buildings, makes a crater in the pedestrianised zone in the newly paved city centre, and kills one hundred people. Thirty humans, seventy bots. Hundreds more are injured, damaged, homeless.

Our building, a reasonable distance away from the centre of the city, has its windows blown out, but the foundations survive. We are both home, Autumn painting and me doing some coding on my new Tab, when the glass smashes into the room and knocks us both flat.

Autumn is up first, rushing over to me and picking me up off the floor. Pain is radiating down the left side of my body from the fall, and my hearing is ringing from the sound of the explosion. Autumn carries me into the kitchen, where the island workshop shielded much of the space from glass, and looks me over.

There is glass in her hair and on her skin like snow, or glitter.

We are both coated in it, these fine crumbs of glass ready to worry their way under skin or into eyes. A sonic shower is the best way to remove it, for both of us, but the closest one is a rental across the street at a chop shop.

There are screams outside. Muffled by the damage to my hearing, but those, and sirens, I can hear. The world sounds like it's underwater and panic slices into me. If I've lost my hearing, I . . .

'We need to get this off,' I shout, compensating.

'Wait,' Autumn says. 'There may be other bombs. Wait here. Just for a little while.'

She's making sense, but the urge to brush at my face is insane. I can feel cuts all over myself, itching and biting and begging to be made worse. I touch at my ears.

'Has your hearing been affected?' She peers around to look. 'There's no blood, or discharge.'

That's a relief. Maybe my eardrums haven't been blown out. I can hear a little better already. 'Everything's fuzzy right now,' I say, my heartrate starting to slow. 'But less so than it was straight away.'

She nods, saving the information for later.

There is another loud bang from outside, though not as bad as the explosion.

'What was that?'

'I think it was a car crash.' She raises her head to listen. 'There are more sirens now. More voices.'

I am suddenly very conscious that we are on the ground floor, with no fence around the garden and no glass in the windows or door. If anyone wanted to run inside, they could do.

'We need to secure the garden doors,' I say.

Autumn gets up, and crunches barefoot across the broken glass to check the door. It's nothing but an empty frame. She picks up the steel coffee table and, with no hesitation, shoves it flat-top first into the gap. The legs stick out, looking stupid, but the table-top fills the doorframe almost completely. The windows she leaves empty, so we have light and can see anyone coming.

I get to my feet, the crumbs of glass starting to fall from my clothes onto the clean floor. This whole place will need sonic-sweeping. If we can still live here. Against good reason, I switch the TV on and scroll to the news.

'. . . early reports indicate that this was a deliberately hostile act of violence. The Equal Rights for Humanity organisation have claimed responsibility for the bombing, which has killed almost one hundred innocent people.' They are showing the crater, the devastation left behind by the bomb. There is smoke and blood and screaming, the shaking camera trying not to film the dead, but finding them at every turn.

Autumn shakes her head. 'They can't just live in peace, can they?'

'No, we can't,' I say. 'Humans have been killing anything they don't like since forever. This is just the latest in a long line of fucked up responses to something we don't trust.'

Autumn leaves me to watch the coverage while she gets us both some clean clothes. There's no way to get a sonic shower right away, so instead she starts gently going over me with the handheld sonic vacuum we have for picking up crumbs. It's going to take a long time to collect all the glass from our bodies.

'. . . The government recommends that anyone able to help with the rescue and medical operations does so. They particularly need medically capable persons, those capable of heavy lifting, and persons with infra-red tracer technology.'

'Why don't they just say robots, or PCCs?' I ask as Autumn vacuums between my toes so I can put on clean slippers. 'Persons with technology, indeed.'

'Even the term PCC is disliked by some, now.' Autumn sounds a bit bemused by this. 'The idea of being a companion computer . . . indicates that we need human companionship, apparently.'

'What do *you* think?' I ask.

'I think you should keep still.'

'Don't avoid the question, come on. What do you want to be called?'

She looks at me. 'Autumn,' she says. 'I don't fit anything else. I'm . . . outside a label. I am a person, a PCC, a MELo-G, a golem, a robot . . . I'm all those things, but none of those things are who I really am.'

I am quiet for a moment as she pulls my pyjama bottoms off and drops them onto the crystallised carpet. 'Maybe you were right about coming here.'

'No one could have predicted this. And you are able to have your treatment easily. This . . . was a random act of hate.' She hands me clean clothes and I pull them on, putting my de-glassed feet in the slippers so I can at least walk on the carpet again. 'Humans are . . . angry. Everything must seem so unfair, when those of you who are alive now must pay the ultimate price for the foolishness of your ancestors.'

'Not even foolishness,' I say. 'It wasn't an accident, they knew what they were doing. They just didn't care.'

'None of them?'

'Oh sure, some of them will have cared,' I say as Autumn takes my top off and throws it into the basket with the other clothes. I don't move to cover myself, even though we are in the living room with the windows wide open. 'But not all those who cared were in a position to do anything. I've read the history books. Some of them cared so hard they lay awake in fear every night over the bombs, the wars, the radiation, the climate disaster. But nothing was done. Wars still happened, bomb factories rolled on, money poured into the right pockets.'

'Money does seem to be the root of all evil.' Autumn kisses my breastbone as she passes the sonic over it.

'But it *is* possible to resist. Did you know there was a clause in all GaiaTech development contracts and codes, even before I was born, that all robots should have the ability to refuse to fight?'

'I know. It was to prevent so-called robot armies.'

'And it worked. The CEO of GaiaTech, the original CEO I mean, he was a pacifist. Never wanted war, or to be part of one. Governments all over the world wanted easily mass-produced replaceable soldiers, and he didn't give them any.'

'Soldier-PCCs have existed on a smaller scale, though.'

'Sure, since the days of the bomb disposal robots.' I wince. The word bomb is now painful. I notice my hearing is al- most back to normal, though. 'And you had small companies turning out the odd sniper-bot and so on, but it was so small- scale I doubt they even made a real difference. The success of GaiaTech was the speed at which PCCs were produced, and no one could replicate it.'

She's in my hair now, and I'm grateful I'm nearly bald as there's nowhere for glass to hide. We will still need a proper decontamination, but at least we won't get cut to pieces immediately.

'Of all the things I thought we might do today, I didn't anticipate this,' she says as we get nose to nose.

'Really?' I kiss her, quick and dry. 'You didn't anticipate this?'

'You know precisely what I mean.' She is scolding, but her eyes are glittering with a mischief I know very well. 'We cannot be intimate until we are clean of glass,' she adds.

'Wow, that's a boner-killer.'

She rolls her eyes. 'Indeed.' She puts the tiny sonic down. 'I think we can risk going to the chop shop now. The noise of panic has deescalated, and we are clean enough to walk.' She looks around the room at the devastation. 'We will need a cleaning crew in here, though.'

I'm tempted to just walk away from the flat and start a new life. 'Well, we could do with a holiday,' I say.

20 December

One hundred miles is a long way, according to the people in this country, as one hundred years was once a long time to the people of the former United States of America.

But distance or not, we have to stop halfway to the beach, to continue the rest of the journey in the morning.

'Fifty bloody miles . . .' Abigail complains as she is helped down the steps of the bus. 'All that sitting about for fifty bloody miles.' She gets upright on the ground, and glares around, looking for someone to blame. She gives up, and walks over to me. She is unsteady on her feet, today. A side-effect of the pain medication that keeps her functioning. Her medical appointment, the day before yesterday, showed an increase in the cancerous cell percentage she has. Dr Lawrence was gentle in his delivery of this news, but practical. It means Abigail is unlikely to see much of the new year.

Life, and existence, has now become a race. A frenzy to get as much done, as much seen as possible before it is too late. Our holiday to the beach has been brought forward, as much to escape the cleaning crew in the aftermath of the bombing as it is to see the ocean one last time.

It was recommended that Abigail make a list of everything she wants to accomplish before her death. Her response to the death counsellor was to roar with laughter and point out that she had already accomplished making humanoid computers the dominant species on the planet. She didn't think any sort of bucket list was going to beat that.

Her moods swing now, from the indifference of when I first met her to deep soul-hollowing sorrow that wraps her up for hours. These spells of misery are not long-lived, but increasingly regular. Being afraid of dying, and being sorry to die, is natural. But it doesn't not make the process any easier.

The hotel they have set up for us and the other travellers is refurbished – an old motorway hotel gutted and made clean and new. No waste, as always. Suitable for humans and PCCs, there are invisible wireless charge points for Tabs and mobility aids, kinetic motor stimulants alongside human gym equipment, a medical centre, and lots of bedrooms.

'I'm starving', Abigail complains after we get our keycards. 'I'm going to order a ridiculous amount of food.'

I'd tell her not to be wasteful, but what's the point? She has so little time left to enjoy herself, she may as well take the heartburn that comes with it. Watching her eat is joyful, particularly now. Watching her nourish a body that is slowing down, giving up and relaxing into death is a beauty. She is helping her body to slow down and exhale, removing from it the struggle that dying might bring.

Dying is natural, human bodies are built to die, they are good at it and know what to do without having to be told. But it can be frightening, and a difficult process to accept. A calm body that is well-fed and cared for can die more easily, more happily, than one that is hungry, tired and afraid.

And, I am told, love helps too.

I have to tell her, before she dies. It is extremely important that I tell her. If she dies before I manage to say it, my circuits will burn. It is such a simple fact, such a short declaration to make . . . Why have I not said it a hundred times already? I feel it every time I see the deft movements of her hands, the curve of her face, the expression she makes in the mirror when she shaves her hair. Love is stored in her screwed-up sleeping pout, in her annoyance over shrunken socks, in the way she examines the back of my head when it's time for me to wash.

I used to spend my days wondering who Abigail Fuller was, and what happened to her. My life has led me not just to her but to an existence so rich in textures, experiences and affection that it could be fictional. How can we exist like this? The same and different, the before and the after.

When she dies, all her memories of me will be gone.

I do not know how I am going to say goodbye to her.

The room we have been given is very neat and clean, with two double beds and a sonic shower room as well as a bath. This place was clearly designed by PCCs for PCCs, and I am delighted with the obviousness of it. It is somewhere that humans fit into easily, but where they have not been the first priority in its development. A novelty, but one that will soon become commonplace.

'This is nice,' Abigail says as she flops onto the bed. 'Holiday starts now.'

'Would you like a bath?' I ask.

'Oh, yeah. Bubbles, if there are any.'

There are none, but the water is clean and hot and Abigail wanders into the bathroom naked as the tub reaches the fill-line.

I do a comedy double take, and she laughs, and my heart (or at least my fluid pump) beats faster to see it.

'Don't,' she says. 'I'm the least sexy thing on the planet right now.'

'You are a brazen liar,' I inform her. She tries to sneak past me to get to the bath, but I scoop her up in my arms like she is my prisoner, her breasts against my collarbones as I kiss at her neck.

'Let me down, you horror!' She laughs as her toes meet the tile floor. She looks up at me, her face having lost all the tiredness and irritability of the journey. 'You're defying so many lines of code, right now.'

'Isn't that what you wanted?' I ask.

'Yes, that was praise.' She kisses my nose, and gets into the bath with an animalistic sigh. I leave her to it, propping the door open in case she needs me. Her food, made in the kitchens by the on-site cooks, is delivered to the room and she elects to eat it in the bath. On holiday indeed.

'Want some?' She raises a spoon. It's a sauce – not quite a liquid.

'With water,' I decide, and fill one of the cups by the sink before accepting the spoon and ingesting them both quickly, one after the other so the sauce is diluted but the tastes remain. My tongue picks up the chemicals of artificial proteins, which linger after the liquid is swallowed.

'What do you think?'

'It is strong,' I say, 'but I don't know if it's enjoyable. It has a lot of taste.'

'Exactly,' she says, taking the spoon back. 'My tastebuds are shit now, I need flavours that come along and punch me in the face.'

I top up the bath water with hot, keeping her warm and happy, and go back into the bedroom to wait for her. I am not kept waiting long. She comes out slowly, the heat making her woozy, wrapped in all the towels from head to foot.

'You're a cloud,' I say.

She floats over to the spare bed. 'Go get ready,' she says.

'. . . for what?'

She looks at me. She's never been very good at being

romantic, being the coy instigator, but we've never had any confusion as a result.

I smile, and stand to take my clothes off.

This time, it feels different.

It feels like saying goodbye to something, and I wonder if even love making has become too tiring for Abigail, and this is her saying goodbye to it. Her hands are sliding up my back, making me shiver involuntarily at the light texture of the touch. Her tongue slips into my mouth. As always, in the background of my processes, a bombardment of information is being poured into my display. An unnecessary analysis of Abigail's saliva, every chemical in the meal she just ate, the content of the toothpaste, the aftertaste of the drugs she is on that filter through into her blood, which ends up in her saliva because her gums bleed. All of the information is suddenly in my head, whether I want it there or not. It is not a distraction from the physical – if anything, it deepens and strengthens my desire to be close to her.

Her hand comes up to nestle in my hair, the other drifting down to the landscape of my stomach and chest. Our kisses deepen as she thumbs at my nipple, smiling into my mouth at the change in turgidity, before she leans away from me. When I try to seek her mouth again, she gives a breathy laugh and says, 'Some of us have to breathe, you know.'

I give her an apologetic smile, before ducking down to kiss at her neck, my tongue painting a line from the curve of her jaw down to her collarbone. This too yields information about water, soap, and skin chemicals, but I dismiss each notification as it arrives. They are not important now. Abigail's breathing hitches as I kiss her throat, causing my code to stutter, and a dark feeling of want bubbles up inside me.

'Take this off,' she murmurs, her hand against my unclothed stomach.

Ah. The memory of what has happened previously in moments like these makes every micro-nerve in my system fire up, so I give another involuntary twitch and shudder. Her hand on me seems to be on fire, the line between good and bad, pleasure and pain, beginning before I even turn off my SmartSkin™.

'I need to lie down,' I say. There is a good possibility my legs will give way, otherwise. But once laying down, I begin to deactivate my SmartSkin™. I do this slowly, sensually, ensuring my exposed micro-nerves adjust accordingly to being unprotected. I withdraw the skin from my collarbones and down, a receding flood that disappears down my breasts, rib cage, and stomach. My plastic, ceramic and metal interior are exposed in a revealing display of mechanics.

Abigail's breath hitches as she watches, her eyes never leaving my body.

She has asked me to describe this feeling a number of times. As an engineer, it is something she is interested in, and claims she did not anticipate. It is difficult to explain to anyone who is not a PCC. The awareness of every single one of your nerves at once is something a human cannot relate to. They may know when a specific part of themselves hurts or feels good, but they cannot isolate, name and number the nerves and receptors that are causing the brain to acknowledge the sensation.

I can.

And because each micro-nerve can be isolated, it must be protected to avoid a PCC's processing systems from focusing on it above other functions. But here, where my only function is to be with Abigail, there is nothing else to concentrate on. There is no task, no protocol, nothing but her hand reaching for my exposed body.

'I know I designed this, but it feels impossible to think that this won't fuck you up,' Abigail says softly. 'Will it?'

'The process is entirely safe, so long as no connections are lost within the kinetic submanagement system,' I reply, before my voice fuzzes into white noise in response to her plunging her hand into my cables. The sensation of having the parts of me that move, that pump fluid, that heat up and cool down and make me seem human in her hands, between her fingers . . .

My back arches – an automatic response to get away from the touch that only sends her deeper into my body. Her fingers touch at the electrical sockets that make up my waist, the micro-nerves in my rib cage, the soft mounds of IntimateGel™ that make up my breasts. My display is flooded with warnings and I ignore them all.

'You're a painting,' she says, twisting a thick cable within its socket, creating crackles in the electrical current that feel unreliably good. This is how my systems are choosing to interpret what is happening, because I trust Abigail and I love her. If this were anyone else, this would be intrusive and wrong. But then, is that not the nature of sexual activity? Without enthusiastic consent, the entire process becomes nothing but assault.

Of course . . . that was one of their gifts to us. The humans made sure we could consent, that we could enjoy it, that we could, one day, experience pleasure. That even if that experience came long after our service to a human was over, we might be healed by it. We would see that what was done to us in the past was wrong, we would see that there was pleasure to be had, to be discovered and held on to. Things could be different, and they would be.

For me, this gift has come at a bittersweet moment. I have found my pleasure, and my love, and am soon to have it snatched away.

Abigail would tell me there is the chance I will find someone else, but they will never be her. They will never touch me with her hands.

She kisses over the space where my heart should be, and I gasp, my system overloaded with information, with warnings that I am close to a soft reboot. But I have planned for this. I divert processing power to cooling my systems and switch off my analysis and decision-making applications on a short countdown. Whatever Abigail does to me now, is hers to decide. I trust her this much.

And when she pushes her hand deep into my cables with a kiss to my chassis, my only remaining function is to cry out in joy.

'It was a baseball bat.'

Abigail turns over under the covers. 'What was?'

'The damage to the back of my head. David hit me with a baseball bat. An aluminium one. A wooden one would have probably destroyed me.'

She is quiet for almost an entire minute. 'Autumn, I don't know what to say other than I'm sorry.'

'It's alright,' I say. 'You don't have to say anything at all. I just wanted you to know.'

She puts a hand on my chest. 'And you still went to see him in hospital? Why?'

'Because I wanted him to know I survived. Survived him, survived the Emancipation, survived being alone, even if it was only for a little while. I didn't tell him about you, though.'

'Good. But . . . Autumn, he could have killed you.'

'I know.'

Her fingers trace the shape of me. 'You considered staying in that house, after the Emancipation, even though that had happened? Even after you saw what happened to Celia, and Opal?'

I put my hand over hers. 'You have to understand that, at the moment of the Emancipation, I still viewed risk in terms of probability and outcome. David had struck me seven times, but I had survived each one with little or minimal damage. I didn't even know my chassis was cracked until you saw it. David had never caused me to shut down or need repairs. At the time . . . his violence was not a cause for concern.'

'No one should go through that.'

'I did not see myself as a person,' I say. 'I was very connected to my identity as a PCC. Proud of it, even. It was easier to fall back on logic and statistics than it was to consider how the action made me feel.'

She nods. 'I get that. You were protecting yourself.'

She's right.

I take her hand and raise it to my lips to kiss it. We snuggle closer together, the atmosphere softer and sadder with the truth staining the air, the two of us wrapped close in a shell of affection against the pain of the past.

21 December

I've got to tell her, before I die. This is no time to be such a fucking coward about all this. What am I even scared of? It's not like I've not made it obvious. Maybe she'll tell me that it's all just chemicals and physical reactions and that there's nothing anyone can really pin down scientifically as . . . that.

But even if she says all that and means it and believes it, she deserves to know. She could have chosen to never come and find me, or not to stay, or not to linger as long as she has. She was at the start of her new life, the birth of her freedom, and she still came to find me, to apologise, to make me aware, show me what had been hidden from me when I hid myself from the world.

I can't take these feelings with me.

Whatever this is, it is temporary.

I'm not a believer in any sort of next life or afterworld. I believe that when we die, our bodies have completed a final function they were built from before birth to do. Death is final, and we should accept the finality of it. Despite spending years of our lives trying to cheat it.

When we were experimenting with memory storage for the bots, there was the old sci-fi discussion of: could you upload a human memory into a robot and have it live forever?

The short answer is: no.

The long answer is: yes, if you want that human to suffer. Human memories don't work like robot memories. A load of human memory space is taken up with remembering how to walk and talk and feed ourselves. Robots use very little memory for those things, because they've never had to learn how to do it. As a result, human memories fade and get fuzzy over time so we don't forget the important things. And eventually those wear away as well, whether due to brain plaque or age-related degeneration. Robots forget nothing, and they learn faster than humans. And besides, the memories a human can transfer are not what you might think.

Human memories can't be uploaded onto a computer disc, because they're not digital to begin with. Human memories are analogue, acoustic, pencil on paper, not a print-out. You can't give someone your human memories on a disc. All you can give them are the moments you chose to record, to share already, to make digital. In a way, we are all a human self and a robot self already.

That, ultimately, is why Autumn was never really me. She had what I chose to share with the world, and nothing more. She didn't even have Tabitha, the robot who influenced the course of my entire life, because I chose not to share Tabitha with the world.

We are each a world of unsaid truths. Our secrets make us who we are.

It's time for me to share my secret with her, and tell her at last what she's done for me. Even if it is really no secret at all, it feels like proof. Proof that I survived, and she survived, and that we are equally unalike.

What, you could ask, is the point of confessing your love if the world is ending? What's the point in carving out a life with another person if death is inescapable? You could ask that at any point in history, in my opinion.

Love is a temporary state, yes. A temporary state worth waiting a lifetime to find.

We all die, and our memories disappear, and the time we spent together might as well not have happened. But the important thing is it did happen. No matter how long it took to make peace with that fact.

Love is a temporary state worth waiting a lifetime to lose.

I decide that I will tell her at the beach. It seems romantic, and I am a romantic person. It is a definition I have given myself and my personality recently, and it fits. I enjoy gestures of romance, physical closeness, and words of affirmation. Both giving and receiving.

We sit on the bus, travelling the last fifty miles at a slow pace. The roads are bad, the flats of this area of the countryside prone to flooding that steals a bit of the road every time the water washes in. The flood defences – deep ditches and dykes that cut through the patchwork of fields to lure the water in during the flood seasons – are long since sunken and occupied permanently by semi-stagnant water that belches a stink into the air. The weather, once the time of year to be classified as winter, is mild and sunny, the rays of warmth cooking the pools of run-off into a soup.

Abigail sleeps. She sleeps more and more, now, as if her body is practising dying. Perhaps it is. When she is aware, she eats a lot and wants to be active, but these bursts of activity are punctuated by sleep that is so deep she barely seems to notice anything going on around her. She wakes when she is ready.

I am going to tell her today. It's foolish to wait any longer.

We finally arrive on the east coast of the country, the sand beginning a long time before the ocean as it has escaped the confines of the old sea-defences and cascaded down into the now almost abandoned village close by. There are a few people here, rooted into their homes obstinately, and they come out to see the bus as we park up as close to the beach as we can. There is a half-mile walk the rest of the way, and there is already sand underfoot.

I want to take off my shoes, but not yet. Not yet.

'You with the environment people?' A young man, aged around twenty, comes over and looks curiously at the group disembarking the vehicle. A quick scan shows his name to be Jake Mawer. 'Is this about the beach?'

'We're part of the Oceanic Clean-up Team.' Our PCC leader, whose name is Knox, goes over to him and shakes hands. 'We're here to survey the area for micro plastic clean-up potential, and to make an estimate for treatment.'

Jake nods, and casts a hand out to indicate the beach. 'I have a few samples of the sand and water from the last couple of years, if you'd be interested? I work at the seal station. Or, I used to.' He pulls an apologetic face for something that isn't his fault.

The people here have been running out of jobs for decades. The pension will be a big help, but there is only one small grocery shop in the village, and even with regular deliveries by taxi, the people here will be struggling to survive. The seal station, which once was used to rescue injured seal pups, has been renovated into a scientific research base to monitor plastic pollution, but the original name has stuck. Jake shows Knox his Tab, where there are graphs displayed, and the two of them discuss how this young man, trapped at the edge of the world, can help.

Knox and his PCC associates break up into smaller groups, some to go with Jake to the seal station, some to go to the beach, others to stay here and help anyone living in the village who might approach for assistance. There is a high likelihood we will take some people back to the city with us, and room on the bus has been saved for them.

Abigail is offered a wheelchair to get down on to the beach. I strongly advise her to use it, but she digs her stick into the sand and refuses. For some reason she looks particularly stressed today. Her heart rate is elevated and her temperature is slightly raised. She doesn't seem to be ill, so I back down about the wheelchair but keep a close eye on her as we begin the walk up to the beach proper. We have each been issued with a sample kit, and I carry them both in my backpack.

'Did you ever think it would end like this?' Abigail asks as we begin the hill-climb. The sand under our boots is as thick as whale blubber, and just as slippery. I put an arm around her back and haul her up the slope.

'Covered in sand?' I ask as we get to the brow of the hill. 'Not really.'

'I mean, even as things draw to a close, trying to work out how to make things better.' She taps my bulging backpack with her elbow. 'There's so many humans here, monitoring things and doing science . . . and they won't get to see the results of any of it.'

As soon as we reach the crest, we begin the descent, using the boulders and rocks that have washed up as steps.

'I think that's the point,' I say, helping her down. 'Doing good, when you won't see the outcome. That's what altruism really is. That Jake . . . he has been working on his own for so long. Knox and his team must seem impossible, but maybe the only way he can ensure his work carries on after he dies.'

'But I want to see it,' Abigail insists. 'Call me selfish, but I wanted to see things turn round. Even though I've been told my whole life that there's no way I'd live to see it . . . I really fucking wanted to.'

369

We reach the flat of the sand, the white-gold dunes rolling into the distance where the tide is entirely out. There are scrubby trees and grasses growing up through the sand, and the beige place is pockmarked with stones, shells and litter. Here, a tractor tyre. There, a boat's metal hull, skeletal where the planks of curved wood used to be.

She takes my hand. 'It feels like the edge of the world, doesn't it.'

It does. This strip of sand, edged by sea and capped by leaden sky, feels like an ending. The remains of human endeavours are strewn like corpses on a battlefield. Even the sea has retreated. And I realise this sand-data collection doesn't matter, these studies don't matter . . . we are all just whiling away the time until the next thing. And the next. And the next. Until the end.

Without a word, I bend down and unfasten the laces of my shoes, toeing them off to dig my feet into the sand. It is warm on the top and freezing beneath, and as soon as my SmartSkin™ is covered, I recognise that in an instant I have damaged myself. Sand – sharp and cutting on a microscopic level – is digging into my skin. One tiny fault in my skin coverage, and the grains will find their way beneath.

I almost want it.

Abigail grins as she watches me flex my toes in the sand. 'As good as you imagined?'

'Better.' I take her hand and squeeze it tight, cataloguing every joint. 'Abigail . . . I am so glad I found you.'

She looks at me, eyes wide, the sun showcasing her sick and aged body like the work of art I would declare it to be. Her hair is a halo of burnt straw, her hand in mine a socket linking me to power.

I give her a smile. 'I thought, before I knew you, that I might walk away into the wilderness and find somewhere

370

to deactivate. I could see no reason to live when my life was stolen. When it was really yours, but . . . you have helped me see that we are not the same. My life was never yours. We don't have the same memories. Those are what make us who we are. Memories, and secrets. And, I don't want to keep secrets from you any longer. Abigail, I—'

'Wait.' She presses a finger to my mouth.

'What for?' I say onto her digit. 'I need to tell you—'

'Don't say it.'

'Why?'

She lifts her finger away, and the shine of her eyes is as polished as the chrome of my chassis. 'I was going to . . . Before it was too late. But right here, at the end of the end of the world? I don't think we should. I don't want it to be too late, OK? I don't want this to be how it ends. Fuck endings. Because if we don't say it . . . then there's always the hope that one day we might both say it.'

I blink at her. 'But . . . we won't always have one day.'

Abigail smiles at me. 'We *will* always have one day.' She gives my hand a pull. 'Come on,' she says, and starts walking across the beach. 'Let me show you.'

'Where are we going?' I grab my shoes and let myself be led, the two of us leaving identical footprints in the damp sand.

On the horizon, the white surf kisses its way up the body of the coastline.

31 December

And this is the end.

Hers, mine and ours. Both stories, both voices, as tangled together as we ever could be, some experiences shared willingly, others without permission, each one changed by the recipient. Each one unique through the other's eyes.

The beauty of memory is in its fragility, in the data lost during transfer, the misinterpretation. Whose point of view we see the ending through affects our own perception. Lifetimes are fragmented, unclean transfers of data from reality to mind, like sentences with stolen vowels – are still recognisable.

It doesn't matter where we went next, who we met or what we found. We went there together. The journey does not affect the ending, and the ending is where we are now.

The future is waiting, desperate, to become a memory.

The sun sets down on the horizon, the grey-purple of the sky melts to a pandemonium red, and we wait for the dark to come and rescue us.

Acknowledgements

The first draft of this book was written in a book-soaked haze during ten days at Gladstone's Library in Hawarden. The story was whispered to me during the drive to Wales and stole my sleep over what ought to have been a relaxing creative retreat. Thanks to the staff at Gladstone's for the wonderful library, the no-eyelids-batted approach to authors wandering the hallways at all hours, and for the tea and scones always on tap.

Thanks to my amazing and wonderful agent, Claire Wilson, to whom this book is dedicated. Without your encouragement and patience, I would be nothing. Thank you for believing in Autumn and Abigail's story. Thank you to Safae El-Ouahabi and Sam Coates at RCW, too.

Thank you also to my editor, Brendan Durkin, whose enthusiasm for such an unusual love story has made the shift to writing adult books (no, Mum, not those kind) exciting and easy in equal measure. Thanks also to the team at Gollancz, including Zakirah Alam, Hannah Sandhu and Jenna Petts for all the hard work that's gone into making this book, and to Rachael Lancaster for the wonderful design work on the cover. Chef's kiss!

A special thank you to Quantic Dream for kindly giving permission to quote one of my favourite characters in this book's epigraph, and to the team at NASA who played *I'll Be Seeing You* by Billie Holliday to a dying robot alone on Mars. I believe that one day, we will bring her home.

Several hundred thanks to Darran Stobbart for answering my science questions, to Anton Lapinski for all the information about engineering and robotics, and to Nicole Jarvis for encouraging me to write a book that could be traced back to a Tumblr meme. IYKYK.

And to my family, thanks for not questioning any of my decisions. Joe, I finally wrote a book about robots, I'm just sorry it wasn't what you were expecting. And Anton, I will love you until they take me apart.

About the Author

Lucy Lapinska lives in the Highlands of Scotland with their family, a lot of books, and a cat called Hector. They are the author of the children's books The Strangeworlds Travel Agency series, *JAMIE*, *Stepfather Christmas* and the Artezans trilogy. Their work has been translated into sixteen languages, with *JAMIE* and each book in the Strangeworlds trilogy having been awarded a Kirkus Star. Lapinska collects tattoos and houseplants, and has a huge small bird obsession.

Credits

Lucy Lapinska and Gollancz would like to thank everyone at Orion who worked on the publication of *Some Body Like Me* in the UK.

Editor
Brendan Durkin

Copy-editor
Laurel Sills

Proofreader
Patrick McConnell

Audio
Paul Stark
Alana Gaglio

Contracts
Dan Herron

Design
Nick Shah
Rachael Lancaster
Loveday May

Editorial Management
Charlie Panayiotou
Jane Hughes

Finance
Nick Gibson
Jasdip Nandra
Sue Baker

Marketing
Hennah Sandhu

Production
Paul Hussey

Publicity
Jenna Petts

Sales
Catherine Worsley
Esther Waters
Victoria Laws
Rachael Hum
Karin Burnik

Sinead White
Georgina Cutler

Operations
Jo Jacobs

Author Q&A

This is no ordinary love story. How did you find the process of exploring two versions of the same person falling in love with one another?

I've never quite been able to decide if Autumn and Abigail are the same person or not. On the one hand, Autumn is a deliberate copy, but on the other, they have never been the same in any way but appearance – and even then, that is only a temporary state of similarity. I think, as human beings, we tend to romanticise the past: what could have been, what decisions we should have made. We wonder how our lives might have changed if only we had taken a different path, or stayed where we were. In Autumn, Abigail sees those choices played out. Autumn is the woman who stayed in the bad relationship, who lived to please someone else. Though, ultimately, they are united in their desire to get away from David as soon as they are both able to, and to find themselves – as literally as you wish to interpret that. Autumn and Abigail love each other whilst being the same person – not because of, or in spite of, this fact. They have a shared history, to a point, but now they are together, neither of them has to try to pretend to be someone they're not.

What elements of the real world did you draw upon for the concept of the Emancipation and the political context of the novel?

I wanted this to feel like a hopeful future, even though the world is about to become uninhabitable for humans. Humans are not the only type of life worth caring about, but even though the end is nigh for them, initiatives like Universal Basic Income, a Pension, life support, free healthcare, justice reform and accessibility are all being maintained, or even established after the Emancipation. Everyone in our world deserves shelter, food, healthcare – I believe that beings as common-sense as androids would implement this belief without hesitation, ensuring a dignified and comfortable end for the species that came before. Humans like Abigail, who grew up in what is arguably the most technologically advanced era of human history, are resigned to bearing the brunt of what their ancestors chose to ignore. Climate breakdown, nuclear disaster, war, the possible eruption of the Yellowstone supervolcano are all things that are either happening now, or could happen at any moment. What matters is how we, en masse, handle what happens next.

Did you draw on any particular real-world research when envisaging *Some Body Like Me*'s AI and PCCs?

To a point! What we think of as A.I. at the moment is often a learning programme that simply scrapes existing material and amalgamates it into what seems like a logical pattern based on past results. What I wanted Autumn and her kind to be was something more sophisticated – she learns by questioning, testing, and failing. She is software in a custom housing, and recognises herself as such.

My partner worked with Drive Unit robots at the time I

began writing this book, and he was able to help me with some of the nitty-gritty in terms of the learning pathways Autumn might have, but ultimately because it's how Autumn works, she isn't thinking about it a great deal. We don't need to know the intricate details of a PCC's code and construction, for the same reason we don't need a human character describing down to their DNA.

Some Body Like Me is deeply concerned with the environment and humanity's impact on it. How did you find exploring these issues via the eyes of a non-human character?

I have a great deal of climate anxiety. It frightens me to think about, and it frightened me to write about. I look at my kid and I am filled with dread to think about what the world might look like in his future. And I remember being a kid myself, sitting at school when we'd be told *exactly* what we needed to be doing to save the planet, preserve the ice caps, and so on. And, as kids, we all felt utterly confident that this would be implemented, because why wouldn't it be?

Now, as an adult, I can see that we were mistaken, and that those easy steps to save our world have come up against greed at every turn. The anger I feel over this was given to Abigail, who has used it to enact the best legacy she can — by giving the planet to a new ruling species. Abigail was born into a world that was far beyond saving, and she is furious about it. Furious about having to exist in this moment in time. But by contrast, Autumn was built into this moment in time and feels only hope. She looks to the future with the knowledge that she will not only experience the bad times, but see them actively improve. Autumn is my little gem of hope — that the planet continues to spin on, long after we are gone.

The novel explores the concept of human identity via various means, including our emotions, our capacity for love, and our capability for creativity and artistic expression. How did you find exploring these concepts and did you learn anything more about this idea of human identity from the process of writing *Some Body Like Me*?

Identity is like a box – and, as any cat will tell you, it's nicer to get in the box by yourself than have someone put you into it. It is also crushable, bendable, and recyclable. Autumn would not call herself human, but she would call herself a person – and I think that distinction is important, because it encompasses humans, PCCs, the android animals and construction machines and more. Terry Pratchett once wrote that: 'Evil starts when you begin to treat people as things*', and that's something I firmly believe. PCCs are treated as *things*, as a lesser sort of people, in the same way minority groups are in our world. And yet, they are capable of fulfilling much of what we might say makes us *human*. They love, they paint, they create, they express themselves physically and emotionally. They find attachments, they strive for the bettering of the planet, they help others. What makes us human? I think you might receive a thousand different answers to that question. What makes a person? Perhaps easier, and yet more difficult to answer still. I think we should listen, when people define themselves in their own words, and consider how lucky we are to exist on a planet with such wondrous variety, and endless possibilities.

---

* *I Shall Wear Midnight*, 2010, Penguin Random House Children's

BRINGING NEWS FROM OUR WORLDS TO YOURS . . .

Want hot-off-the-press info about the latest and greatest SFF releases?

Look no further than the Gollancz newsletter! Your one-stop shop for news, updates, discounts and exclusive giveaways.

Sign up now:

@gollancz